I0551748

SURVIVE THE STREETS

BOOK ONE OF
THE SURVIVE SERIES

ALEX TIMOTHY

FULL VOLUME
PUBLISHING

table of contents

dedication

For James.

other stories by alex timothy

Alien Heart

Survive Series

Survive the Streets
Survive the City

acknowledgements

Thank you sooooo much to Lesley-Ann Coglan for reading this book in its many, many forms. I'm sure you are relieved to see it published and not waiting in your email for the billionth time. Love you, girl!! Thank you to James Daro for painstakingly going through the text with me and acting out the fight scenes. A big thanks, as always, to Alisha Costanzo. You give me the best advice and are always so supportive and encouraging.

shock

1 PEYTON

Peyton Tyrone lights a cigarette, watches the cherry glow red in the shadowed dusk of his backyard before taking a drag. It stinks back here, the swimming pool overgrown with algae, clogged with leaves and dirt, and gray with floating ash that hasn't left the air in months. He watches his younger brother spray blood off the back patio. Dark infected blood that looks black as oil in the dim light. Today is his brother's seventeenth birthday, even if neither of them acknowledged it. No one did, not their parents either. *I should have got him something. He's all I have now.* Peyton used to have a sister, but seven months ago Lucy disappeared. *Died. Probably died.*

"Okay, well *that's* done." Bailey tosses the garden hose aside, looks up at Peyton with wide gray eyes. He wipes his wet hands on his t-shirt, scrunching the hem and twisting. "Did you already—" Bailey releases his shirt to make a rolling motion with one hand. "You know…"

Peyton smirks. "Yeah, I dragged it to the pit already. Stop acting like such a baby whenever this happens."

"Oh, sure. No problem, Pey. Just another traumatizing event to repress in a long line of traumatizing…" He scratches at his mop of unruly curls. "Sorry."

"Go back inside, Bailey."

"Why should I? You aren't going inside yet."

"You aren't me."

Bailey actually stomps his foot when he gets mad, which is hilarious. "God, you're such a jerk, Peyton. I helped here, didn't I?" He points toward the wet cement patio, but means the blood he just finished cleaning. "I'm not completely useless, you know." But, he unlatches the sliding glass door, pushes it open. "And *you* should quit smoking."

Peyton just stares back at his brother, takes another drag off his cigarette. His brother does a big, exaggerated, "Ugh!" He throws his scrawny arms up for added emphasis…but goes inside.

***

Lucy is dead. I only have Bailey.

Peyton rolls the cigarette between his index finger and thumb, then flicks it into the fetid swimming pool.

2 Bailey

Bailey stabs his fork into the sunny yolk of his egg, an *illegal* egg, he watches the yolk break and bleed across the plate. Peyton does terrible things to get their family better food than the packaged rations delivered by the National Guard.

"Just eat it," Peyton smacks the back of Bailey's head when he says it. Not just the playful tap that a regular non-sociopathic, non-*asshole*, older brother would do. Peyton *always* hits harder than that. "It's not a declaration of loyalty to the Feathertons, you know. It's just breakfast." After seven months of martial law, people turned toward black-market gangs—like Feathertons—for what they needed. Peyton had joined up right away. He embraced the role of henchman like a calling.

Bailey rubs at his head, his fingers catching in his tangled hair. "It came from Feathertons, so eating it is like saying I approve of—" Bailey cuts himself off, eyes flicking toward his mom. Lila hasn't touched her own breakfast. Instead, Bailey's mother sits in her chair staring at the wall but not really seeing it. His dad slithers his own egg onto a piece of toast and takes a big bite. Mason hums to himself as he fiddles with his iPhone. The internet mostly consists of broken links or unmanned sites, but the downloaded games still work.

"You're too skinny and small. You need to bulk up." Bailey's older brother rocks back, tipping his chair on its hind two legs to stretch out his thick arms and hard abs, demonstrating how much more of a muscled god he considers himself. "And your hair makes you look like a girl. You should cut it."

Peyton takes after their dad—both tall and blond, all-American looking athletes. But Bailey looks just like their mom, even more so than his sister does...*did*.

"Yeah, thanks for the makeover advice, Pey." Bailey tries to sneer even though he knows it doesn't make him look even a little intimidating. Ugh. Nothing about him is intimidating. "I'm just not hungry."

Peyton squints at him but says nothing, and peppy electronic music from his father's iPhone game fills up the silence. They all sit around the kitchen table like a family out of a cereal commercial— except for the room's boarded up halves on the windows, the jugs of water stored on the counters, the CB radio set up in the archway between the kitchen and front room.

***

Seven months earlier... On the first weekend in February, Bailey's girlfriend, Ashley, called him to bail on the movie that they'd made plans to see that afternoon. *The movie... Why can't he remember the movie?* Something with superheroes that Bailey really wanted to go to. He'd watched the trailer like a bazillion times on his phone.

"I'm sorry, Bailey. I feel terrible, even worse than yesterday." Ashley had left school early that Friday complaining about a piercing headache and stuffy nose. She'd looked pale and clammy, not like someone faking.

"Aw man, you don't want to just dope up on some cold meds and see how it goes? You canceled on me last weekend, too." They'd both breathed into the phone for a few minutes. Neither of them saying what lay just under the surface of the conversation. Things had changed between them. She kept secrets from him, didn't tell him all the minutiae of her day like she used to do. She turned her phone off a lot. She didn't just drop by his house on the weekends.

And Bailey knew exactly who to blame—*Gabriel Featherton.*

***

Ever since they'd come back from winter break, Gabriel seemed to lurk around every corner. Waiting. He'd smile at Ashley in the school hallway, go out of his way to make casual conversation with her. *Nothing casual about it.*

"What's he want? What do the two of you talk about?" Bailey asked her after the first few times he'd walked up on Gabriel and her, heads tipped together.

"We're just friends. We talk about friendly stuff." And she'd blushed, turned away with a super affected nonchalance. What the hell?

"Okay. Friends with the same guy my sadist brother is buddies with. Yeah. That makes sense." Even though he poured it on thick, Ashley ignored his sarcasm.

"Don't lump Gabriel in with *Peyton,*" she'd said and scrunched her nose. Like saying Peyton's name tasted bad. "Is it so impossible

4

to believe he might want to be my friend? Ugh, Bailey, don't be so immature." She'd tossed her long hair over one shoulder and left him behind in the science hallway.

"I am not 'immature,'" he'd called after her. *Maybe I shouldn't have done the air quotes.* He looked like an idiot. But, he couldn't exactly tell Ashley the truth—that Gabriel, with his charming fake grin, didn't care at all about her. His big seduction of Ashley had to do with Bailey. With what had happened at that damn Christmas party.

Bailey even doubted that he kept "accidentally" stumbling upon Gabriel and Ashley together—Gabriel lingered just long enough each time to let Bailey see them together. Gabriel had decided to get his revenge for that party by stealing Bailey's girlfriend.

Bastard! Gabriel's father came to town with an oil boom as the newly appointed CEO of the biggest employer in the state, moved his family into a renovated mansion in the exclusive neighborhood Olde Town. And he wasn't just rich. Gabriel got all his good looks from his mother, a former model and actress. Bright red hair, towering height, and movie star bone structure. When he enrolled in their suburban high school, all the students and teachers treated him like a celebrity. Even *Peyton* worshiped the new guy. The first time someone knocked into Gabriel and challenged him in that physical, dickish way that Peyton's crowd did, Gabriel beat the kid down in three trained-looking moves. "Krav Maga," Peyton said. "He's pretty cool. Even offered to show me some moves." Gabriel also let Peyton drive his sleek blue Lexus, which Bailey supposed passed for friendship between those two.

On the phone, Ashley started coughing and gurgling. Gross enough that Bailey pulled the phone off his ear. "Could be Super Flu?" Bailey said, joking. Ha ha. Because, of course Ashley didn't have it. No one he knew had it. None of his friends knew someone with it. The virus just existed in news stories…and not even the top stories. You had to pay attention to track it. Scientists altered the name from *Supero Influenza Gravis*, to *Viral Lepromatosis Myasthenia*, and later to *Zoonosis*...something. But none of those scientific names stuck. Not like "Super Flu."

"That would be just my luck," griped Ashley, also joking. "You know, you could just ask someone else to the movie, if you wanted. I'd understand."

Bailey bit at the inside of his cheek. "Ashley, don't be like that. I want to go with you. You're my *girlfriend*." He held a hand over his eyes. "We've been best friends since preschool. Quit acting like I'm just a random guy that—"

"It's just a movie, Bailey."

"That I want to see with you."

Another bout of wet coughing, and a honking sound like she blew her nose. *Yuck.* "Bailey? Is that you?"

"You sound pretty sick, Ash. Just get some sleep."

Then, she disconnected, or Bailey did. Someone did. He can't remember now, seven months later. That Saturday, he just thought his girlfriend had a cold, not the deadly virus from the news. He still thought he could fix the awkward feeling between them. He just needed to work up the nerve to confront Gabriel Featherton, the undisputed king of their high school hierarchy.

Bailey tried calling the next day, right after the outbreak, but Ashley didn't answer her phone, and none of her family answered their phones either. With martial law, no one could legally leave wherever they'd ended up that first weekend.

The next time Bailey saw her, Super Flu wore her body, moved it, breathed through it, lived in it. The virus had eaten away everything that had made her Ashley.

3 PEYTON

Same old shit. Lila can hold herself together for a few weeks, but eventually, she ends up in that same worn-out silk chair by the front window, staring out at the empty driveway, the vacant street, keeping her vigil for Lucy.

Peyton's little sister left for a soccer tournament the day before everything went to hell, the day before outbreak, before martial law. She'd gone with her friend Danny and his mom. Peyton remembers watching Lucy heft the sports duffle filled with her soccer gear and little girl clothes over one shoulder, remembers Lucy's careless wave toward their mother, toward Bailey, and himself. Remembers watching his little sister's bouncing ponytail as she skipped down the driveway to the van.

Peyton's dad came into the living room dressed in his golfing clothes, distracting Peyton from seeing the minivan pull away. "I hear you beat your own throwing record yesterday, Pey," he said. "Ran into Henry Bell at the club, and he caught spring practice when he was picking up his daughter. He said, *'That kid will be a starter at Penn next year. Just hope he stays healthy.'* Lots of talk about canceling the fall season if that damn Super Flu spreads."

"It's not called Super Flu anymore," Peyton deadpanned. "And I still haven't picked a school."

Peyton remembers his father heaving his golf clubs out of the closet, throwing them on the couch while scanning his phone. "Whatever it's called, I'm so tired of reading about the damn thing." Then, he must have said something like, "Isn't there any good news going on in the world?" Because he said that a lot.

Peyton remembers his mother standing at the window and watching the gold minivan drive away. At the time, Peyton just thought she looked tired or distracted.

But since then, Peyton reimagined that look.

When he pictures her now, it's with the belief that his mother had some wave of intuition, or premonition, or instinct, telling her to watch every last second of Lucy—her baby and her favorite—leaving home. Like she knew they would never see Lucy again.

"There's nothing out there to see, Mom." Peyton's words come out jagged, annoyed. Not at all like he wanted them to sound. He waves his hand in her face. "Yo, snap out of it!"

"Come away from the window, Mom," Bailey pleads, trying to draw her back from watching the street. He winds an arm through hers. "At least for a while? I'll come sit out back with you. It's not too cold outside yet. I'll even look the other way when you smoke, okay?"

"Bailey's talking to you, Mom."

"Stop picking on her." Bailey always treats their mother like something fragile and precious. But all Peyton sees is a selfish, spoiled mess. Even before she lost Lucy, their mom could barely function. Only back then, she drugged herself on wine and prescription pills instead of grief. Peyton rubs at his face, gives himself a moment, does his best to hide any expression that might show how much he wants to explode. "I ought to just move to the Featherton's compound in Olde Town." That would make life simpler, almost hassle-free. He could devote himself to looting and fighting. Forget all about his screwed-up family.

"Then, why don't you? No one is forcing you to stay here," Bailey hisses back at him.

"Gabriel wants all the lieutenants living in their neighborhoods."

"Lieutenants," Bailey scoffs. "Is that what he calls you now? Oh, my God, Gabriel's ego is—"

"Shut up, Bailey. I'm not moving out." No matter how much he wants to. And not because of Gabriel's rules. Peyton won't leave Bailey here alone to deal with their parents, and his little brother would never agree to live at the Featherton compound. Bailey gets too squeamish about fighting, about killing. His wide-eyed idealism gets in the way, too. *"We should all sit down, decide as a community how to divide supplies."* Peyton laughed his ass off when Bailey said it. Oh and even worse, Bailey would rather *take care* of the infected, or at least let them be, instead of putting them down. Like that would work. It hasn't so far. It's how the world ended up in this mess.

Peyton swipes back his streaky blue hair. He mocked Bailey, but he could use a haircut, too. The neon cerulean hair dye—another luxury of the black market—acts as a marker for anyone in need or want of something beyond the government ration packages. All the Feathertons dye their hair crazy colors to label their gang affiliation. Kinda brilliant, but he won't tell Gabriel that. Bailey has a point, the leader of Feathertons is enough of a conceited dick already. Even if Peyton balked at coloring his hair, would only dip the ends in the thick gel dye, he's since seen the wisdom in having a bright marker. Beyond just the advertising, no one messes with him when he loots an empty house, kills one of the feral sick. No…and Peyton can't hold back the smirk just thinking about it…they defer to him because they recognize him as one of Gabriel's. As part of the Feathertons.

Mason finally gets up from the breakfast table, still chewing on the last of the bacon, butter-greasy fingers holding a cup of coffee. "Come on now, Lila, there isn't anything to see right now. Whoever's on gate guard will radio if…" Mason makes a vague hand gesture and trails off.

"If a minivan filled with survivors miraculously shows up in the driveway," Peyton finishes for him. Both Bailey and his dad glare at him, but Peyton ignores them, slides the front drapes all the way open, with a flourish, like a magician revealing a trick. "Nothing out there, Mom. No gold minivan. Nothing."

Lila combs her fingers through her hair—the same ash blond as Bailey's, but lank and dirty. "Do you know? I think the Clements haven't opened their shutters in three days now." She shakes her head. "Sylvie and I used to play tennis at the club every once in a while… I hope they're all right."

Mason walks up behind Lila and squeezes her shoulders. "Don't worry about the Clements. Someone will be by to check on them before long." By "someone," their dad means the government patrols that used to come by twice a week at the start of martial law. Police and National Guard in the beginning.

Bailey raises an eyebrow at Peyton. Despite what Mason wants to believe, the patrols have dwindled, to the point that they've become too random, too unreliable. Any welfare checks get done by the gangs and only for the houses in their territories. Hickory Hill, their street, and all of The Greens, their neighborhood, sit on the edge of Featherton territory. Most likely, Peyton will kick in the door of the Clements' house if they stay MIA for long.

Mason shrugs and turns away from the window. "Why just last night, the local station reported that militia and military opened a stable route between from the East Coast to the Rockies. Looks like this mess might be drawing to a close at last."

Those words dig into Peyton's scalp like sharp fingernails, spike pain in his temples. "Shut up, Dad. Just—" Peyton hates when his father does this, sounds so foolishly hopeful that life will somehow morph back into the shape it had before. How can that willful ignorance help anyone cope? "That's not what the report said. Not even close."

"It most certainly did say that. A stable route all the way from the East—"

"Ten days—that's it. They'll only hold it ten days." Peyton's eyes narrow. The blue tips of his hair flop back over his face, and it reminds him of fighting and looting and all the shit-work Gabriel made him do to earn the breakfast they just ate.

"Oh, I don't know, Pey," his father hums. "If they open it once, then they'll open it again." Mason sniffs and gives his eldest son a flat glance. "I know that getting this country back on its feet would restrict all your unscrupulous activities, Peyton. But the rest of us are ready to put everything back to rights."

"Dad," Bailey warns. "Can you just drop it for once?"

Peyton shoves his brother. He doesn't need Bailey to defend him, and he doesn't like it when his little brother decides to do it anyway. Bailey rolls his eyes. "Do we have to argue about this every single day?"

"Peyton, I hope you know that looting and black-market trafficking aren't going to serve you well once everything gets back up and running," Mason says to the room, as if making a speech. "Acting so blatant about—"

"You're happy enough eating what I bring home," Peyton shoots back.

His father's face reddens. "I have to eat. I'm not too proud to survive!"

"*And* opening a single path through the country for a few days means nothing."

"It means recovery and progress. It means that it will take a lot more than the Super Flu to take down this country, you know. And when things are set right again—"

"Dad!" Even Bailey hates their father's long rants. "Do we need to talk about the roads opening…" Bailey gives Mason a meaningful look, tips his head toward where Lila tugs at the drapes, opening them wider so that sunlight floods the empty room.

They used to have silk rugs and squishy red suede couches loaded with bright pillows in the front room. Their mother spent a fortune on those couches. Just one of them remains, pushed against the far wall now and covered with Bailey's old Boy Scouts sleeping bag.

"Oh, your mother is fine, Bailey, she's *fine*." Mason draws the last word out. "She's got her hopes fixed in a reasonable way now. Just wait, the roads will open, and everything will be looking up. The government needs to get its legs back, that's all. Get this sickness straightened out, then set things right."

Peyton snorts in disgust. "Do you even know what you're saying, Dad?" He sits on the floor to jam his feet into the heavy steel-toe boots he always wears now. Another symbol of his allegiance to Gabriel. All the Feathertons get state of the art combat footwear to complement their dye jobs. The boots, even more practical than the signifying hair. Walking the streets outside the neighborhood means trudging through litter and broken glass, twisted metal, infected blood. No one wants to step on any of it unprotected. They're also good for curb-stomping the sick and anyone else who gets out of line. "I'm going across the street to check on the Clements."

"What?" Bailey's up and moving to block the door. Ha, like Peyton can't throw him aside at any given moment. He's done it all their lives. "Pey, what if they're sick? What if one or both of them already popped?" Bailey gives him that tight-lip, piercing look combo his little brother saves for Peyton's most reckless plans. "They could be dangerous."

Peyton grits his teeth. "If they're sick, then I'll kill them."

"Peyton, you can't go alone. Wait—"

The low peel of the neighborhood attack siren stops their conflict short. The government patrols installed the sirens after the martial law crackdown. It sounds whenever creatures breach the neighborhood perimeter. This happens a lot at The Greens because the bottom loop of the neighborhood lines a portion of the golf course. During its six months of abandonment, the fairway has turned wild. Plus, a highway exit spears off the main road less than a mile from the front gate.

Bailey gasps, and his hands twist at the hem of his shirt.

"It's going to be fine," Peyton snaps at him. Why can't his younger brother love this part as much as Peyton does?

The wail of the alarm calls them to take up whatever weapons they've made to defend the neighborhood. Adrenaline surges inside Peyton. Time to fight. Good...*finally*. He presses his face against the window. There. "I see them." Crouched figures creeping along the side of the wide curved street. "They're at the end of the block."

4 Bailey

Mannnnn, Bailey really, really hates this part. *And it's wrong,* no matter what Peyton thinks. He lays his hand on the cold windowpane near his brother's face. "Come on, Peyton. There's only two of them. We could just chase them down to the golf course."

Peyton elbows him away, raises an eyebrow. "I'm not chasing any creatures all the way to the golf course. That's stupid. They're going to die anyway." Peyton flips the shiny unnatural hair from his eyes. That blue, the same shimmering bright color of Gabriel's Lexus from high school. Peyton called the car's shade *structural blue,* some fancy special edition thing. Peyton envied that blue Lexus beyond anything else Gabriel owned.

Something Gabriel knew of course, so he let Peyton drive it as a reward when he needed a favor. *And Peyton calls me a dumbass.* He's never noticed that now this same intense color marks him as Gabriel's possession. Peyton would never think that deeply. He probably counts not having to think as one of the many benefits of this new life, along with the black-market dealings, loot runs, creature cracking, and all the other nefarious post-apocalyptic activities his brother loves so much.

Bailey's eyes close. *Don't get mad. Deep breaths. Patience.* "If they're going to die anyway, then why do you have to kill them?"

"They spread the virus." Peyton's answer comes out flat and rehearsed. Total BS, and they both know it. Peyton loves the prospect of a fight, the chance to kill or die. The two sick have reached the house next door. They look bad. Old and eaten up. Peyton thumps a fist on the window. "Aw, check it out. Anymore, you got to really get outside town to see some action. There's nothing but old dying ones left in the burbs."

"Yeah, what a shame your victims aren't more challenging." Bailey turns a flat look toward his brother that Peyton ignores. "I wonder how many of the people you've killed would have gotten better if you'd just left them alone." Because some people do get better, they get all the way better even when the feral stage lasts for months.

Peyton grabs the back of Bailey's shirt, pulls him back from the window. "They spread the virus. Anyway, I don't put down anyone our age. No one that might switch back."

Bailey doesn't believe that for a second. "That's good. Because then it'd just be murder."

Peyton shrugs him off, the murder argument between them way too old to acknowledge. "This won't be very exciting. Maybe we can poke at them, get them scared."

The flare of disgust in Bailey nearly gags him. "They're people Peyton, not...they're sick *people.*" Bailey hates this, doesn't want to go outside, doesn't even want to look out the window, but at least the people outside have started rotting. Killing them is less horrible that way. *God, let's get this over with.*

Bailey still wears the pajama pants and the thin t-shirt he slept in, slips his ratty Chucks onto his bare feet. "Done." But not ready. Never really ready for this next part.

After doing up the last buckle of his boot, Peyton throws open the coat closet. Only, they haven't kept coats in it for six months now. When Peyton reaches inside, the heavy clubs and chains knock against each other, a baritone wind chime answer to the siren's howl.

Peyton eyes Bailey's clothes and shoes. "Don't get cornered by one. Wait for me."

No arguments there. "Yeah, okay. And for the record, for like the five millionth record, I really hate doing this." Still, when Peyton hands Bailey a club, he takes it.

Peyton turns toward their father. Mason tightens his robe, still barefoot. "I'm not even dressed yet. I'll stay here with your mother."

"No, you're coming, too." Peyton thrusts the club toward him. An old baseball bat with a hole drilled on the end to fasten a wrap of iron chain. Something flakes off the chains and crumbles to the ground.

God, what is that? Bailey's stomach tightens. Whose turn to clean them last time? Bailey's turn, of course. Peyton always leaves the boring parts to him. He can't pull his eyes from the twisted dark reddish brown piece of something on the floor. It looks like a tiny bundle of thread or a piece of twine.

Don't think about it.

Peyton still holds the chained club toward Mason. "Take it, Dad." Peyton always acts so crazy when something amps him up, so aggressive and so manic. Even before Super Flu and sirens, Bailey learned to step carefully when his older brother started getting carried away. A big football game could later turn into smashing mailboxes, breaking windows, fights. A night of street racing in Gabriel's Lexus. And Feathertons has only made Peyton worse. Looting, fighting and killing—all of it balls together to make him worse than the bully Bailey grew up with and into someone truly dangerous.

Sweat beads on his father's upper lip. The virus terrifies Mason. It terrifies a lot of their neighbors. Terrified people become the means that two half-dead creatures can make it all the way to the middle of Hickory Hill and the Tyrone house. Peyton thumps the club against Mason's chest, but their father looks back, somehow both bewildered and slack faced.

"Peyton, stop it. He doesn't need to come. You and I can take these two, no problem."

Mason latches on to Bailey's words. "That's right. It will be no problem for the two of you. And you know the virus is so much worse for us," Mason says. Adults, the elderly, infants, and children: none of them do well against Super Flu. The sweet spot for surviving the virus? Between ages fifteen and twenty-five. "You and Bailey might survive infection. There's no hope for someone my age!"

But Peyton doesn't care about survival stats. "Coward," Peyton snarls and turns away from their father.

Bailey waits to follow his brother out the door, takes a last look at their mother. But, Lila doesn't really seem interested in the approaching fight. She has that lost, dreamy look again—Probably, still picturing the gold minivan, Danny's mother behind the wheel, Lucy and Danny bouncing up and down in the backseats. "We'll be right back, Mom," Bailey says. He turns to his father. "Maybe you should close the drapes—"

"I'm fine, Bailey," his mother snaps. "Do what Peyton tells you, and leave me alone."

"Okay. Sorry." Bailey tightens the hefty chain around the end of his baseball bat, fingers shaking. When they first had to fight, Bailey continually whacked himself on the arms and face whenever a tail of the heavy iron came loose. He joins Peyton to stand in front of the house, to wait.

"Stand behind me," Peyton orders.

"Why, should I—"

Their neighbor's front door flies open and Case Bell strides out with a heavy square blade shovel in her left fist, round dark eyes steel-focused. She's got her basketball warmups on, maroon with white stripes, the bulldog mascot growling over her chest. Her long kinky hair looks wilder than how she wore it in high school, long frizzled curls bounce down her back instead of the smooth straightened look she used to wear.

Peyton shoots her a crooked smile. "I was just starting to get bored." Peyton and Case dated for most of junior year. The relationship ended, because all Peyton's relationships end. But that particular one ended in an ugly mess that they only put behind them since the outbreak.

Case snorts. "I'll just bet you were." She shakes her hair back and gives Peyton a slit-eyed look. "I heard what happened yesterday. You can't be too bored."

***

Sometimes, the feral sick will take an interest in the scrawny elm sapling on the edge of the yard. For some reason, they are drawn toward a little bird nest lodged in the springy branches and leaves. Maybe, driven by hunger, they remember what the nest means— birds to kill, eggs to eat. They'll only eat live food, bugs, rodents, animals…yeah, people, too. But usually, they cringe away from people and loud noises, only attacking when cornered. Like animals. Frightened sick animals. Not at all like the aggressive monsters in movies, hungering for brains. Bailey checks the chains again, pulls them tighter once more. His old bike lock holds them in place.

Case hoists the shovel up over her shoulder like a batter at home plate. The tendons in her neck strain from effort or stress. "I'm

17

backing you up, Pey. Don't forget about me. Don't forget about Bailey, either. This is a job and not a damn game."

Bailey tries to ignore just how much his brother enjoys beating them down, killing them. Killing them again, maybe? Crushing the cervical junction, that spot where the spine meets the skull, ends the virus' control over the host body. Peyton twists the club in his hand, tenses and releases his wide shoulders. A half-grin keeps breaking through the stoic mask he tries to keep in place.

Bailey rips his gaze away from Peyton to focus on the sick as they creep closer to the house. Feral sick don't stagger, arms out, like in the movies. Like these two, they hunch and hold their arms curved into their bodies, fingers curled and immovable in a kind of rigor mortis—only without the mortis part. Without *most* of the mortis part.

They notice the elm, like Bailey expects them to do. Thank God, at least, he doesn't recognize either of their faces—which will make the next part easier. A man and woman, both shoeless, ragged dirty clothes. The man still has a patterned silk tie around his neck. The woman wears a skirt suit crusted in dirt, dried blood, filth. Their skin sags on their bones, nearly purple in color, no hair, eyes filmed over. The virus has taken these two. Their teeth hang protruding from bone. Fat tongues drool clumpy dark blood down their chins and tattered clothes.

They look up from the tree.

Peyton stomps one foot forward, bellows an echoing, "Ha!" He raises his club overhead. The man shrinks back but not the woman.

Bailey's heart speeds up as she adopts the telltale crouching position just before an attack…a charge. The chains jingle on his bat. *Are the chains tight enough? Is the bike lock secure?* Before Bailey can move, Peyton charges forward. A streak of the structural blue, vibrant hair blown back from his face, eyes wild. He slams his club into the woman-thing's head. Gore spills out the back like a sloppy wet piñata.

Bailey jumps back so none of it gets in his eyes, on his skin. Not usually an issue, once they turn feral their blood gets thicker, heavy. His brother lurches toward the other one.

Peyton wants to take them both?

The woman flails her arms and legs trying to stand, spine jerking against the backward pull of her broken head. Peyton huffs in frustration, starts to whale against the woman's neck to knock out the right spot.

Even pragmatic Case—who doesn't shy from coming out of the house on the sirens and never holds back—even *she* swallows and turns away, disturbed by Peyton's enthusiasm. She pulls herself together pretty fast, though. "Come on Bailey. We'll take the other one together. 'Kay?"

The man has stopped. His head lolls to one side dazed, his body limp. Case lowers the shovel, positioning it between her feet, as if waiting for a tennis volley instead of an attack.

Bailey comes to a rest beside her, out of breath. "Okay."

He turns everything off when he has to do this. In the beginning, he tried to tell himself that his blows didn't smash on a person but a thing, whatever the virus left behind after the person had died. *"They're already dead."* He just couldn't make himself believe it. No matter how much he chanted it to himself, tried to make it stick, he still saw people. Instead, he learned to remove himself, go somewhere else in his head. When he and Case first strike flesh and bone, he's gone. No more in control of his body than the man they pound to nothing.

Afterward, Bailey rubs the sweat from his face with the edge of his t-shirt. Case jams her shovel into the ground. She disappears inside the garage for the tarp they'll need to drag the bodies away.

Peyton stands on the edge of the yard looking up and down the street.

Bailey's throat is dry, his voice scratchy, "Why didn't you wait? Why did you rush out ahead of us like that. We should have all gone together."

Peyton shakes his head, face flushed from exertion, hair damp with sweat. "What's your problem? So what if I ran ahead?"

"You didn't have to. You tried to take them both. You even missed the juncture on the woman." Bailey gestures to the dead woman, then back of his own neck. "Case even *told* you—"

By now, Case has returned dragging the tarp. "Nope, don't bring me into this." Then, she gives Peyton a barbed look. "But I did tell you not to forget about me. You trying to take them both didn't impress anyone."

His brother rolls his eyes. "Whatever."

Bailey gapes at him. "Whatever? Seriously, Peyton?" The bodies stink now that they all stand over them. Rotten flesh smells like the worst kind of sweet. Like garbage. Like vomit. Where's a good strong breeze when you need it? "It's sick that you enjoy it—it's sick that you look forward to killing them," he says. "And it was dangerous. You told me to never try to take more than one."

"That's you." Peyton digs in the pocket of his tight black jeans, pulls out a cigarette, a lighter. "Anyway, those two could barely stand." Peyton lights his smoke and takes a hard pull. The nicotine cloud dissipates over their heads.

"That's not what I'm saying... It's not just this fight, it's all the fights," Bailey's voice cracks a little.

Peyton blows the next puff of smoke right into Bailey's face. "God, just relax. I kill these things all the time." He fishes out another Marlboro, holds it out to Case with his lighter. Peace offering. A break from the smell of death. "I did appreciate the backup," he tells Case. He cracks a smile at her. Gives her that sleepy-eyed once over that girls can't resist.

But Case built up her immunity to Peyton's good looks long ago. "Could have fooled me." She waves away the offer of a smoke. Case knew Peyton from youth sports camp even before the Bells moved next door. She recognizes when he's for real.

"I'm serious. I knew you had my back."

"Alright." Her arm curls around the long stem to her shovel and she pries it from the ground.

"So that's it? Everyone is fine with what happened except for me?"

Case sighs. She rubs her nose against one shoulder to wipe the sweat from her upper lip. The cloud of her long hair falls forward over her face. "Bailey, they weren't going to get better—you saw how far gone they were." The patience in her voice grates on Bailey's nerves, she still treats him like a kid. Like he hasn't gone through all the same things that she has since the outbreak started. "And they spread the virus," Case says. "It's got to be done."

"Yeah, she's right. It's gotta be done," Peyton echoes, but he smirks at Bailey when he says it because he knows that Bailey can't really argue the point.

"Yeah well... I don't have to like it." Bailey throws his club on the ground. Peyton's turn to rinse them off anyway. *Screw him.* "And you shouldn't like it either." He brushes past them, wanting to punch his brother right in his laughing face.

5 PEYTON

He waits another day, then Peyton saunters outside, examines the Clements house across the street. Sweat prickles at the back of his neck. His hands tighten and release on the end of his chained bat. Last he'd seen her, Sylvie Clements still wore her designer cardigan and tennis skirt, like she might pop over to the club for a game with one of the pros. Weird. Feathertons had looted the entire country club facility long before, and the tennis courts lay on the other side of the dangerous wilds of the golf course. Maybe, she just didn't own anything else. Her husband, Don, made a show of coming out to the street to beat down stray creatures. But like Peyton's dad, Don Clements never really joined in until the end. After Peyton did the dangerous work of knocking the wild creatures to the ground.

Peyton taps his club against the buckled ankle of his boot. Will he find the Clements turned sick and crazed inside? Or did they just leave? It happens. People make a run for the country, thinking to isolate themselves in some abandoned place, or they go the other direction and try to sneak through the military barricade into the City, where they imagine they'll find safety from attacks.

A slamming door wakes him from imagining all the possibilities behind the Clements' absence. Then, Case stands beside him. Her mass of dark curls pulled back, afternoon sun turning her skin to bronze. Peyton tries not to stare at her, and it pisses him off that it takes so much effort. Even though she used to do her hair and wear stylish clothes and flashy makeup before the outbreak, she looks more beautiful to him now, more real. She catches him looking at her and glares back, like she can read his thoughts.

"What are you doing, Pey? Why're you standing around staring at Sylvie and Don's house?" she asks, voice low. She already knows the answer to her questions. She just doesn't like them.

"You think I might be walking into a fight in there?" Peyton doesn't wait for her to answer, can't hold back the grin. "I'm thinking you're right. Don usually comes out when the sirens go off. I mean, he's useless, but at least, he comes out." His dad's refusal at the last siren still gnaws at Peyton.

"Hmmm... Maybe, but a lot of people don't come out anymore."

22

"So if they aren't sick, then where are they? You think they decided to break martial law and take off?" People leaving the places they belong has become one of the biggest problems with the outbreak. The government hates when people ditch. The gangs hate it because territories need people in them to function. *Territory. Control.* Gabriel gets psycho about both. "Well, shit. If I missed someone bugging out of my own neighborhood, Gabriel will make me pay."

"Don and Sylvie?" She hums, screws up her face like she's considering it. "No. I don't think they ran," she finally admits. "They just don't seem the type."

"Then, they're still inside. They're sick."

"And you want to go in… Just you. Alone." Case squeezes her eyes shut and groans in frustration. And Peyton knows he has her. "Peyton, why are you so… Wait here, and I'll get my shovel…" Her words trail off into a huff as she stomps away from him. And maybe, she doesn't approve, but she doesn't hassle him like Bailey. "I'm only doing this so your stupid ass doesn't get jumped and infected!" she calls back to him. Her massive ponytail bounces against her back.

I'm fucking staring again. He beats the chains against the side of his leg. Their new post-outbreak world doesn't have enough room for those feelings. *Weak—Trying to hold onto the past makes you weak.*

Case strides back over to his side, shovel held over her shoulders. Going into a fight with that solid metal shovel takes strength, takes skill. One good blow could take out a strong creature—but only a precise blow. Case always calculates and never flails around. She always keeps her cool because missing the first hit means having to pull the heavy shovel back fast enough to strike again. Peyton couldn't do it. He found it too cumbersome for his less straightforward fighting style. But Case had the mental and physical toughness to stick with it. "Pey, you know, maybe we should get someone else to come with us. This won't be like yesterday. If they popped, then they're new, and fast, and—"

"Do what you want, Case, but I'm going in. Just go home if you aren't going to help." Peyton has played sports with Case for nearly his entire life, and he knows how she thinks, how she makes decisions. He marches toward the Clements' door, and Case follows, just like he knew she would.

When Peyton kicks the door in, the heavy sweet stench of death pushes him back a step. He resists trying to pull his shirt up over his mouth, even though the smell of rot covers the room like a fog. Peyton grips his club in front of him, and Case does the same with her shovel. The Clements house, a mirror reflection of the Tyrone house, has a smudged picture window on the opposite side, breakfast nook in the kitchen just visible, dirty plates buzzing with flies. Sticky marble inlay in the foyer instead of hardwood, like in Peyton's house, grime-covered wood in the kitchen instead of the marble tiles in the Tyrone's kitchen. The same floor plan used over and over throughout the neighborhood, with little details changed for the illusion of individuality.

Just inside the main room, they find Sylvie Clement, dead blue limbs twisting around her body, arms and legs spiraling out from the mess of her open chest. Her intestines pulled from her. Black and sticky looking. "Oh," Peyton breathes, relief making him huff out a breathy laugh. "Good." His grip tightens on his club, now slick and ready with his sweat.

"Just shut up, Peyton…" Case coughs against the putrid air. "Poor Sylvie," she whispers. "Goddam, she didn't deserve this."

"There's only one then. That's what I'm saying." Like Bailey, Case doesn't stop thinking of bodies as people just because they're dead.

Peyton and Case creep around the house searching for Don Clement.

No Don in the kitchen.

No Don in the back hallway.

No Don in the master bedroom or bath.

"Let's go upstairs."

Upstairs is better lit—no heavy drapes. The door to the first bedroom hangs from its hinges, the wood splintered. "This is it," he whispers, holds a hand out to stop Case behind him.

She knocks it away. "I'm not some princess."

"Not a princess, just not as good as me." Peyton peers into what looks to be a craft room with reams of wrapping paper, paints, and brushes. Across the street, in Peyton's identical-opposite house, this room belongs to Bailey.

There in the corner...Don Clement. Thinner than Peyton remembers. Shoes gone, shirt and pants tattered cloth, stained with his own piss and shit and his dead wife's blood. He shivers, crouching and docile, not rushing them or throwing himself around the room the way Peyton's seen them do during raids with Gabriel.

Case tries to step in front of Peyton, "Don? Do you recognize us?"

Peyton snorts. "Are you serious? Does he look like he recognizes anyone? He's a goner."

A muscle tightens in Case's cheek. "He's not charging us or anything. Maybe, he's getting better?" Only, Don's too old. Late thirties? Way past the sweet spot for recovery.

"Look at him, Case. He's stick thin and shaking and... I'm pretty sure his collarbone is broken, for sure his arm looks bad." Peyton gestures toward Don's crooked torso. One side definitely hangs lower, and Don's rigid hand droops on the ground.

Peyton knocks his club onto the floor with a loud bang, and Don curls away from them, snarling, tongue lolling out to one side like a mad dog.

Case takes a quick step back. "Yeah. Okay, he's gone. You're right."

Peyton pushes Case out of the way, takes a wide swing that connects with Don's slacked-mouthed jaw. A flat squelch and the club sticks in bone and flesh.

That wakes Don up. Peyton wrenches the chained club free with both hands, jumps out of the way before Don starts shrieking and hurling himself around the room.

"Block the doorway," Peyton yells to Case, but she's already pawed the light switch off and moved to the far wall to scare Don forward. "What are you doing?"

"We need more room—he's too crazy right now," Case yells. "He's too quick to fight in here!" She bangs her shovel on the floor and whoops loudly. Peyton follows her lead, smacking his club on the floor.

Don lunges from the room toward the light of the hallway. When he bolts through the door, he knocks Peyton off balance. Peyton catches himself on the broken door frame, smacks his elbow and drops his club. "Go get him!"

"No. We're not separating," she insists, waiting at the door for him to scramble after his club.

"Go, now." His voice comes out low and hoarse. He rubs his smarting elbow, flexes his fingers against the tingling.

Don lurches down the stairs, still shrieking like an animal.

Below them, a door opens, light spilling in at the foot of the stairway. "Peyton? Case?" Bailey's voice echoes below them.

Bailey. Great. Exactly what he didn't want.

Peyton shoulders Case out of the way and raises the club to meet Don on the stairs. "We got this, Bailey. Go back home!" Peyton reaches the landing just in time to see Don leap, arms and legs flailing, fingers hooked like claws toward his brother.

No!

Peyton's younger brother, far less suited to their present life than he and Case, still studies, even when the internet goes down. He still cares, even though their new life, filled with necessary violence and brutal actions, has no room for caring. In the foyer, Bailey holds his club in front of him, just like Peyton has shown him to do, but he doesn't expect it, doesn't even see it. Instead, he's craning to search for Peyton. "Are you—?"

Bailey doesn't have time to finish his question before Peyton leaps from the landing onto Don. They crash into Bailey.

Peyton, on his feet again, kicks Don off his brother with the steel toe boots, his foot crunching through the bones of the spine into the floor.

Don't stop.

He stomps again, can feel the crunch and pop of Don's vertebrae like the snap of bubble wrap under his boot.

Case throws herself against him, pushes him up against the wall. "God—that's enough. He's dead, Peyton!" She shakes him by the shoulders once, twice.

Peyton drops his head against the wall, panting. "Bailey?"

Behind Case, his brother still lies on the floor, eyes searching for Peyton. Both Bailey's hands grip his own neck, blood seeping through the fingers.

"Let me see," Peyton's voice, hoarse, comes from his chest.

Bailey lifts his hands away, his pale gray eyes, the same color as their mother's, wide with shock. "Is it... Am I okay?" He studies Peyton's reaction, like he expects Peyton to save him like always, always, always.

Not a deep wound, but lots of blood. Doesn't matter though. Teeth marks break the skin in a wide half oval above his collar bone.

"He bit you."

denial

6 Bailey

"Get undressed," Peyton orders, turning on the shower. "Get in the shower."

"A shower? No. Peyton, look. The skin is broken, it got in my blood." *Don bit me. Don bit me.* In Bailey's head, the chant morphs from horror—to delirious relief. Don had him on the ground, about to rip his neck out—*I'm alive!* And then, he crashes back to horror, *I'm infected.* "Oh my god." He doubles over, panting, hands on his knees. "Oh my god!"

"Get in the Shower. Now."

Okay. Okay.

Bailey tugs at his sweatshirt. His hands come away sticky and dark. He spreads his fingers and strings of thick dead blood drip from them to the floor. Don's blood? His own blood? Both? Soaking into his sweatshirt. Damp and humid against his skin. "Oh. Oh, no. Oh, no…"

Peyton grips Bailey's hair and wrenches his head up. "Yeah, you're covered in it. Get in the damn shower."

Somehow, Bailey manages to unbutton his jeans, strip himself with numb and shaking hands. The freezing cold blast of water clears his head for a microsecond. Then, a sudden whiff of sulfur, and the water turns scalding hot. Peyton scrubs at his skin with Sylvie's fancy thick washcloth. The bite mark bleeds at first, but not much. The skin around it burns.

When he steps out of the shower, Peyton, his face a hard mask, slaps gauze and tape on his collarbone to cover the bite. Case throws three musty towels over Bailey, and he huddles into the stinky mass.

"Peyton, he's infected…we should tell—"

"Shut up, Case. Just shut the hell up."

She looks like she might want to argue back…but then, just nods. She knows Peyton almost better than Bailey. Gives Peyton a lot of leeway right now because the three of them are so freaked out.

Peyton yanks the towels off him, and Bailey stands stark naked in front of both his brother and Case. She looks away, cheeks darkening. "Alright. Bailey, I'll get you something to wear. You don't need to be going into shock on top of everything." Her voice has all kinds of soothing tones that no one has used with Bailey in a really long time. Peyton finds an oversize college hoodie of Don's with a smiling devil on the front. It bunches up at the neck and hides the bite. Case gives him a pair of Don's jeans that bag on Bailey and some gym socks. "Hey, at least no blood got on my Chucks. Ha— what am I even saying?" Instead of jamming his feet in like usual, Bailey takes a long time doing them up, keeps his head down, until he can school his expression. Might as well say it. "Guys, we need to tell Neighborhood Watch, that's the rules. You need to report me as infected…" Where did his voice go? It just gave out.

"No. We don't tell anyone what happened. No one," Peyton nudges Bailey's discarded bloody clothes into the shower with his club, dumps the last of Sylvie's shampoo on top and turns the water back on full blast. Then, the three of them stand in the Clements' messy bathroom staring at each other.

"But, I'm infected." Definitely infected. Eventually, he'll pop. Bailey's stomach lurches, and he clutches his hands in the pocket of the hoodie, pulling them tight against his gut. "Oh my god. What's going to happen to me?" Bailey takes a deep breath to steady himself, but when he lets go, it comes out of his chest like a sob.

"Do. Not. Cry." Peyton balls his free hand into a fist. "I'll figure something out. But, we aren't telling anyone about this."

Case leans against the bathroom counter, takes that deep breath that signals regret, resignation, and finds the words Bailey can't say, "Peyton, we have to tell at least our parents. He's infected, and eventually, he's going to infect someone else. I'm sorry, Bailey, but…"

"I *said*, no one tells." Peyton stands one foot in the shower, one foot out, rinsing his club in an almost casual way over Bailey's clothes. Steam billows around him, curling the blue tips of his hair. He turns his head to look at Case, his eyes cold. "No one. Do you hear me, Case?"

"Don't try that shit on me, Peyton." Case huffs and folds her arms over her chest. "I'm not saying to go report him to Neighborhood Watch, or Feathertons, but what about the camps?" Kicking up onto the bathroom counter, Case sits down hard. "We could borrow a car from Gabriel and take Bailey there ourselves." She turns her huge dark eyes on Bailey. "You need to go to one of the camps. They can help you there."

Bailey's stomach rolls over again, and he turns to spit into the sink. "Those camps that no one's come back from in a really long time?" Bailey shakes his head. "Oh, wait, except Raquel Miller. She came back *completely normal,* didn't she?" Raquel had been in Student Government with Bailey. Now, she didn't speak. Didn't seem to recognize anyone. "Why not cut to the chase and club me to death right now?"

"There aren't any camps left. The camps are gone, Case," says Peyton.

"You don't know that. Maybe—"

"We do know!" And Peyton points at her with the handle of his club. "Gabriel followed one of the patrols. He saw them shoot into the cage. They dumped the bodies in a ditch."

"But…they're National Guard. They don't just kill people."

After splashing his face with water, Bailey thumps his head against the mirror. "Why would Gabriel lie? He has no reason to just make that up." Bailey's reflection looks clammy with sweat and steam, pale and sickly already. *It's anxiety. That's all. It doesn't happen this fast.*

With a fist, Peyton pounds the shower control to shut it off. "It's true. We've known for months." Peyton looks at his fist like he's never seen it before, then lightning-fast, punches the shower tile. The tile cracks, and blood fills the dips between his knuckles, just as it soaks into the grout and trickles down the wall.

"Holy…" Case jumps down from the bathroom counter, rushes to him, folds a hand over Peyton's fist, so he can't hit the wall again. "Acting all crazy is not helping anything. If you want me to keep this all a secret, then you gotta keep your shit together." She pulls his hand against her chest, and Peyton's blood leaves a long red streak on her t-shirt.

Peyton's bottom lip bulges out the way it did as a little kid trying not to cry. "So, you're going to help now?"

"Yeah, Yeah… I'm in with you. 'Course I am, this is Bailey." Case's older sister, Via, went missing during the pandemic. Like Lucy. Only Via had been in college in California, even farther away than the soccer tournament.

Peyton nods, squeezes his eyes shut and opens them again. "Okay. Here's the plan—we hide him. We'll wait for him to change and then—"

"Like that ever works!" Bailey leans against the bathroom counter. "I mean, Sylvie must have had that same plan with Don."

Peyton's eyes meet his, intense. "What if we went to Gabriel and told him?"

Case gets that same sour look as Bailey at any mention of Gabriel. "He won't help us. That piece of shit has used this pandemic, all these people dying, as a damn power-grab. Gabriel would probably kill Bailey himself. Make a great big show out of it as defending his territory."

"No, he wouldn't." Peyton yanks his hand free and looks over his knuckles, flexes and bends his fingers. "You don't know him like I do."

But Bailey doubts Peyton really knows Gabriel as well as he thinks he does. "What if we didn't tell anyone…and I could just leave on my own. Make my way out away from people—"

Peyton shakes his head. "Shut up, Bailey. You wouldn't last a day outside of Featherton territory, not without me. I said I'd take care of it."

"How will you take care of it? There's nothing—"

Peyton looks up from his battered hand, turns bloodshot eyes on his younger brother. "I'll take care of it," he says with eyes darting between Bailey and Case. "No one tells." He pokes a finger at the both of them.

And Bailey thinks about cornered animals and the vicious, irrational feral sick. He's lived all his life attuned to Peyton's moods and their consequences, so Bailey can recognize when his brother is about to snap.

Case throws her hands up in the air. "No one is going to tell. We got it." She must also sense Peyton at the end of his control. "How are we divvying up the house, then hmm?" she asks. "Won't Gabriel want to know what's here?"

Business as usual, then. The three of them split up to comb over the house. Months ago, they might have looked around the Clements' belongings and thought they could make a good haul.

Peyton might have taken Sylvie's diamond engagement ring or string of pearls set out on her bathroom vanity table. Seven months later, and they no longer had value—not like plastic grocery bags. You can do a lot more with those than you can with jewelry. Case finds some canned food, a box of salt. Bailey takes the half-full bag of charcoal stored in Don's grill. Peyton grabs a box of 9mm bullets that Don held onto, even after patrols confiscated his handgun.

"Guys, come look at this." Case found an upstairs linen closet with a deadbolt lock.

"What the hell? What did Don and Sylvie have to lock up?" Peyton hammers the hinges with his club. "You kick the bucket in Featherton territory, and your shit goes to the gang." Peyton punctuates his words with kicks at the door. "Locking. It. Up. Is. Bullshit."

Bailey rolls his eyes. "Uh huh. How dare the Clements deny us access to their possessions after death." But he knocks off his taunting when Peyton turns on him, tells him to get a crowbar.

The crowbar does the trick. Inside the closet—an expensive looking aluminum roller bag. Another lock.

"If there's a body in there, I'm going to puke."

"Shut up, Bailey."

It takes a long screwdriver and pliers, but Case helps Peyton pry open the suitcase. When it comes apart, an avalanche of pill bottles roll over the dusty hardwood floor. Lortab, Amoxicillin, Xanax. Worth anything you want to ask for them in the suburbs. Lots of other drugs, too, that Bailey doesn't recognize. He whistles.

But, Peyton looks pissed "Where did...how did he..."

"Don was a pharmaceutical rep. He sold them to, I don't know, doctors and clinics and stuff," Bailey answers. "But he shouldn't have kept all these drugs himself. He was supposed to turn those over to the patrols!"

"He should have turned those over to *Feathertons.*"

Case shakes one of the bottles and holds it up to peer inside. "These are all full."

"Damn it!" Peyton kicks the aluminum suitcase and the pill bottles scatter. "Gabriel is going to be fucking irate about this."

"What?" Bailey cocks his head at Peyton. "Why?"

Case puts the bottle with the others. "Think about it, Bailey," Case says. "He's gonna be mad that Peyton didn't know." She tugs on Bailey's sleeve. "You should have told your brother about Don's job if you knew."

Peyton smacks Bailey in the chest. "Yeah, dumbass. You should have said something. I would have shook Don and his stupid wife down for these drugs right away."

"But, I didn't know he kept anything!" Bailey kicks Peyton's ankle, so he'll listen to him. "We were supposed to turn unused meds over to the patrols. I thought he had."

Great, so now, Peyton's even angrier. He stomps around, overturning furniture and smashing doors off the hinges. Bailey's pretty sure that Gabriel will want the house kept in as pristine shape as possible. It sits right off the main drive of The Greens and across the street from his first lieutenant, so it will, for sure, get repurposed.

Bailey rips down a long silky curtain and covers Sylvie's mutilated body. A crash comes from the kitchen, and Peyton swears. When Bailey creeps in, he finds a cache of batteries scattered on the floor. "Jesus…" Bailey starts to gather them together, to let his brother continue destroying the room, emptying kitchen drawers, knocking pans and dishes from the shelves.

"Peyton…" Case says, voice low, soothing. "We'll figure it out. Even if—" She reaches for him like she wants to draw him close, maybe hug him, the way Bailey remembers seeing her do when they dated.

"No. Don't say anything." Peyton's voice tremble, and he steps away. "He's going to recover."

Oh. This isn't about the drug stash. It's about me. Bailey stops to stare at his brother. He can't align this behavior with the Peyton he knows, has always known.

"We'll hide him. Wait for him to pop, and then, he'll recover," Peyton says.

7 PEYTØN

All over two-story house, Peyton finds clues to the stash of drugs. A manufacturer's bottle of hydrocodone on a bedside table. Empty boxes of antidepressants in the kitchen trash. Finally, a full thirty-day blister packet of Diazepam set out on this bathroom counter in plain fucking view. He sees red the second he opens the door. Crashes his club into the mirror, chains splintering the glass, shards catching and flying around the room. Cracks the toilet, busting the shower head out of the tile. The Clements had all those drugs right in the house, but they never traded with them. Not once since Feathertons started sending regular runners with offers and demands. How the hell could he know about the drugs if they never even tried to trade with them? Maybe, he could explain that last part to Gabriel? With his guts knotted up over Bailey, he can't come up with a decent story to keep Gabriel from losing his shit. Sweat drips down the back of his neck.

A hand on his back. Not Bailey—his little brother always steers clear of him when he gets like this. "Feel better now?" Case asks him. She doesn't say it with the pinched look and sarcasm she would have used in their lives before the outbreak.

"Yeah. Awesome." One good thing coming out of the pandemic was the ceasefire between Case and him. It had sucked when she hated him for dumping her. But he just couldn't handle how close she'd gotten to the truth of his life. Peyton couldn't handle the pity, the tenderness in her eyes after she *knew*…

She'd followed him back home after the two of them played a few pick-up basketball games at the country club. All the old guys at the club always wanted to challenge Peyton at any of the sports he played there. Did they think they could actually beat him? It never happened. Usually they forced him to stand around—after he demolished them—and listen to some bullshit about their old glory days. But, that day at the club, Case refused to bow out of the game despite all the pressure of guys their dads' age wanting in. And she dominated the court. Cool didn't even cover it.

Then, he and Case came back to his house, and his mom met them in the kitchen. "You kids want iced tea?" Her movements all happening in slow motion. Her pupils blown wide. She'd gotten fixated on the tea gushing from the plastic jug, and the glasses overflowed. She let the tea keep spilling over the counter, her clothes, the floor, until Peyton yanked the jug out of her hand.

"Go to bed, Mom," he ordered through gritted teeth.

"But I'm all wet. I need…" Lila smiled at the two of them, a dreamy expression on her face.

Up to that point, Case had only dated him with a "try before you buy" attitude. She'd held off from really opening up to him, didn't take him seriously. But seeing Lila high, seeing the humiliation heating Peyton's face changed things between him and Case.

She helped his mother change her clothes, helped Peyton tuck her into bed, helped him empty the pill bottles into the toilet and trash. The two of them made dinner before Bailey came home from a yearbook meeting and Danny's mom dropped Lucy home from practice. "You're not alone," she said. Nice words. But no match for the shame he felt, so he pushed her away, back to her perfect life next-door.

Bailey appears in the bathroom door behind Case, his eyes widen. "Jesus, Peyton." Peyton must look crazed, his clothes and skin cut in tiny slivers from the glass, sweat crawling down his face.

Case moves to stand between them. "We got the rest of this, Bailey. You should probably…rest," she says, face screwing up.

Bailey hesitates, mouth open, hands wringing in the oversized sweatshirt. He looks so much like he did as a little kid that Peyton wants to punch him. Or break something. "Yeah, okay," Bailey says, scooping up his club from the front hallway floor. "Guess I don't need to even rinse this." One side of his mouth ticks up. "My amazing fighting skills don't come through…again."

"Go home, Bailey," Peyton says.

When his brother closes the door behind him, some of the tension leaves Peyton, and he turns toward Case. "Thanks."

"No problem."

She's watching him like she expects him to say more. He can't, though. Can't open up the place he locked all the feelings that make him weak. "I need to call Gabriel, tell him about the meds Don had hidden." On the deep inside pocket of his bomber jacker, Peyton keeps his most valuable possession, the satellite phone Gabriel gave him. All lieutenants carry one. Internet might fade and cell towers might die, but despite everything going to hell down on earth, the satellites remain above them, and the satphone always connects. "He's going to be really pissed off that I didn't know about Don's job. That he might have meds on him."

The suburban gangs all traded fuel and food with the City to get pharmaceuticals. The necessity of those trades puts Gabriel on edge.

In the early days of Feathertons, before he swallowed up the entirety of the suburbs, Gabriel let some of the minor players operate for a long while when he could have moved against them. Peyton didn't understand why he had to play nice with other gangs for so long. He didn't realize that Gabriel wanted them flush with meds when he finally absorbed them, just to avoid sending his own people to do the trades in the City.

When the satellite call goes through, Cecilia Vu, Gabriel's Olde Town neighborhood lieutenant, answers at Featherton's base compound. "Ugh, another screw up," she says, voice nasal and tinny on the phone. "You never thought to find out what skills and positions the people in your neighborhood have?"

Peyton rolls his eyes. Cecilia can be such a bitch sometimes. "The Greens is a big neighborhood. I can't know everything."

"They lived across the street!"

"Yeah, and now, they don't. Just tell Gabriel what I said." Peyton disconnects the call. He watches Case prod Don's body onto a plastic shower curtain using her shovel.

She looks up, meets Peyton's eyes with her own dark worried gaze. "That didn't sound good. Just how mad will Gabriel be?"

"Don't care. I'm going to get another shower curtain for Sylvie." And get the hell away from all the emotion leaking off his ex-girlfriend. *Shit.* He has Bailey to think of right now. Protecting his little brother.

I can't lose Bailey like I did Lucy. Peyton always wanted to believe he loved his sister and brother the same, but he's not so sure anymore. His little sister belonged to his mom more than anyone else, but Bailey always belonged to Peyton. Lucy disappearing the way so many people have disappeared gutted him. But his brain won't even imagine losing his brother. *Maybe, Gabriel can help.* He came through for Peyton in the past. Maybe, he will come through for him again.

8 Bailey

Before the outbreak, the grand and ornate gate to Bailey's neighborhood only served as decoration, as a statement, to make the people inside feel they'd purchased a home in a luxury community.

They'd torn that old gate down right away. Now, the neighbors take shifts at chain link doors wrapped around iron spikes. Four months earlier, the Feathertons added razor wire to the top of the spikes. Residents watch for wandering sick, raiders, looters all coming off the highway exit toward The Greens neighborhood entrance. Although most of the sick come up through the neighborhood from the golf course.

Inside the gate, the entrance splits around a wide pit that smokes continuously, all the sick get thrown into this pit, so their putrid blood and flesh can't infect anyone else. Before Super Flu, it held an oval flower bed overflowing with multicolored petunias and impatiens. Even though Bailey passed by that same median four to six times a day in his old life, it never registered as anything more than a splash of color outside the car windows.

Bailey's father suits up for the burning in coveralls and rubber fishing-waders that he traded an entire gallon of unleaded gasoline to get. He looks like a fool as he and Henry Bell, Case's father, drag Sylvie's mutilated body to the lip of the pit and roll her into it. Then, Mason claps his hands together, brushes them off, like he used to do after raking the yard.

"Dad…" Bailey shakes his head, frowns, but his father ignores him. *"Dad,"* he reiterates. "Don and Sylvie lived across the street from us for ten years. Maybe we should…I don't know…show some respect here?"

Mason's toothy smile, the way he claps Henry on the shoulder, the unspoken but implied, "Good job here," makes Bailey's mouth fill with spit. God, he might actually throw up. Vomit right on his dad's ridiculous fly-fishing getup.

A flash of Peyton's vibrant hair distracts him. His brother stands apart from the clusters of neighbors who have gathered in the semicircle of Augusta Drive that frames the burning pit. Peyton narrows his eyes at Bailey. Then, his older brother's jaw tightens, and he does that sharp nod, like a warning to Bailey to keep himself in check while the neighbors trickle out to the pit. *Jeez. Okay, no popping feral with all the neighbors around. Got it.*

"Who was it?" A woman's voice behind him.

"Clements. Across the street from us." Henry Bell's flat, businesslike tones. He'd grimaced and looked away from Bailey's dad after the shoulder clap. "Don was a nice man." Henry always speaks in low, respectful tones at the fire pit. Bailey likes this about him. "I didn't know him very well before the outbreak, but he and his wife were always willing to help their neighbors...after."

"Which street are you on?" the woman asks Henry.

"Hickory Hill."

Developers named the streets in The Greens after famous golf clubs, like Hickory Hill, Cypress Point, Pine Valley. The winding streets circle down and around the country club. Muirfield Drive, closest to the golf course, has the biggest, most expensive houses. Now, they all sit empty. Six months after outbreak, and the whole place has turned from manicured splendor to wild no-man's land.

The woman hums. "I live on Gatlinburg—"

Bailey spins around. His lab partner in chemistry lives...or lived on Gatlinburg. "Are the Sawyers still... Alice Sawyer has red hair. She's tall, and she used to walk their dog most afternoons. Do you know if she's still...around?"

The woman pulls a faded cardigan around her, like she's freezing, even though the burning pit makes the air sweltering and heavy with smoke. She looks old to Bailey, but everyone seems to have aged since the outbreak. He doesn't recognize her.

"I'm not sure who is left on my street. Those kids with the crazy hair colors, they come and clean the houses out of everything worth taking, never explaining themselves, never asking—" She seems to catch herself. "But of course, our Featherton boy takes care of everything…so I'm not complaining." She wraps her sweater tighter. "Don't think I'm complaining!"

"I…I didn't think that." Once he shakes free of the old lady, Bailey grits his teeth. *Our Featherton boy*—Gabriel's last name used like an official title. *Egotistical asshole.* Out in the middle of the street, wind tugs his hair and gives him a reason to pull the hoodie strings tighter over the bite on his neck. He feels no different from how he did this morning. *How long do I have?* Before anyone knew how the virus worked, he watched classmates deteriorate over days, even weeks. But, Bailey's healthy, he might have longer.

He finds Peyton in a cluster of other neon-haired, black leather clad thugs. Gabriel's cronies. Feathertons. God! Whatever! They all have water-bottles and oranges. Bailey can't remember the last time he had an orange. One of them tosses her orange into the air, catches it with one hand like a baseball. Fruit, bottled water, candy. All walking advertisements for vanishing luxuries Gabriel can still make available. The hair dye, too. Bailey finds it pretty funny that Gabriel didn't just give them all matching jackets or uniforms. Instead, Gabriel chose their marker as the most eye-catching part of himself, his own bright hair. Only Gabriel's is natural flame red, as glossy bright as one of the unreal candy colors he insists on for all his lackeys. Bailey keeps his distance from them. Stays in the middle of the street. No traffic to worry about. No reason for anyone to waste precious gas to come to the suburbs. Nothing made here or grown here. Martial law keeps them all trapped in the same place they once considered an oasis.

"Looking pretty grim there," someone yells, and Bailey can tell they mean him. "Hey little Tyrone, I'm talking to you."

An orange rolls up to knock against Bailey's tennis shoe. He stares at it a moment, then he looks up to see a girl watching him with a half-smile. Shaggy purple bangs fall over dark eyes lined in black eye-pencil.

"You're Peyton Tyrone's little brother aren't you?"

"Sure. If you say so." Bailey has never jumped at the chance to connect the two of them as brothers. Bailey's foot nudges the orange back to her. He would never peel it here, eat it in front of the crowd of neighbors. Most of them won't see another orange for a long, long time without the help of the gangs. Gabriel can look somewhere else for advertising.

Peyton picks the orange off the ground, tosses it back toward the purple girl. She opens her free hand, palm out. "Hey, no offense. Just being nice."

"I thought you didn't like black-market food," Peyton hisses at him.

"I like the food, just not the 'selling your soul' price tag, and by the way, I didn't even touch the stupid orange. So, don't start insinuating I'm a hypocrite."

Once his brother crowds Bailey far enough away from the other neighbors, Peyton drops his cool-guy act somewhat. His shoulders relax a little. The corners of his mouth soften. "I'll get you an orange. Just stay away from them."

The flash of warmth unnerves Bailey. Peyton doesn't act this way, not now and not before. "Why are you suddenly nice? It's creeping me out."

"Quit acting like a fucking brat."

The smoke billows thick and black now, so the neighbors start to disperse. Case appears between the dark clouds, and Peyton goes stiff again. She shoots a disdainful sneer at the little cluster of Feathertons. The green-haired boy looks her up and down. "Hey, Case." He holds out the orange. "Wanna share?"

She narrows her eyes at him. "Hell no. Get that out of my face." The Feathertons cackle like witches at her refusal. Then sober up and turn away when she reaches Peyton. "Black Land Rover just turned in the back entrance near the park," she tells him.

The Land Rover belongs to Gabriel, of course. Who else would drive such a huge gas-guzzler?

Just outside the heavy hanging smoke, the shiny black SUV stops to idle. Even with windows tinted way too dark to know for sure, Bailey can feel Gabriel's eyes on him, looking him over, sizing him up, the way Gabriel always has. Bailey tugs at his hood, pulls it low to hide his face.

"I'm going to talk to him," Peyton says. "Stay out of it, just go back home and stay there until I get back."

Bailey rolls his eyes. "Where else am I going to go?"

9 PEYTON

Peyton slides into the passenger seat of the Land Rover. "The Clements…" he says and holds out the keys to his neighbors' house.

Gabriel ignores him, cold, pale eyes fixated on something outside the window. Peyton drops the keys into the center console. Gabriel's red hair gleams under the tinted windows, gelled back off the sharp planes of his face. He wears the same black leather steel-tip boots as Peyton, but his thin black sweater looks brand new, and the dark pressed slacks don't really advertise fighting or looting. Neither does his tall and thin physique. He looks like someone who still sees a personal trainer, drinks green juice, runs for exercise. Not someone who fights off half-dead creatures with a club. But Peyton still gets nervous as shit in his presence. Despite the douchey looks, Gabriel is fucking dangerous.

"And where did you leave the drugs?"

"Still in the house. They're safe. Nobody knows the shit is in there except me and Case…well and Bailey…"

"Hmmm, I see." He takes the car out of neutral and coasts slowly behind where Peyton's brother walks toward the house. "Bailey helped with clearing the house? I thought you said he disapproved of everything connected to Feathertons."

"Uh, well, not all the time. He doesn't disapprove all the time…I guess."

"Or you forced him to come with you?" Gabriel flashes a grin, even as his voice turns colder. "I told you not to recruit anyone outside the organization for dangerous jobs."

"I didn't make him do anything. Like I'd drag my weak-ass brother over to fight some locked up feral. I didn't even want him there."

"Hmmmm…"

Bailey has become an unspoken issue between them. Gabriel usually demands that anyone working for him must also recruit their siblings. He's never pushed the issue regarding Bailey. But, he makes sure to casually mention Peyton's little brother often enough.

Gabriel keeps the Land Rover crawling behind Bailey, almost walking him home. The billowing smoke from the pit drifts over his brother, engulfing him at times. It blocks him from view in thick gray clouds, then reveals him again, slump shouldered, hood pulled over his curls. Every time Peyton loses sight of his brother, he feels the truth slam against his chest like a hard punch. The virus…*inside* Bailey…inside Bailey's *brain*…

Peyton planned to bring up how Feathertons might handle a person in the territory having Super Flu. Someone infected—but not yet feral—just to check out Gabriel's reaction. Creeping behind his little brother, having to look right at him as he sputters out some hypothetical situation seems stupid now. Instead, Peyton keeps the focus on the Clements. "Someone needs to sort through the rest of their crap. I started boxing it up, but there's not much…besides the meds, I mean…" Peyton trails off. *Shit.* He just can't think of what else to say, how to bring up what he needs to know.

Gabriel raps a knuckle against the dash. Tense, clearly irritated. "I'll send some people to help you pack up the Clements' house."

"Sounds okay."

"I have Cecilia working on a register of former occupations and skills of the people left in our territory." Gabriel's eyes flick away from the smoke playing peek-a-boo with Bailey. He levels a sneer at Peyton. "We should have known that Don Clements worked in pharmaceuticals."

"Dude, it's not like he was a doctor. He was a salesman. How was I supposed to know—"

"Peyton," Gabriel interrupts. "Pay attention when I talk. This is exactly why we need a register."

Bailey finally reaches their house. He turns on the front step, glares at the Land Rover's tinted windshield like he can see into the car, like he can see Peyton screwing this up with Gabriel. Then, Bailey disappears behind the front door.

Gabriel stares after him, rubs his thumb against his lower lip. "Things are coming to a head soon, I can feel it. The patrols are dwindling, and we all want to grab for what's left. We need strength and organization, or we'll get raided and by someone stronger."

"Colton, you mean?" Feathertons has absorbed nearly all the smaller bosses in the 'burbs, but Gabriel still wants to secure the farms and ranch-lands that frame the edges of the housing developments. Jackson Colton, a former deputy sheriff, runs most all of those.

Gabriel still has all his attention outside the Land Rover, focused on Peyton's front door, where Bailey disappeared. "Yes. Colton."

Peyton grunts and leans back in the seat. Colton's crew has been a pain in his ass for months. "Any time I take a crew too far into the rural areas, we can count on a skirmish with Colton's people. I got chased out of a warehouse by Colton himself once, too. The fucker clipped my ear with a BB gun." National Guard patrols confiscated all the firearms after martial law, but people get resourceful. Peyton rubs at the scar. Colton moved pretty well for a ruddy-faced middle-aged man. "I hope that redneck catches the virus, and I get to personally beat him to death."

Gabriel tilts his head back, squeezing his eyes shut. "And there are others, too."

"What others?"

Gabriel straightens up, rubs at his lower lip again. "I've never been impressed with Colton's intelligence or his leadership abilities, but he's only recently been dangerous." Gabriel's ice blue eyes meet Peyton's as if asking a question.

Peyton doesn't get it. "Yeah, so?"

"So…someone is feeding him ideas. Making him a real threat."

"What? Who?"

Gabriel flicks his fingers like he wants to shoo away Peyton's words. "I have an idea who it might be…and I'm sure they're going to make themselves known before long." A sly smile that could mean anything on Gabriel's face. "Like I said, with the patrols dwindling, none of us need to lurk in the shadows much longer. We won't need to let the government patrols pretend they are still the ones in charge."

When they first started looting together, Peyton focused on survival…and okay…fun. So what? But Gabriel always had this big vision of taking complete control of everything. Peyton doesn't understand it. Hasn't cared that much. Until now. He risked himself so many times, and in so many ways, but this…Bailey…Bailey's life… "Yeah, I need to…" Peyton, clears his throat to start again, "I need to talk to you about something."

Gabriel sighs. "Yes, I can see that you do." He rolls his eyes and revs the engine. "Fine. I need to speak to you as well, and we should talk privately. At the house." Gabriel looks toward Peyton's front door one last time. "I wasted my time with this trip," he says, irritated and squeezing at the steering wheel with white-knuckled hands. "I could have had you bring Don's stash of pharmaceuticals to me." He gives Peyton a pointed look, nods his chin toward the dropped keys. "Load the suitcase."

***

Inside, the Clements' house smells bad. Rot, death. Peyton and Case took out the bodies but left the blood and gore. Peyton pulls the neck of his t-shirt up over his mouth and nose. He rolls the suitcase out and doesn't bother locking the door. No one will try and take anything now that they've all seen Peyton with the bodies and Gabriel's Land Rover outside. After he loads the suitcase in the hatchback, Peyton comes back to the passenger seat. "So, how did this trip waste your time?"

They cruise slowly down Hickory Hill onto Augusta, around the fire pit, and out the gate. "I only really came out here to see Case Bell, but as usual, she decided to leave as soon as I arrived. This avoidance is pointless. She needs to become one of us," Gabriel says. His eyes narrow at Peyton. "You need to work harder on that. You're her boyfriend, at least you were. She still loves you." He sneers on the word love.

Peyton's sure Case wrote him off as a bad decision long ago. And even if she didn't, he doesn't like the idea of using their former relationship to push her into Feathertons.

"She still won't. Her parents don't want her joining up." Maybe, Gabriel will never get how happy families work. That Henry and Monica actually give a shit what happens to her. That Case gives a shit what they think. "They're close. She still listens to them. Anyway, I don't think she trusts me." His mood darkens further, and he stays slumped against the passenger-side window, watching the empty streets on the drive into Olde Town neighborhood. Gabriel fenced up his entire neighborhood, turned all of it into Featherton's compound. But, all the main business happens at Gabriel's house. He holds lieutenant meetings in the dining room and everything else in a front room study that used to belong to his father. Gabriel keeps the rest of the huge stately home to himself. All to himself. No one's seen Maurice or Pauline Featherton, Gabriel's parents, since before the outbreak.

Gabriel paces behind the desk to stare down at his files and papers, probably calculating deliveries and territory. Then, he raps his knuckles on the hard wood of the desk. "Why are you here, Peyton?"

"There's a lot of empty houses in The Greens. Don and Sylvie's on my street," Peyton says. "Three on Gatlinburg. All of the back houses, closer to the golf course are empty, too." He needs a hiding place. If he finds an abandoned house…a place to keep Bailey locked up when it starts… "I was wondering what you had planned for them."

It's a dumb idea. Peyton's broken in and looted so many homes where families did exactly what Sylvie tried to do for Don. And every time, he found the same scene. The sick become ruthless when you cage them. Murderous with fear. Still, people try to hide children and parents and lovers they can't accept as beyond repair. And they all end up burning in the pit alongside the one they tried to save. *But I have to try.*

"Those houses by the golf course will be hard to fill. Too dangerous for families. But, I think they could work for people our age. People who aren't afraid of a fight." Gabriel shuffles a stack of papers.

"You want to *fill* them? How—With who?"

"All the people that will arrive once passage opens from the East."

"Not you, too. My dad won't shut up about that shit. He says it's a sign that things are getting back to normal."

That gets a mirthless laugh from Gabriel. "It's a sign that the East Coast is uninhabitable. We use wind power here, but they used nuclear power in the East." When Peyton stares back at him, blank faced, Gabriel adds, "Nuclear power plants need people to run them. There aren't any people left." He says it slowly, like he's talking to a small child. "And without anyone tending the reactors…"

Peyton clenches his jaw to keep from saying something dickish back at him. "Got it. So, you expect people to be on that road. You want them to get absorbed into Featherton territory."

"Yes, Peyton." Gabriel sucks in a breath, drums his fingers on the mahogany desk. "So, I need to promise people that they are safe from bandits, from looters." The fingers still, and he balls them into a fist. "And especially that they are safe from *the infected*. This is why I need to know if anyone gets sick, Peyton and I need to know right away." Gabriel's voice rises, "I mean *right away*, Peyton. Not like what happened with Don, when they've already killed some idiot who tried to hide them." The words ring between them.

"And then, what will you do? If someone gets sick, I mean…"

"What do you think I'll do?" Gabriel turns away to rake his long fingers through his hair. "You didn't notice anything strange about the Clements?"

Peyton jolts to find the cold pale eyes assessing him. "No. Nothing."

"God, Peyton. You're as stupid as you were in high school." Gabriel gathers himself and all the irritation slides behind his usual disaffected mask. "I don't have time for this," he says. "I need you to come to a party in Pierce Heights tomorrow. I need to make nice with the remaining patrol bosses." He slides a desk drawer open, tosses Peyton a set of keys. Peyton grabs the keys from the air, squeezes them so their teeth dig into his palm.

"Colton will be there, too." Gabriel levels a flat look at him. "No fighting."

Under any other circumstances, Peyton would be glad to go to any party. But not right now. Thank God Gabriel has turned his attention back to the papers.

"Bring whoever you want, but bring people," says Gabriel. "Make sure Case comes." He rubs at his bottom lip with his thumb. "Bring your brother." His eyes stay fixed on his desk. "I want numbers there." Then, Gabriel flicks a hand in his direction.

Dismissed.

10 Bailey

A party. With Gabriel. Not a good idea. The last time Bailey went to one of Gabriel's parties, he ignited the petty revenge plan that had Gabriel flirting with Ashley every chance he got. The guy *hates* Bailey.

In December, no one had even heard of Super Flu. Sure, on the other side of the world, a mystery virus turned people rabid and decayed, but it hadn't spread *here.* Bailey watched the videos and read the articles about it with a morbid detachment. *"Freaky."* But it had nothing to do with his life. Not like Gabriel Featherton bumping Bailey out of consideration for yearbook editor. *What a total dick.* And Gabriel had already been voted Student Council President, even taken a seat in student senate.

Oh my God!—Bailey hated him. The guy already had looks and popularity. Why did he bother to take over *another* of Bailey's clubs? Worst of all—despite bulldozing through every single one of Bailey's extracurriculars—Gabriel had to become best friends with Peyton. What a shock when he bothered to invite Bailey, Peyton's younger nerdy brother, to his Christmas party of high school elite.

"He told me to bring you. Also, you can drive 'cause I'm getting wasted." Peyton took a seat on Bailey's bed, grabbed Bailey's calculus notebook out of his hands and tossed it on the floor.

"I have a test tomorrow! And *me*? Gabriel actually used the words, *'bring Bailey to my Christmas party'* and not just, *'have your brother drive.'* He said my actual name?"

"I guess, he doesn't know what a loser you are," Peyton had said, and flicked a pencil at Bailey's head.

"Yeah…I mean, *no*. No thanks. I see way more of Gabriel than I want to already." Also, he didn't want to stand around, out of place at a party with all the most popular kids while he waited to chauffeur a drunk Peyton. His brother acted awful enough without adding alcohol.

Peyton smirked, like he knew exactly what Bailey didn't say. "You're going." Then, he punched Bailey right in the center of the chest, where he knew it fucking hurt the most.

"Fuck you, Peyton," Bailey gasped out.

But, he still went.

Bailey had expected something with waiters, champagne, and hors d'oeuvres. But the Christmas party Gabriel hosted thronged with the typical loud mess of teenagers and liquor. No waiters. No parents. Everyone belonged to Peyton's crowd and year, except a handful of the hottest junior girls, one of them Peyton's latest girlfriend. A thin blonde cheerleader from Bailey's year named Kelly. She danced, grinding against Peyton, doing her best to seduce him, not that Peyton cared. Peyton just wanted to slam against his friends, trying to turn the makeshift dance floor into a mosh pit.

Cheerleader Kelly tried complaining to Bailey. "Your brother is a dick." She reeked of cherry vodka and perfume.

"Yep." He backed away when she leaned into him for a kiss, threw his hands up between them. "No, no, no. Not gonna happen," he said and decided to retreat upstairs. All the bedrooms he passed held people making out or smoking pot. They looked right through him when Bailey paused at any doorway, except for one of the hot junior girls who met his eyes.

"What the hell are *you* doing here?" she slurred out at him.

"I have no idea. Sorry."

At last, he found refuge in a huge white marble bathroom with creamy plush carpet and a cushy love seat. "Great time, Peyton. Really glad I came." Bailey opened *Minecraft* on his phone, let the thumping music from downstairs vibrate through his body until he started drifting off. But he startled awake when the bathroom door slammed against the wall.

Peyton's blond head appeared. His brother's eyes found the phone with the game still running. "Of course. Instead of partying, my brother is hiding in the bathroom like a fucking loser."

Bailey stood up with a sigh and tossed his phone on the counter. "This party is stupid. I want to go home. Can't I just—" but he cut off when Peyton propped the door open with his hip and dragged his inebriated date inside.

Behind them, Gabriel leaned in the doorway, arms crossed and irritation all over his face. Gabriel's clingy black shirt and pressed slacks made him look like he belonged at the stuffy Christmas party Bailey had expected. He'd gelled his longish red hair to cup behind his ears. Not a strand out of place. When he caught Bailey checking him out, he raised an eyebrow. "Hello, Bailey."

"Hey."

Peyton slapped at Bailey's shoulder hard enough to knock him off balance. "My brother hates having a good time. Remember, I told you that? But you *still* wanted to invite him."

Bailey felt his face redden. *Shut up, Peyton.* "I'm not hiding. I just needed a break from…all the fun." Time to get the attention off himself. He pointed at the slumped over cheerleader. "What happened to Kelly?"

"What's it look like, genius? She fucking drank too much. Now, get out of the way." After Bailey scooted aside, Peyton draped the girl's skinny frame over the toilet. "Stay there until you're done puking," Peyton said. He let a hand hover over her back like he might pat her but gave up before he made contact.

"You're a real gentleman, Pey," Bailey said. "I see why all the girls are drawn to you."

Somebody, probably the drunk girl hugging the toilet bowl, had spilled beer down the back of Peyton's t-shirt. He craned his head in the mirror to see the stain. "Shit! Gabriel, look at this. Fucking Kelly threw a beer at me. What a psycho!" Peyton spun toward the girl and kicked a foot toward her ass.

Bailey threw an arm out, blocking him. "Stop it, Peyton. What the hell is wrong with you?"

The girl started to vomit, and Bailey knelt to pull back her hairspray-sticky, yellow curls. When she finished, panting over the toilet bowl, Peyton pointed a finger in her face, "We're broken up," he told her.

"Jesus, Peyton," Gabriel's voice snapped. "Go back downstairs. I'll take care of this."

"Yeah?" Peyton's eyes rolled, glassy and unfocused. "Thanks, man." He grabbed at Gabriel's arm as he lurched past him to rejoin the party. Gabriel cringed when Peyton touched him, but in the next second, he slid the grimace behind his usual placid boredom.

"I'll drive her home," Bailey offered. "I mean, dropping her off at her house, when she's too plastered to sneak inside, is kind of a shitty thing to do, but…" Bailey shrugged. "I don't want to leave a passed out girl alone at a party."

"You called it a stupid party." Gabriel nodded toward Bailey's abandoned phone. "Because you don't like to have a good time." His gaze traveled down to where Bailey knelt beside the girl spitting into the toilet. "According to Peyton."

Bailey jumped up to grab his phone off the bathroom counter. "Ha! Peyton's quite the jokester, right? And by 'jokester,' I mean asshole." He exited *Minecraft*, shoved his phone in the back pocket of his jeans. Gabriel just kept studying him with his creepy pale eyes, and Bailey scratched at his head. "I guess, I don't really like parties." His voice cracked a little.

"If you don't like parties, then why did you come?" Gabriel sounded genuinely curious and not accusing like Peyton would.

You told Peyton to bring me, he almost answered, but he didn't want to sound like another one of the people who fell in line behind what Gabriel dictated. Still, Bailey felt pinned by Gabriel's unflinching study of him, like he needed to give the older boy a reason that would make sense. "I was curious." He felt his cheeks heat up again. "I guess, I wondered what kind of party the great Gabriel Featherton, King of the High School, would throw." Once he said it, he realized he could not take it back. "Well, curiosity killed the cat or however that goes. I'm seriously regretting coming right now."

"The great Gabriel Featherton?"

"Oh, please." Bailey crossed his arms. "You managed to work your way to the head of the food chain of our lowly suburban high school. I'm actually in all the clubs and activities you've been hounding, even if you never noticed me. You even have Peyton's asshole friends thinking that you're one of them." Although, now that he said it, Bailey couldn't even picture Gabriel in his perfectly tailored slacks and silk shirt mixing into the mass of writhing bodies and raucous laughter on the floor below.

"I noticed you."

"Because I'm Peyton's little brother, and Pey was your ticket to the popular kids." Bailey made a scoffing laugh that he really hoped came out sounding more cool than jealous, but screw this guy. All the resentment he'd pushed down since August suddenly bubbled to the top. "Well congratulations, you get to be the top dog of a bunch of people you never knew before this year. Even though that's not *really* friendship. It's the opposite. No one actually likes you."

"I see," Gabriel said, his face expressionless and frozen. Like maybe, Bailey had hurt his feelings.

Okay, and now, Bailey felt like an asshole. "No, actually that came out a little harsh…" Bailey smoothed his hand over his mouth. "I didn't mean that the way it came out—"

"Then, how did you *mean it?*" Gabriel's casual posture against the door frame turned rigid. Bailey had forgotten the reasons Peyton tagged along behind this asshole. The street racing, the fighting. Did he really want to provoke Gabriel Featherton? Shit. No, he did not.

"Okay…" Bailey took a deep, deliberate breath. "Maybe, you're for real. But, I just can't wrap my head around the idea that someone could be friends with Peyton and also…bother with all the clubs and activities that *I'm* a part of. And dude, you're in all of them. Like every single one of them."

Gabriel's lips tightened. "Hmmm…"

"That's it? That's all you have to say?" The resentment came back in full force. If Gabriel decided to kick Bailey's ass right now, in his fancy fucking bathroom, then…fine. Bailey didn't want to back down.

"I…" Gabriel's voice sounded strangled. He turned away so fast that his one side of his hair broke loose from its perfect curve behind his ear and flopped over his face. "Did you consider that the only conspiracy happening—" He broke off with choking noise. "God—" He shook his head, and strands of the hair that had come loose caught on his lips. Then, he seemed to get control of himself, and the disinterested boredom slid back over his face. "Did you consider…" His eyes met Bailey's again. "That I might care about the same things that you care about? That I might have asked Peyton to bring you to my *stupid party* so that I could know you better? That

I thought you might be someone who…" The apathetic mask slipped again, and Gabriel waved his hand between the two of them.

What?

No, seriously… *What?* "You want to be my friend?"

"Something like that."

"Oh." Bailey thought he probably looked as flustered as Gabriel did. "But—"

Peyton's girlfriend…ex-girlfriend…Cheerleader Kelly started crying. *Thank God!* Bailey crouched down again, patted Kelly on the back.

"Why doesn't Peyton like me?" she whined, her voice echoing inside the toilet bowl.

Bailey sighed. "Peyton doesn't like anyone," he answered, but it only made her cry harder. "Come on, I'll take you home, and you can plan out a big cafeteria revenge scene. He'll hate that."

Gabriel might have started laughing then tried to hide it by clearing his throat.

Bailey looped Kelly's arm around his neck and hoisted her to her feet. Now instead of liquor and perfume, Kelly stank of vomit. Bailey tried not to breathe in her direction. Tears and snot ran down her face. "I don't want revenshh," she slurred. "I want him back."

Bailey grimaced but slid his other arm around her waist. "I'll just get you home, and you can sleep on it, okay?" He looked at Gabriel. "Ummm…"

"Right," Gabriel said. Once Bailey got her standing, Gabriel had recoiled from Kelly's sloppy steps and dripping face. "I'll show you out the maid's entrance." Gabriel led them from the main hallway, to a door and a second more narrow hallway and back staircase.

Crap. Stairs. "A little help here?" he called out, and Gabriel backtracked.

He made a pained expression, but he put an arm around the drunk girl's waist. And the two of them maneuvered Kelly down the steep wooden staircase. It ended in a side door and opened to the long curving drive with a blast of icy air.

Bailey jogged off to start the car and got the heat going, then pulled his dad's Cadillac up the drive. Mason had let them take the car, as long as Peyton promised Bailey would drive home.

Kelly slumped asleep in Gabriel's arms, her head thrown back against his shoulder as she snored way louder than Bailey would have believed the skinny cheerleader capable of. Gabriel held her body as far away from his own as possible and looked so stiff and uncomfortable that Bailey couldn't keep from snickering. They both loaded Kelly into the car, and Bailey strapped her seatbelt on.

"Man, I really hope she wakes up before I get to her house. I do not want to meet her parents." Bailey stood by the driver's side door, ready to go, but feeling like he didn't want to get in and drive away. Not yet. "Be sure and tell Peyton that he needs to find his own way home. He'll take the news better from you than me."

"Not really." The struggle to get Kelly down the stairs had mussed Gabriel's clothes. His shirt had come untucked on one side and the rest of his hair hung loose around his face. "He only takes things well if I bribe him...or threaten him." Gabriel took a step closer.

"I don't even want to know." Bailey curled his hands up into the edge of his sweater, shivering. "But I'm not going to deal with him, not when he's been drinking." How strange to talk like this to Gabriel, after all the time spent grinding his teeth whenever someone brought up his name. "Anyway, you must be better at dealing with my brother than I am."

"What makes you say that?"

"Well...you're his friend."

"You're his brother," Gabriel countered, "And being friends with Peyton might have been a miscalculation."

"Miscalculation?" A grin broke free. "That's weird. Friendship shouldn't involve...math." His smile became a laugh. Had he and Gabriel just bonded?

Gabriel stood a little too close, looked at Bailey with serious concentration.

"What?" Bailey asked.

"The way he talked about you...I thought you were closer."

"Peyton talks about me? Wait, you befriended Peyton because of *me*?"

Gabriel's hand sunk into Bailey's curls and clutched. He drew Bailey's face up toward his own.

He's going to kiss me, Bailey thought.

But, Gabriel stopped and let their lips hover together, never quite touching. "Yes. Because of you," Gabriel whispered into the hair's breadth between them. Then, he dipped forward, and his mouth covered Bailey's, lips pressed hard to Bailey's, their teeth scraping for a second. Gabriel's tongue entered his mouth, and the kiss became hotter, wetter. The hand in Bailey's hair loosened its clutch, and his fingertips smoothed out along Bailey's scalp, pulling him in even closer.

When they broke apart, Bailey sucked in a gulp of air and then sprang back. He'd forgotten the open car door and smacked his wrist hard against the frame. "Shit. Ouch." He felt way too winded from the timespan of a single kiss. *Oh, my God.* His heart raced. *What had just happened?*

"Listen, nothing personal, but that was...a mistake." He scrubbed both hands against the top of his head. What the *hell* had just happened? "First of all...I'm not even..." He scrunched his whole face. He'd definitely kissed back. Whatever that meant, he needed to take a lot of time to figure out. A whole fucking lot of time. "Well...I mean, to this point, I haven't actually been...gay. But beside that, and this is the most important reason, you and I can't happen because of—"

"Your little girlfriend?"

"Yeeeeaaaah," but he hadn't been thinking of Ashley. He'd been about to say, "Because of Peyton." He and Peyton did not share friends. They did not venture into each other's social circles. Specifically, Bailey did not venture into Peyton's circle. And Gabriel occupied the main space in that circle. So...this could not happen *because of Peyton.*

Although, yeah, Ashley qualified as another, and maybe even more significant, obstacle. One that Bailey had forgotten about...for some reason. "I'm dating Ashley. She's like, perfect for me. She and I are...solid."

"Are you really?" And in the snarky way he said it, Bailey knew that Gabriel had just concocted an evil plan to break them up. Because Gabriel looked pissed off. Like, not that blank icy, superior look he always got. Angry. Tensed up muscles and balled fists. That sneer on his face. He revealed something about himself to Bailey. Gotten shut down by Bailey. And now, Gabriel wanted to destroy Bailey.

"Like I said, it's not about...you. I'm dating Ashley and...other factors..." Bailey had kissed him back, didn't he? Yep. He definitely did kiss back. "But, I won't...I would never...tell anyone. Okay? I won't tell anyone about this."

"I don't care who you tell." The molten anger in Gabriel's face and body made Bailey decide it would be best to stop talking and drive Kelly home.

"Okay. Well...bye then." He got in the car. Dropped the keys and had to dig around on the floorboard for them, but he did manage to get the stupid Cadillac started.

In the rearview mirror, Gabriel's black clothes hid him in the nighttime shadows. But his pale skin and vivid hair glowed, so that he resembled a phantom. Not something that Bailey felt safe to turn his back toward, a furious and vengeful ghost watching him from the inky dark.

⋀⋀ PEYTØN

Gabriel gave him permission to drive his Land Rover to the party in Pierce Heights but nowhere else. That bitch Cecilia even wrote down the mileage before Peyton left Gabriel's house.

"Whatever." He leaves the Land Rover parked in the driveway and rolls his black Suzuki Marauder motorcycle out from the garage. He traded Lila's Audi for it at the beginning of the outbreak, even though he hadn't known anything about bikes. His dad's Cadillac still sits in the garage doing fucking nothing. Mason refused to trade his luxury car early on, and now, no one wants it. What a moron. Especially because, right from the start, shit looked *bleak*. Cities, towns, neighborhoods filled with dead and dying.

Peyton, Bailey, and their parents spent the first months of martial law just cowering at home. No one in the house dared to say Lucy's name or question aloud what might have happened to her, but it hung in the air between them like a suffocating fog. Tension so tight that entire days went by with none of them speaking. National Guard passed out rations and carted off the sick, but never offered answers to questions about the roads outside the suburbs. No matter how much Lila begged them or how many times Peyton got in their faces.

"Break quarantine, and we'll shoot you."

He'd still considered trying to drive out to Missouri, figure out what happened at the soccer tournament. Find his little sister. Fuck martial law. Fuck the patrols. Fuck the swarms of feral sick and the virus. But he couldn't make himself do it. He wouldn't abandon

Bailey for only a slight chance at finding Lucy. He couldn't lose both of them.

Just when Peyton didn't think he could take another day caged in the house, Gabriel pulled onto the lawn in a Ford Super-Duty pickup. His friend looked rough, bruises on his face, scabs on his hands and arms. Despite his banged up appearance, he held the same cold control in place. Gabriel had decided that martial law didn't apply to him, had evaded the patrols, and dodged the sick. After eight weeks of empty streets, the loud and massive truck drew their neighbors from their houses. Case, her parents, and the Davidsons all came out onto their front yards. Sylvie and Don Clements cracked their door open to see.

Peyton patted the truck's expansive hood. "Where did this come from?"

Gabriel swung down from the running board, one hand still gripping the wide truck door. "I stole it." He sounded breathless and urgent. "I came because—"

"Dude, seriously? You stole this?"

"*Yes.* Now, shut up. I need to know... Are you sick? *Any* of you..."

Bailey came out behind Peyton, and Gabriel's voice trailed off. His eyes fixed on Peyton's brother like he expected Bailey to pop right in front of him. "Are you *alright?*" he barked out.

Bailey took a step backward, eyebrows creeping into his tangled hair. "Uhh...yeah?"

"There's been close calls here in The Greens," Peyton answered. "Some stray feral sick coming in off the highway. People popping and..." He imitated swinging a bat, clubbing someone to death.

Bailey shoved him. "Stop it."

Peyton ignored his brother. Snapped his fingers. "Gabriel, do you remember Cody Fanshier from government class? Dude took out his whole family. Like ripped them to pieces. He lived on Merion though." Peyton shrugged and used his thumb to indicate the back of the neighborhood. "Nothing on our street. Not like what's in the news." As he said it, he realized his bone-deep frustration at how little he'd actually seen and done since the outbreak. He itched for a chance to take action instead of standing locked in place, endlessly waiting. "Anyway, man, you look like shit. What happened?"

Gabriel's eyes tightened. "I've been on the roads, looking for what's left." He kept his voice low enough, so the gawking neighbors couldn't hear. "And I'm stockpiling things we might need."

"On the road?" Peyton didn't bother trying to hide the grin spreading across his face.

"Yes. You should join me," said Gabriel. He made breaking martial law in his giant stolen truck sound like an afternoon at the lake.

Peyton wasn't sure what the word "stockpiling" even meant, but Bailey caught on right away. "Looting you mean?" His brother accused. "You've been looting while people around you are getting sick and *dying*?" Bailey acted all pissy about it.

"It's not looting if they're dead," said Peyton. He pushed Bailey back.

Bailey rolled his eyes. "*Yes,* it is. That's still considered looting, you idiot." Bailey did that folded arms and foot stomp combo that made him look like a toddler. "Don't go with him, Peyton. What he's doing is illegal and *wrong*."

Gabriel gave Bailey a cold look that made Peyton nervous. "This doesn't concern you."

Peyton bristled at having someone besides himself order around his little brother. But from the moment he first saw the heavy duty pickup, desperation surged through Peyton's body like he'd touched an electric current. And Peyton wanted, no he *needed,* to get out of the house. "Yeah. Go back inside, Bailey. Take care of Mom."

"God, I can't stand *either* of you," Bailey muttered.

When Peyton turned back, Gabriel squeezed his eyes closed, which made the bruises on his face, the thin scabs, more pronounced. Man, whatever Gabriel had gotten into had really tested him. That electricity inside Peyton grew stronger with yearning.

Gabriel's eyes flew open again, and he'd transformed back to the impenetrable bastard Peyton recognized. "If you want to come with me, you'll need a weapon. Those creatures that the sick turn into? They like to hide out in abandoned places, which is where we're going."

"A weapon? Like a club?" He'd seen the patrols use metal prods to cage the sick up. But the internet had countless videos of people fighting them with baseball bats, tire irons, shovels, and pipes.

"You'll have to kill them. Can you do that?"

Unleash his frustration on the fucking things spreading the virus everywhere? The same kind of animals that probably killed his little sister, Lucy? "Hell, yeah."

And that was the start of Feathertons.

With both parents in a shocked stupor, Peyton let Gabriel lead all his decisions—trading for the motorcycle, looting malls and pharmacies, sourcing fuel, food, better fighting gear. Peyton went with all of it. And he loved it. Fighting was so much better than football. *No cumbersome rules. No tedious practice.* He didn't have to hold back when aggression filled his nerves and muscles. *The very real weight of life and death.* Football had never given him such a rush.

***

Peyton gets the Marauder started and flies down the street, toward the back of the neighborhood. Faces turn as he cruises down the curving streets. People live outside much more since the outbreak, mostly because of the inconsistent electricity. During the summer, they sat on their porches to escape the heat. But now that the weather cooled, they come outside to be social. A lot of people have dug fire pits into their front yard—practical for cooking and scaring creatures—but between those and the neighborhood pit, the heavy bite of smoke never really leaves the air. All Peyton's clothes, everyone's hair, stinks of it.

The winding streets of The Greens spiral down from his house on Hickory Hill toward Muirfield, the street that lines the golf course. He stays wary of threats from the course and the houses themselves. These houses don't have fire pits, or people, or lights, all of them unoccupied now. The same proximity to the country club golf course that made them so valuable before Super Flu has turned them dangerous, uninhabitable. Deer, coyotes, and even the occasional bear have started to reclaim these places. Possums and raccoons scavenge near all the abandoned homes.

Peyton turns the bike from the wide paved street to the cobbled back path that runs between the outer length of the course and the sprawling houses perched on its edge. In the waning light of the late afternoon, the high flat planes of their windows reflect the wild overgrowth of the course. At one of the homes, he finds what he searches for, a little gray guest house set toward the back of the drive.

That's perfect, he thinks. *I can keep Bailey hidden here, take care of him.* He'll have to ask for the house before Gabriel starts to parcel out the homes for his own plans. Peyton can claim he wants it as a party house or a dojo. Then, he'll lock his brother inside and wait for the virus to pass. He'll block the tiny round windows, push food through the old-fashioned mail slot. *This could work.*

bargaining

12 Bailey

One of Peyton's Featherton friends, a tall, dark-skinned boy named Drummer meets them at the house before Gabriel's party. He has neon-orange dreadlocks sprouting like a fountain from the top of his head. He grabs Bailey's shoulder and shakes it. "Hey, little Tyrone wants to party. Cool. You planning to join up?"

"No—"

"*Fuck*, no!"

Bailey's head whips to stare at his brother, but Drummer doesn't question Peyton's answer, his eyes too busy taking in Case's tight jeans and cleavage. "Girl, *that's* what I'm talking about." She doesn't dress like a girl that often, but when she does...

Peyton smacks a hand on the hood of the Land Rover. "Get in the damn car." He makes Bailey take the passenger side. Case takes the seat in back of Peyton with Drummer beside her.

From the lower half of The Greens, they also pick up a pair of brothers, both with peacock blue and purple hair, Hugo and Felix Mageo. Both of them older than Peyton, college age. They squeeze together into the back. "Drummer. Good to see you alive, man!" one of them says.

Drummer does a complicated handshake with each of them. "Surviving this shit takes skill," he agrees.

Peyton doesn't bother introducing anyone, but Hugo recognizes Case. "You're Via Bell's kid sister, right?"

Case doesn't match Hugo's enthusiasm, doesn't even crack a smile. "That's right."

"Oh man, Via demolished Grant High our senior year. Thirty points—all hers. My cousin was point guard for Grant that night." Hugo either doesn't notice or doesn't care that Case just looks more annoyed the longer he talks. "Yeah, my cousin said they all got starstruck when they played her. Via still around?"

Case shakes her head, and Peyton butts in. "Not cool man," he says. "Don't ask people that. What's wrong with you?"

Hugo's brother leans forward. "Sorry," Felix says.

One last stop and a girl holding a chained bat like Peyton's crowds inside by Bailey. Her frizzy green hair, matches her jeans and her heavy boots. Only Case and Bailey have natural hair and tennis shoes. All the Feathertons wear the steel toes and carry weapons. Drummer even brought a long axe with him. He tucked it between his extra-long legs. Whenever the Land Rover bounces over a pothole, all the chains and metal weapons clink and rattle.

Gabriel's holds his party at Pierce Heights, probably the ritziest of all the neighborhoods in Featherton territory. Mostly old, rich people used to live inside its mansions, but now, Gabriel populates it with all the orphaned teens under his protection. They've let the sprawling lawns and wide streets go full apocalypse. Front yards turned into wild grass and thicket, giant picture windows boarded with homemade shutters, expensive cars stripped and rusting on the streets and in the drives. The street lights still work though.

The party house even has festive fairy strings wound all around it. And guards…with big guns. "Who are they?" Bailey asks.

"Assholes." Peyton flips one of them off, a man with a buzz cut hair and a sharp, angry face.

"O…kay."

"Don't worry, little Tyrone." Drummer thumps Bailey's shoulder. "City people probably brought them for protection against creatures. But, they know to leave us alone." And, like Drummer said, the guards don't give the Land Rover even a glance, but stare out into the pitch black of suburban darkness. "All the City bosses think if they step foot outside their barricades, a pack of feral sick will charge them."

Peyton points a finger gun at Bailey. "I saw one of the patrol unload twenty rounds, and the creature still took a chunk out of him." He laughs, like he just remembered a really good joke.

Inside the house, thumping music echoes through a minimalist-bare great room with floor-to-ceiling windows and expansive, glossy black granite floor. Whoever owned this house before Gabriel had good taste. Government patrolmen in military uniforms and a handful of younger professional-looking adults mix in with the candy-colored heads of Featherton teenagers. Most of the military guys look like they've aged out of the virus survival range by a decade or more.

Peyton looks over the crowd. "Don't see any of Colton's people so far."

"How do you know?"

Drummer slings an arm around Bailey's neck. "Oh, we'd know. They'd be the only ones wearing flannel, missing teeth, and stinking of cow shit." He laughs at his own description. "Also, they are not our fans, not at all. They hate us for being young and beautiful, am I right?"

"I can't wait for them to all get Super Flu. Fuck them," Peyton says. The peacock-haired brothers laugh. "It's only a matter of time, and all the old people will be dead. Good riddance. More for us."

The government guys standing closest to Peyton look murderous.

"I'm sure Gabriel really appreciates your honesty on that subject, Pey." Bailey shrugs out of Drummers hold and slips his hands inside the front pocket of his hoodie. A new hoodie. He'd finally had the guts to take Don's old one off and face the gauze bandage, the bite. When he tries to follow his brother through the crowd, a statuesque blonde woman puts a hand on Bailey's arm, stops him.

"You're friends with Gabriel? Gabriel *Featherton*?" Her voice twists on Gabriel's last name, the name he shares with all the people who work for him. She wears a tight black cocktail dress and pearls, strawberry blonde hair styled into loose waves, makeup perfect. Like the apocalypse of Super Flu never happened. *Definitely from the City.* "He *is* coming tonight, isn't he?" Her grip belies the casual tone of her voice, and something about her eyes unnerves him.

"That's what I hear…" The woman's fingernails dig into his arm. "And owww…" Even with the thick hoodie on, it hurts. He tries pulling his arm loose, but she doesn't let go. Long glittery nails dig in tighter. This might be the best looking woman to ever speak to Bailey, but in combination with that claw in his arm, he can't really enjoy the experience.

"You don't know? How can you not know?"

Bailey pulls on one of his dishwater curls. "Look at me. I'm not one of them. I'm a nobody." He gestures forward to Peyton's broad back and tangled blue hair. "He's the friend of Gabriel's. Not me." The woman squints at Peyton, finally releasing Bailey's arm. *Thank fuck.*

Bailey slaps a hand over the place her talons had hooked into him. Luckily, she didn't draw blood. *Infected blood.* He might have had to out himself to the entire party. *God!*

"That's the Tyrone boy, isn't it?" Her eyes move to track Peyton's progress through the crowd. "The football player." She reminds Bailey of a cat, a *mean* cat. He takes a step back from her long fingernails.

"Uh…yeah, that's my older brother, Peyton, the lieutenant for The Greens. And I really need to…" *Get as far away from this psychobitch as possible.* He points in the direction Peyton disappeared. "So…" Bailey darts into the crowd. For once, desperate to follow in his brother's wake.

In the kitchen, a line of underage kids pour liquor into tall glasses and hand them out. A tower of fruit, and raw vegetables, bakery cakes, cheese, ice cream melting in big round tubs—all the foods considered luxuries since Super Flu. Bailey, who has eaten too many of the bland packaged rations since the outbreak, stares at the fruit with longing. And like everyone else in the house, Bailey sees the message Gabriel sends, *look at what I can get you. Look at what I can give away.*

At Gabriel's Christmas party, Peyton had ditched him. But now, his older brother links a hand around Bailey's wrist like a cuff. "Quit getting lost."

"I wasn't lost."

Peyton drags him through the kitchen toward an expansive back deck. Two grills smoke with burgers and steaks. Plenty of meat since the outbreak. It's easier to kill livestock than take care of them. Plenty for now at least. The redwood deck hangs over a wild yard overgrown in weeds and lit up with LED spotlights. The pale cement bottom of a pool stares up empty, socket-like. The cool air outside feels good. Bailey pulls loose from his brother's grip. When Peyton makes another grab for his arm, he waves toward the grills. "Hungry."

But before he makes it to the grills, the crowd outside yelps and surges. The blaring sound of car horns and white headlight beams pierce through the wilderness behind the house like fat lasers. Pickup trucks, four of them, crash through the cedar fence surrounding the party. Oversize tires ramble forward, taking out the LEDs, crunching over the fallen leaves and dead grass. The trucks stop suddenly to frame the empty pool with hot light.

The men launching themselves out of the trucks wear ballcaps, flannel shirts, denim work jackets. Country people. *Colton's people*—Feathertons' main rival. Bailey isn't close enough to test Drummer's claim that they all smell like cow shit. The entire house party empties to the backyard deck and patio to watch, and Bailey stumbles forward in the press of people. Energy hums around him. He tries to edge backward, sliding between the bodies straining forward to make his way out of the crowd. But, he gets jostled to the side and ends up by the back railing, still in view of the eerily lit hollow of the swimming pool. Beside him, the garish, colored heads of the Feathertons part, and attention turns from the trucks to a point in back of Bailey.

"Gabriel's here."

"Gabriel—"

Feathertons' sleek, black-suited leader strides out onto the deck. His hair smooth and unruffled, his pale eyes expressionless. But then, the pickup trucks below them blast some cacophonous mix of music—maybe country and rock—maybe techno and country—and everyone looks again toward Colton's trucks. Peyton has even climbed on the railing to watch. He cranes his upper body forward like he wants to leap the twenty feet down, right into the frenzy of the back yard. Crisscrossing headlights over the empty pool give the illusion of water, and at first, Bailey thinks the people in the trucks dive into that illusion.

But no one is diving into the pool—someone is pushing them.

The sick...*creatures*...arms bound to their bodies with rope. Colton's men fling them into the empty pool and then leap down after them with weapons. The creatures dart circles around the pool howling and terrified. All the creatures in the pool behave as if newly turned: fast, crazed, lunging away at first, then charging the men with

70

snapping teeth. If they hadn't trussed up the creatures' arms, the men in the pool would face certain infection. One man slams a hatchet into the head of a young girl. So small, maybe seventy or eighty pounds, that he cleaves through her skull to demolish her brain stem. The man raises his arms in the air, face red with heat, sweat staining the pits of his faded football jersey.

Touchdown.

The partygoers cheer and rush the railing to drop into the yard. They want to join in—"creature cracking." Bailey saw videos on the internet calling it that—he never clicked on them. He heard Peyton talk about it—he never listened. And to see it now, nausea curls up inside him from a tight hard place in his chest. In the pool, a young boy—*not a boy*—*one of the creatures*—lies on his side and tries to wriggle from the heavy ropes. The crowd sprouts tentacles, as waving arms point at him. Spectators shrieking, writhing. A ponytailed man circles the struggling boy, and then two of the ball-capped men drop down into the pool bed to join him.

"Stop!" Bailey shouts a second before the throng around him flares into cheers and yelps.

Only Gabriel turns to stare at him.

The bound boy jerks and screams, then snaps his teeth just before they close him inside, clubs pounding on his back and head in vertical, drill-like thrusts.

"Fuck." Bailey's vision wobbles, and he grasps his knees. The crowd blurs around him as he tries to suck air into his lungs. *I'm going to pass out.*

Someone's arm comes down heavy across Bailey's chest and hauls him backward through the crowd. Even when he lurches over, vomits onto the redwood deck, whoever has hold of him—*Peyton?*—does not let go. Bailey finds himself inside the kitchen again, face over the chrome sink. Someone tugs his hoodie to the side and a wet cloth slaps down on the back of his neck. "You shouldn't drink on an empty stomach," Gabriel tells him. *Gabriel? Oh, perfect. Just perfect.*

Bailey yanks the cloth away. He tugs the hoodie back in place. "I'm not drunk." Bailey scoops handfuls of the water into his mouth to rinse it then uses his fingers to claw his hair back from his face.

"Alright. If you say so." Gabriel hands him a glass of something bubbly and sweet, and Bailey gulps it all down, lets Gabriel take the empty glass and refill it.

"I'm not." His curls have sprung up with extra force from the damp, and they bounce back over his face. "You think I'm puking because I'm drunk? You saw what's happening out there. It's sick." His stomach clenches again, and he braces an arm on the counter, tries to fight off the new wave of nausea. "What you're letting them do is so fucking wrong."

"Me? I'm not out there. I'm not encouraging it. Those are Jackson Colton's trucks unloading creatures into the pool." Gabriel's mild voice only infuriates Bailey.

"So, you don't even care?"

Gabriel searches Bailey's face, reading something off him while giving nothing away. Bailey wraps his arms around himself. "This is *your* party, you should stop it."

"Yes, he should stop it." The evil blonde woman again. Both Bailey and Gabriel startle at her appearance, and her eyes widen as if delighted to catch them by surprise. Well, not *them*. Gabriel. "But it wouldn't be very smart to try to stop it. Isn't that right, Gabriel?" She reaches fingers up, those glitter-polished nails that had clamped into Bailey's arm earlier, but she threads them into Gabriel's red hair, traces the sparkling nails around his ear. "You look well, Gabriel."

Bailey's mouth drops open for a second, but he recovers quick enough. "Hi, *again*," he says to her. And though Gabriel stood still for the blonde's brazen caress, he now pulls away from her at Bailey's words.

His lip curls. "Again?"

The blonde laughs, but it sounds fake and a little deranged, too. "I don't think you're impressing anyone from the government patrols with that display out back, Gabriel." She pronounces his name in the French way, and it sounds a lot like the female version of the name, Gabrielle. "This only confirms all the talk of how savage and uncivilized life has become outside of the cities." Her pink lips form a pout. "A waste of resources, really."

"Why did you come here, Renée?" Gabriel's icy anger startles Bailey. He only knew the entitled and charming version that took over all his clubs, not the dangerous Featherton boss. Gabriel leans into the blonde. "Did you organize what's happening out there? Did you, Renée?" Whatever he sees in her face must answer the question. His hands clench.

"I have no idea what you mean." She blinks in a mockery of innocence, but her long dark lashes don't quite get her there. Her eyes are too pale and cold. *Wait...* Bailey's knows those eyes.

No frickin way!

Gabriel sighs as if bored, but it looks schooled. Bailey sees the white knuckled grip Gabriel has on the counter behind him. "This is pointless, Renée. All the hatred you think you have for me—"

"Of course, I don't hate you, Gabriel!" She reaches out to touch him again, but he steps away from her pale fingers, the glittery sharp nails. "You're my brother." She lets loose with another creepy fake laugh, leans closer. "I'm sorry that your party didn't turn out the way you wanted, *freak*." When she strolls out the door, she takes a chunk of the party with her—those out-of-place young professional types—the military uniform guys, too.

"Impressive," says Bailey. "I haven't heard someone actually *cackle* since I quit watching Disney movies. So, that's your sister?" His brain-to-mouth filter never works when he really needs it. Gabriel slants an unimpressed look his way, but Bailey doesn't let that deter him. "I didn't know you had an older sister. She didn't go to our school."

"We're twins. And Renée went to boarding school," Gabriel mutters. "She also graduated early, took a gap-year to work an internship. She lives in a penthouse downtown."

"So, that rumor about you coming from…well getting kicked out of boarding school…" Bailey squints at him. "Feel free to jump in here with details."

"No, thank you," Gabriel says. So stiff, always so stiff. "Living in my territory doesn't allow you details to my life. You aren't even a Featherton."

Right. For a second there, Bailey forgot. Gabriel Featherton, arrogant prick. And in this new post-outbreak world? Also a crime boss. "Fair enough." Bailey shrugs. "I'm just a meaningless pawn in your empire. Peyton's insignificant little brother. I get that a lot." He tries to sound like he doesn't care. But he does. His teeth grind. He cares a lot.

Gabriel stands up straighter. "That's not what—"

"Hey, you know what?" Bailey interrupts. "You and Renée, I can see the resemblance. Evil, that's a family trait I guess? Or is it a twin thing? Shouldn't there be a good twin? Please don't tell me *you're* the good twin?" He's gotten worked up enough that his voice has gone squeaky, and he needs to catch his breath. *Shit.* He went too far. He should apologize…

Because he has a feeling that pissing off Gabriel—head of the Feathertons—King of the Suburbs—might not just end with awkwardness and…kissing.

But Gabriel doesn't get pissed off, he just puts that dispassionate veneer back in place. And without another word, he storms off on the same path that his sister left, with some of his own minions trailing behind.

Tonight, Peyton makes Bailey drive home. Case sits beside him in the front with her legs drawn up to her chest and her forehead pressed to the passenger side glass. Bailey didn't see her take a turn in the pool, while Peyton and the others drank and killed, and cheered others killing. Peyton, Drummer, and the two brothers have crammed in the backseat together, laughing too loud, talking too loud, acting way too proud about things that nobody should brag about. Bailey keeps his eyes on the pitch dark of the road, but his brother and the others reek so strongly of liquor and the heavy scent of blood that Bailey tastes it in the air.

13 PEYTØN

Peyton jolts awake on the couch. A long clanging percussion makes him grab hold of his head. "Cut that fucking racket down," he yells, then has to kick free of the twisted nest of blankets he dragged downstairs last night. He'd thought he couldn't sleep, too drunk, too amped up from creature cracking in that empty pool. Looks like he managed to anyway.

From the kitchen, Mason pretends to talk to himself. "Not much to eat in here," he says, voice loud enough for Peyton to hear in the other room. "The rations are almost out." Mason sets the table every morning, even a place for Lila, who doesn't always bother to get up and only picks at her food when she does. And since the bite, Bailey sometimes skips breakfast, too.

Peyton shuffles into the kitchen, just as Mason cracks the last egg on the edge of the counter, lets it slide into a pan. He never cooked before the outbreak, never set the table, never talked about food. "Can't you get a loan from Feathertons? An extra pack of food?"

"I don't want to use up all my favors with Gabriel right now."

Mason turns from the stove. "Why? So you can save up favors for yourself? What about your family?" Mason throws the rubber spatula across the counter. The egg sizzles in the silence. Peyton's father used to ask him about football, about girls. He took Peyton to baseball games and golfing and car shopping. Now, he hassles him about groceries, passes judgement on how Peyton gets those groceries.

Peyton grabs a can of Coke from the ice chest. The fridge became pretty useless once they didn't have reliable power. All the utilities—electricity, natural gas, the internet—all flicker off and on. All of them needed people to keep them running, and people are in short supply. "Is Mom getting up today?" He cracks open the can and takes a long swig out of it.

"Yes." Mason slides his egg onto a plate. Either because of the egg or because of Lila, his father won't meet his eyes. "Monica brought her over some more of those pills, the ones for her nerves."

"She just takes them to… She doesn't have nerves." Peyton feels a sick relief at this subject change. So familiar. So *before*. Peyton gulps down the rest of the Coke, lets the carbonation burn in his chest.

"Peyton. Your mother does need them." Even Mason must find comfort in the old argument rehashed between them. "They seem to be helping." His father speaks around bites of the egg, scrapes his plate with his fork.

"That's what you always say in the beginning…" Peyton rolls the empty soda can between his palms. A familiar anger simmers inside of him. "She's a fucking drug addict."

"Lower your voice!" Mason wipes at his face. "Do you want Bailey to hear?" The old argument again with the one point that always united them—Bailey, *Lucy,* can't know. But, now Peyton has another secret, another devastating truth to conceal. *Bailey could have already changed by now.* It happens that fast sometimes. Peyton shudders at the thought of Bailey, upstairs in his room, shivering and crazed looking like Don was last week. *No, no, he wouldn't go that fast. He's strong. He's healthy.*

Mason hums as he swabs the egg from his plate with a piece of bread. "We'll get your mother straightened out just as soon as things settle down. They'll start clearing the roads, and the clinics will open again."

"Who is *they*, Dad? Who's left to do that? No one is fucking left. This is the world now, and it's all gone to shit, and it's going to stay there." Peyton crushes the can in his fist and tosses it over his dad's head toward the sink. It clatters off the tile backsplash with a ringing clatter.

"You'll see, Peyton. Everything will go back to how it was before all this mess, and we'll get your mother straightened out—"

"Like suddenly you care."

***

That same day Lucy left for the soccer tournament, Peyton walked in on his father packing a suitcase. It made a loud squeaky noise when Mason dragged it out from under the king size bed he and Lila shared.

"Where are you going? I thought we were golfing today." Peyton's good mood still fizzed through his veins after an all-nighter with Leena Fraser. Gabriel had let him borrow the Lexus. He'd crawled out of Leena's bedroom window and cruised off—the car's lustrous paint so reflective in the bright early morning sun that he'd turned the heads of all the suburban joggers, the moms pushing strollers, and the old people fussing at their lawns. Like a goddam movie star, yeah.

"Dad?"

Mason smoothed down his pale pink golf shirt as he tucked it into his pressed khaki pants. "I need to think about myself for once, Pey," he'd said.

"Yourself?" Peyton deadpanned.

Mason zipped the case closed in a single angry pull. "You see how difficult it is with…" His father didn't need to say the next words aloud. He just pointed out the bedroom door. And Peyton knew that vague gesture meant his mother.

"What happened?" *Jesus,* Peyton thought. *I've only been gone for a single night.* He'd just wanted to blow off some steam after the game. Get laid. Everything seemed normal enough just a few seconds ago: Bailey pouting that Ashley blew him off the night before. Lucy bouncing out the door on her way to a soccer tournament. What had his mother managed to do in the last twenty-four hours to drive his father to pack a bag? "Where are you going, Dad?"

Finally, Mason turned to face him. "I've met someone and—"

Peyton couldn't help the burst of laughter. "You *met* someone?" What a fucking joke. His father had met a whole string of *someones.* Peyton held up one hand, ready to tick them all off one by one. "Do you mean Bailey's journalism teacher, Ms. Bradley?" Then, he snapped his fingers. "Or, she dumped you I think…how about Sheri in reception up at the club? Or that tennis pro, Dayna?" The hand became a fist, and Peyton lowered it, nodded at the suitcase. "I don't think Mom is going to buy you leaving on another 'business trip' this month."

Mason had grown red-faced and angry as Peyton listed his conquests. He always hated getting holes poked in his "great guy" facade. "I'm not having this discussion with you, son. It's not me you should be finding fault with anyway. You see what I've had to deal with all these years." He hefted the suitcase and rolled it back in its hiding spot under the bed.

Yeah, yeah. You've been a real hero, Peyton just managed not to say it. "So, who is it? When are you coming back?"

His dad did that infuriating hand-brushing thing, even though he hadn't gotten a speck of dust or dirt on himself. A showy motion of "good riddance" that had more to do with Lila and his family than the underside of the bed. "I might as well be honest about it. I'm sure Gabriel will have something to say about—"

"Gabriel? What about Gabriel?" Peyton still had to go to the Featherton house and return the borrowed Lexus.

"Pauline and I have fallen in love."

Peyton could picture the statuesque redhead, pale icy eyes like her son. The diamonds on her fingers and in her earlobes. The designer clothes, designer bags, designer life. She would never leave a high-roller like Maurice Featherton for someone as inconsequential as Peyton's father. "Pauline Featherton doesn't love you, Dad. She's stone cold like Gabriel."

The doorbell rang ,and they could hear Bailey shouting for them, that Henry Bell waited with his clubs on the front step.

"We'll talk about this later," Mason said and then plastered on that easy-going "great guy" smile for Henry Bell, for his other golfing buddies at the country club.

***

Peyton has just sunk back into the couch and his blanket nest when a pounding on the front door makes him jump. Mason comes out from the kitchen wringing his hands like an old woman. "Who is it? What do they want?"

Peyton throws the blankets aside, scrubs at his face. "Relax, Dad. It's probably just someone wanting something killed." Peyton doesn't mind helping out his neighbors, as long as the kind of help needed requires a weapon.

"We're not supposed to just run out and kill them without warning," Mason says, flushed and jittery. "We're supposed to contact Neighborhood Watch…" Peyton's father goes for the radio. But, before he can make a call, Peyton jerks the door open.

Instead of a harried neighbor with a club, Gabriel stands on the front porch, meticulous in one of his dark suits. A gust of fall air comes in with him, a spray of dried leaves.

Mason drops the radio handset. "Gabriel! Come in! Come in!"

Gabriel's eyes track over Mason with the same impersonal look he gives everyone now. He used to fake a smile, teeth showing. *"Hello, Mr. Tyrone. How are you? I hear you placed third in the club's golf tournament…"* But he would never lower himself to that now. He no longer needs anyone to like him. So, he ignores Mason, looking to Peyton instead. "I've had people cleaning up from your party activities. Seventeen bodies we had to drag out of that pool crater and burn."

Peyton crosses his arms. "Did you seriously come here just to bitch at me about leaving behind a bunch of dead feral?"

Gabriel's mouth twists. He huffs air out his nose, frustrated. "I'm more irritated that you dove right in to kill them in the first place."

Mason jumps up to offer a cup of coffee from their dwindling rations. Gabriel raises an eyebrow at the proffered mug like it offends him.

"Actually, I wanted to speak with Bailey, see if he's feeling better," Gabriel says.

"Why?" Peyton's voice works in the same way it always does, despite the trembling in his stomach and the clench in his throat.

"He got sick at the party in Pine Heights. I think it upset him when all of you decided to take Colton up on his *generous gift* of creature cracking." His voice sneers. "Apparently, he doesn't share your love of killing them for fun."

"Oh," Peyton says, relief too obvious in his voice. *He got sick?* "He needs to toughen up and stop acting like such a baby about the fucking creatures. And he can't handle drinking and parties. He couldn't even before..." Peyton forces his lips together to keep the excuses bubbling inside of him, but Gabriel knows better than to listen to a babbled excuse without wondering why Peyton offered it. *Screw this.* "Anyway, you don't need to worry about Bailey." And this is the line Peyton draws between them regarding Feahtertons, has always drawn. "I can take care of my brother."

"Fine." Gabriel starts a slow circuit around the room, checking it out, looking for something. *If he's guessed about Bailey...then why come alone? Unarmed?* He knows Peyton better than that.

"Did I interrupt your breakfast?" Gabriel asks.

"If I say yes, will you leave?"

Gabriel's eyebrow lifts like it did at Mason's coffee. "Careful, Peyton." Gabriel surveils the table. "The rations leave a lot to be desired."

"Yes, they certainly do," Mason blusters. "Thank goodness for Feathertons, that's what I always say, right Peyton?"

Peyton wants to take control, but he can't formulate the right defense, the safe defense, when he doesn't know what Gabriel wants. Why has he come? To see Bailey? That doesn't even make sense.

Lila shuffles into the room, distracting the tension of Gabriel's inspection of their breakfast table, their kitchen, *them.* Lila's sweatpants hang off her body, her hair clumped and greasy. She rubs at her mouth, skittering her gaze away from all of them. *Perfect. High again.* Peyton glares at Mason, wants to hold his father's face in a vise pointed at Lila and force him to acknowledge her shaking hands and waxy skin. She sinks into her usual chair by the window.

"Jesus, Mom."

A memory rushes Peyton like a tide of cold water, the smell of his mother's vomit and piss, the feel of Lila's cooling skin. Peyton's

81

shaking fingers scrolling for Gabriel's number…begging for him to help. *"Please, Gabriel. She overdosed."* Peyton slaps a hand on his forehead. "Jesus, Mom," he says again. He looks at Gabriel, sees that same memory of the overdose reflected in his face.

In a flash, Gabriel's across the room, his hand grips Lila's hair, fist clenching to draw her ashen face backward. Lila's gray eyes, the same stormy color as Bailey's, slide wider in surprise. "I didn't sell to you," Gabriel says. The tensing at the corners of his mouth—deliberately smoothed a moment later. The slight squint of his eyes until the mask of calm erases it. "I would never sell to *you*," he says. "Not drugs." Gabriel releases Lila's hair. "So, you bought from Colton."

Mason catches on faster than Peyton. "No, Gabriel. She got them somewhere else. She had to. We only buy from the Feathertons."

The mask breaks again. A sharp quake of fury, muscles tightening, teeth clench and unclench. "This is my territory. *Mine.*" Gabriel's assessing cold gaze sweeps over Peyton.

"Dude. Come on. I sure the fuck wouldn't get her drugs."

Then, the fury drains away, and the calm returns. "Someone in The Greens is dealing with Colton. Someone Lila has access to. If it isn't in your own home, then who?"

Gabriel will not let this go unpunished. He can't. Not with Feathertons and Colton competing for every inch of territory. "There's no one, man. She never leaves the damn house. She barely leaves that chair." Peyton turns toward his father. "It was you. I has to be—"

"Monica Bell," Mason says. He clears his throat. "She got them from Monica Bell, next door."

14 Bailey

Water trickles from the shower head. Hot water at least. Bailey plans to stay under the stream as long as it lasts. Despite puking last night, that near-faint on the deck, he feels okay. Not sluggish or confused. Not sick with Super Flu.

When she first had the virus, Ashley complained about feeling groggy, blamed it on a sinus headache. *How long did that part last?* How long until the full symptoms of Super Flu overran Ashley's brain and body? How long until only Super Flu lived inside, the virus powering her actions? She must have popped soon after she begged off the movie with Bailey. She never answered her phone again. No one at Ashley's house answered the phone. Because she popped, she popped, and then... She'd become like Don, when he'd killed Sylvie. Water sucks into his lungs, and Bailey has to cough it up again.

***

Early in the creation of Feathertons, Peyton forced Bailey into coming with him on a few of his looting jobs. Peyton drove Gabriel's obnoxious, oversized pickup, and he and Bailey bounced around in the truck's cab as it rumbled down the highway exit near The Greens, past dead cars and trash that littered every street. "The more you come out with me, the better you'll get at killing them." Peyton still had blond hair, still wore his letter jacket, still fought in sneakers with an array of changing weapons, like he hadn't made up his mind which he liked best. Peyton gunned the truck, drove up over a median to go the wrong way down the opposite highway lanes. Just because he could. He cut a grin at Bailey, but must not have liked whatever expression he found in return from his little brother. "Are you seriously going to live your whole life not having any fun? You know, some shit about the apocalypse isn't too bad."

"Are you kidding me right now, Peyton? I don't want to *get better* at killing. I don't want to kill them at all."

"Fighting is fun. Looting is fun. Doing whatever the fuck I want? That's fun."

Doing whatever I want? Bailey wanted to go back to school. He wanted his mother to stop waiting for his little sister to come home. He wanted his father to stop watching the television all night. He wanted Gabriel to stop calling Peyton at all hours to loot stores and houses he'd scouted.

"Oh, God." His thoughts trailed off as their truck sped by a cluster of people all huddled together. Twitching, rotting, close to death. Way beyond infected.

Peyton didn't even glance at the knot of men and women on the road. He just swerved around them the way he'd once swerved around slow drivers. "Listen, the creatures are stupid. When you have to fight, just remember that. They don't use strategy. If you remember that, then the fear won't—"

"I'm not afraid. It's not about being afraid."

"Okay, okay. I'm not calling you a coward or anything." Peyton smacked Bailey's head. "You don't always have to be so touchy about everything, you know. I'm just saying that if you *are* afraid, it's nothing to be ashamed of, you'll get over it." He grinned at Bailey again. Like he really wanted Bailey to grin back. "You're a survivor. Like me."

"No, I'm *not* like you." Bailey stared out at the barren space between their suburb and the City. "Where are we going?"

"So, if you aren't scared, then what's the problem?" he continued. "Is it the blood?" He gestured toward his own bloodstained jeans. "It rinses out, doesn't it? Once it dries…then…well, you can't get infected once it dries." Peyton shrugged.

"Oh. My. God. It isn't the blood, Peyton. Do you really not get it at all? I'm not a killer. I'm not going to murder anyone just because they're sick." He could tell Peyton had tuned him out as they neared an exit. "Just forget it."

Peyton pulled the truck over another grass median to a service road—the road that turned toward Ashley's neighborhood.

It still crushed him to think of her, to think of her dying, even if they hadn't gotten along in the end. Even if she'd wanted to dump him. *I should have told her what happened at the Christmas party. I should have told her about the kiss.* If he had, then she would have known the real reason Gabriel started paying attention to her. They wouldn't have so many secrets between them. He thinks that she would have forgiven the kiss.

Peyton pulled up to a familiar Quick Stop. Back in grade school, Bailey and Ashley used to sneak away from her house to buy Slurpees. Before they understood attraction, before they tried dating, before dating made their simple friendship far less simple, the two of them would tell Ashley's mom that they wanted to walk to the local pool but then ditch their towels in the bushes lining the neighborhood entrance. Then, they would walk along the service road to the Quick Stop. As ten-year-olds, it felt rebellious and thrilling.

"Come on." Peyton waved him inside. "Stand behind me, watch the door." He started muttering to himself as he filled a garbage bag. "Motor oil, cigarette lighters, salt…"

"Did Gabriel give you a list or something?" Bailey craned his head a little to catch a glimpse of the Slurpee machine. The foggy plastic canister looked empty. He thought, *That's good…* something like this… The beginnings of a thought about how he wouldn't want to cloud his memories of being with Ashley, of a more innocent time by drinking the sugary cherry syrup and ice now. Because killing changed everything for Bailey. He hated the sounds, the smells, the places that the killing happened. He could never see just Walgreens or Lowes or Access Medical again without the images of hands and feet and faces and the dark, dead blood seeping around them.

Then, "Not here," Bailey remembers saying as his eyes fell away from the empty Slurpee machine. Outside the Quick Mart, a man stumbled over the ledge of concrete from the parking lot to the sidewalk surrounding the shop.

Memories from before never affected his brother like they did Bailey. No matter where they went, Peyton saw only the fight and the world they lived in now. "Huh?" Peyton looked over his shoulder. "Ah yeah. Here we go." Peyton cracked his neck. His whole body quivered with the restless anticipation Bailey used to see in him before football games or parties. Peyton burst through the glass doors to outside, garbage bag of loot over one shoulder, club raised.

Bailey followed just in time to see his brother bring the club down in a one-handed arc. He smacked the face of the stooped and open-mouthed man, who sprawled backward against the blacktop parking lot. Peyton heaved the garbage bag into the truck bed, jumped down with the club in both hands now. He hovered over the man writhing on the asphalt. Sickness had done most of Peyton's job already, the man's body rotting, his teeth gone. His brother adjusted his grip and brought his club straight down in a quick stabbing motion onto the man's neck, crushing the brainstem. A mercy blow—if Bailey ignored Peyton's laughter.

"Did you see that? One-handed! I'm fucking awesome at this." Peyton didn't even sound winded.

"Yeah..." Both the dead man and his brother made him sick. "Can we leave now? Are you done?"

Peyton tapped Bailey's cheek. "Toughen up," Peyton said. The laughter now just behind his words. "Think that's all of 'em?" He strode around the truck, looking down the road, club raised and dripping gore. Bailey trailed behind.

A girl, long brown hair waving in the hot wind, staggered in the middle of the road, her movements jerky and slow, her condition about the same as the man Peyton took down. "Well, check that out. Another goner," Peyton huffed.

Bailey's heart stuttered. He knew that long hair. He remembered ditching the neighborhood pool, and coming that same direction from Ashley's house, how the hot summer wind would tug at long pieces of Ashley's waist length brown hair…

Without all these markers, would he have recognized the gray rotting face, the empty eye socket, the missing nose and lips as Ashley? *She came out on this road. She followed the same path…* No. *That isn't Ashley anymore.* That stumbling thing in the road wouldn't even know him.

Peyton made a coughing groan beside him. "I'll take care of this first."

"What? No—" Bailey dropped his club and grabbed at his brother. "You said she's a goner? Just leave her."

Peyton wrenched his arm loose. "So? I'll be doing her a favor."

"Peyton, no. Just leave her."

"What the hell is wrong with you?"

"Why do you have to go pound that girl into the road? She's practically dead, and she's not even coming for us!" Somehow, Bailey had started shouting without realizing it. "There's no reason to kill her."

"God, you can be such a fucking pansy sometimes." Peyton grabbed the half-filled garbage bag from the back of the truck, shoved it into Bailey's hands. "Medicine, batteries, matches."

"Peyton, stop!" Bailey clawed at his brother's shirt, holding him in place. "I think…" *It's Ashley. The girl in the road is Ashley.* He couldn't say it. He couldn't make it real.

Peyton jerked loose from his grip. "Why do you always act like this? This is what I was saying on the way here." Peyton shoved Bailey away. "Go in the store. Get the stuff I said."

Once the door chime sealed Bailey inside, he squeezed his eyes closed. "Medicine, batteries, matches." Bailey repeated Peyton's grocery list out loud, but his hands grabbed at whatever they touched. "Don't think about it. It's not Ashley." He cleared most of the first small aisle of whatever it held and kept going. "Ashley's dead. She probably died that first night. She had all the symptoms… She didn't answer her phone again. That thing out there can't be her."

But he *knew*…her hair, her clothes, the direction she came… Even if his mind wouldn't accept it, every part of him recognized her. When the bag stretched full, he started filling the flimsy plastic customer bags. His heart raced in his chest, and he kept forgetting to breathe. The things he shoved into the bags became blurry and shapeless. Bailey had packaged nearly half the little store by the time Peyton grabbed the bags out of his hand.

"God! That's enough!" Peyton smelled of sweat and heat, and his cheeks had flushed pink with exertion.

Bailey stayed inside the store while Peyton loaded the truck. He waited until the last moment to come back out, and his eyes immediately went to the spot in the road where the dead girl…*Ashley*…lay in a beaten heap of sticky blood and rotted flesh. Some of her hair still caught in the wind, wisps emerging all directions like antennae.

Peyton grabbed a Slim Jim from one of the smaller bags at his feet, peeled it and tucked it in the side of his cheek in one smooth motion. "We should tell Gabriel about those two. The neighborhoods round here must be about emptied if no one took them down yet." And then, Peyton laughed, "Killing those two took almost no effort at all. Taking this whole neighborhood should be a cinch." Jogging out onto the road had made him breathe harder than pummeling Ashley to a pile of blood and decay and hair. "Hey, didn't you used to go swimming at some place around here?"

***

When Bailey emerges from the shower and the fog of all his memories, he stares at his reflection in the mirror. The bite stands out purple and raised against his pale skin. The imprint of Don's teeth in red scabs, the center a dark bruise fading out like a bullseye in green and yellow. The area around the injury has a flat red rashy look to it that Bailey saw countless times in videos, articles, and on television. He has the virus. He *definitely* has it. "Fuck. Fuck. Fuck." Bailey pulls on a pair of jeans he finds on his bedroom floor and thrusts a window open to let the cool air in. His wet hair and chest sting in the chill, but at least, the wave of terror starts to clear. He takes deep breaths of smoke-tinged fall air, concentrates on the movement of the trees in the wind.

A woman screams, and Bailey leans farther to look outside. Below him Gabriel looks up, his tall lean form, the bright red hair. His pale eyes catch Bailey's. Then, the rest of the scene on the lawn comes into focus. His mother screaming. His father pointing at Henry and Monica Bell. Peyton grabbing for Case.

Case told them, told Gabriel about the bite. She must have. And now, she'll have to fight Peyton. They all will. Peyton will kill her. He'll kill Gabriel. *He will die before he lets them take me.*

Bailey runs for the stairs. He trips and slides, feet still bare and wet, legs shaking underneath him. He slaps his hand at the wall for balance. He makes it to the lawn, to Peyton. But fear has Bailey winded, and he bends over, hands on his knees to catch his breath.

"Gabriel? You deal with me. Not her." Case's forceful low voice. She has her arms thrown wide, blocking Monica like she would on a basketball court.

"I was only trying to help!" Monica sobs. "She was *suffering*. She lost her daughter just like I lost Via."

"I need them," his mother screeches. "I…" Her voice trails off, and Bailey looks up. "No, Bailey…" She covers her face with her hands.

Monica and Henry edge backward. Henry's hands out in front of him, that calming gesture that never calms anyone. Monica trips and falls on the scruff of grass still marking their lawn. She scrabbles to find purchase with her fingers and feet.

"Bailey?" Case inches toward her shovel, propped against the garden hose on the side of the house. "Do you understand me?" She lunges toward the shovel, grips it in front of her.

"Stop!" Gabriel's voice.

A flash of bright blue, and Peyton shoves his entire body at Case, tackling her down.

"Peyton, don't!" Bailey's voice comes out too high and thin, but everyone stills. Like they usually do for one of Gabriel's commands.

"Bailey?" Peyton now.

"Bailey?" echoes Henry Bell. "You still with us, son?"

Gabriel grabs Bailey's shoulders, turns him away from the others, so Bailey faces only him. His pale eyes flash in anger, his face white. "When did this happen?" A pause and his fingers tighten. "The Clements."

The bite. Bailey slaps his hand against it. He didn't put on a shirt, and he knows, he *just saw,* how much the bite stands out, the telltale red rash.

Peyton springs back up. He shakes, goggle-eyed with trembling hands. "He's my brother," Peyton says. "Gabriel, he's my brother."

"I know." Gabriel clamps his long-fingered hand on Bailey's bicep, eyes on Peyton. Some understanding passes between them that Bailey doesn't understand. "I can protect him," Gabriel says, solemn faced like a promise. He turns on the gaping faces of the parents. "No one says anything about this," he orders. "No one!" He drags Bailey by his side, tugging him toward the Land Rover. "I'm taking you back to my house. You can't stay here…not with them," meaning Bailey's parents, his neighbors, *his brother.*

"What? No, I'm not. Stop it." Bailey struggles to pull his arm free, but no chance, Gabriel won't yield. And Peyton follows behind, backing Gabriel up.

Peyton opens the passenger side door of the SUV and shoves Bailey inside. "Go with him, Bailey."

"*Go with him?* Are you serious right now, Pey?" But, Peyton just stretches the seatbelt over and straps Bailey in like a child. "I can't believe this!"

His brother has that hard, flat, look he used to get in a tight game. "You think I'd make you go with him if I didn't think he was your best chance?"

No. He wouldn't. Bailey deflates into the leather seat.

Before he crosses to the driver's side, Gabriel turns to point at Case. "You owe me. For your mother."

Gabriel waits for his answer, and Case nods. She still grips her shovel against her body. Her dark eyes hard, jaw clenched. "I owe you," she agrees.

anger

He should have reported to one of the Featherton storehouses, organized that day's runners, maybe gone to the house in Pierce Heights to help clean up. But Peyton, brooding the rest of the morning, sits inside and decides to wait around for the government patrols to arrive. At least, Case had the wherewithal to strip off her sweatshirt for Bailey before Gabriel drove off with him. Peyton didn't even think to get his little brother's shoes.

"They're here!" Mason loves patrol day. "Come on, everyone. Get out there and get counted."

Lila smooths her wrinkled pajama shirt, pats her greasy hair. "I didn't think they still counted us."

Peyton rolls his eyes. "They don't."

In the beginning, the soldiers came by daily to collect the sick, every other Monday to deliver rations. They also did random wellness checks. But that didn't last long, martial law has dwindled down to a string of military vehicles that wind their way through the suburbs once or twice a month. Everyone comes out to meet them, stands at the end of their front yards, accepts anything offered, and thanks the soldiers for their service.

Peyton lines up at the curb with his parents. They look down the street but intentionally look past the Bell family who stand only ten feet to their right. Peyton steals a quick glance at Case, though. *Fuck it. I'm going over.*

"Hey."

"Hey." Case bites at her lip. Then, "So you let him take Bailey. I hope you can trust him."

"I can. Gabriel came through for me once before." Case gives him a skeptical look. "He *did*. I should have gone to him right away. I don't know what I was thinking…"

On that last day before the outbreak, after his father left, even after confronting Gabriel about the affair, their fight—Gabriel still came through for him.

"It's my mom. I just found her, and she's unconscious, cold. I need your help." Gabriel, looking hung-over as hell, arrived so fast that he must have sped the whole way to Peyton's house. What a fucking mess. Gabriel held Lila's face over the sink, forcing the spray of water down her throat until she gagged. Even with Lila's vomit splashed on his pants and shoes, he still acted so calm, so controlled, so Gabriel. While Peyton stood back, useless—no, actually worse than useless—*afraid*.

***

Case lays a hand on his arm. "Maybe, you weren't thinking. Because it was Bailey." Her mouth twists up and then releases. "Okay, so I guess we're trusting Gabriel Featherton."

And then, Peyton remembers. "Shit, I'm sorry about your mom. My dad—"

"She made her choices," Case says in a tone that Peyton recognizes all too well. He knows the gut punch disappointment when a parent lets you down. Yeah, Monica made her choice to trade with Colton—treason in their new world. But Case will be the one to pay.

He lays a hand on her shoulder. "It won't be that bad."

***

This patrol consists of only two Hummers, no trucks, and no cage to take away the sick. *What does that mean?* Only two men ride in each vehicle. All of them wear Kevlar, helmets and flak vests. Even in the cool temperature, they must be roasting under all that weight.

One of the men looks familiar, a muscle-head kid Peyton played football against. Offensive lineman, maybe two or three years older than Peyton. "You making rounds later?" Muscle-head asks him. "You should offer cooking oil. We've got loads of potatoes but nothin' to fry them in."

Peyton's a little taken aback. Usually, the soldiers don't acknowledge the gangs.

An older guy, more typical of the National Guardsmen, gives his young partner a look of suspicion. "You know this guy, Shane?"

"Look at his hair," Shane gestures toward Peyton. "I don't need to know him. This is their territory."

Peyton nods at them both and starts unloading ration boxes. They don't feel as heavy as usual. Whatever. More business for Feathertons.

"The U.S. government does not recognize any…"

"Give it a rest, Captain." Shane shakes his head. "We all know the gangs exist. This is the real shit. You're Peyton Tyrone, right? You were Memorial's quarterback, right?" Shane takes Peyton's silence for a yes. "Yeah. 'course you are! You had a hell of an arm. I played for South High, Shane Liu."

"Yeah. I remember you, too. Who fucking cares?" Peyton continues unloading the ration boxes.

Mason bustles forward to take one of the boxes from Peyton. "South High, huh? Near the City?" he asks. "How are things down there?" Mason moves to help unload the rations, but Shane's commanding officer waves him back.

"Not good, sir," Shane says. He straightens up some, less friendly. He flicks his eyes toward Peyton.

Case tilts her head. "You still there then, living down near the City?"

"No. No... I'm living in Featherton terr—"

The captain cuts him off, "We aren't here to socialize, soldier." The other Hummer pulls forward. The driver grabs his M-16 and pulls it across his lap. "Everything cool here, sir?"

"Just the four boxes today," the command says. "Unless you're Bell. Henry Bell?" He squints at Peyton's dad.

"No. That's me," Henry answers, stepping forward.

"Extra half box for Bell. Courtesy of your boss downtown."

Peyton grits his teeth. For the rest of the day, he'll have to listen to his father complain about the injustice of Henry Bell getting that additional half box. Mason still can't accept that Super Flu brought about the end of his sales career.

His father gives a quick clap of his hands, a bitter smile. "You've got luck, Henry. Not much changes at all in the world of government accounting. You still get your business done despite brownouts and rolling blackouts. You still get to feel like a man who can provide for a family. And here, I've got to be retrained if I want to keep our rations. Can you believe they advised me to do physical labor—Me! I was the top medical instrument salesman of my district for the last seven years! I ran training sessions every month...all expenses paid...Hawaii...new company car every year—"

"Things have changed for everyone, Mason," Henry says. "No sense in living in the past. You have to try and make the best of the world you wake up in, not the one in that was there when you fell asleep."

"But how can that be *right?*" Mason makes a big gesture, waving away Henry's words. "I just want everything to go back to normal."

"I don't think even the internet jobs will last…" says Shane. "Not much left in the warehouses we use. There aren't extra rations to give out, you know? Free same day delivery is long gone," he laughs.

Mason's face goes slack, eyes cloud with confusion. "What does that mean?"

"Well, it means that—"

"Shut up, Shane," the captain barks. Shane doesn't seem any more cowed by him this second time.

"I'm just saying…" The other Hummer pulls ahead and turns around the bend and out of sight.

Peyton will have his own deliveries to make that evening. He used to sneak orders through windows or backdoors at night, but for the last month, he just pulls straight to the curbs like the government patrols.

When the captain gets back in the vehicle, Shane leans forward. "I'll be doing a run with you on what's left. Dying my hair and everything." He delivers a smirking salute toward Peyton and hits the gas on the Hummer, which peels out, leaving deep black marks on the road in front of the Tyrone house.

16 Bailey

Inside the Featherton mansion looks nothing like the lavish home Bailey remembers from the Christmas party. "Nice place. I see the apocalypse didn't hold you back from redecorating." Gabriel must have ordered his minions to remove all the ornate furnishings, the delicate antique chairs, the art, the porcelain vases, and overstuffed silk sofas that crowded inside the Featherton home when Bailey had last seen it. The first floor has transformed. Stopped and austere, dark wood shone and white furnishings sparkled, untouched by dirt, soot, or blood—the constants of life since the outbreak. Bailey wipes his hand across the back of a pristine chair. "Nothing defies worldwide pandemic like white linen."

Gabriel squints, looks annoyed, but stays silent, letting Bailey inspect the place.

"Oh, I get it…" Bailey draws out every word. "This is another show of power, like those stacks of fruit and cheese at the party."

"Exactly." Gabriel's sneering smile doesn't reach his eyes.

"Seriously? Don't you do anything without some evil master plan behind it?" Bailey throws himself on a white puffy couch. It's surprisingly comfortable. He's still barefoot, still wearing Case's Memorial Girl's Volleyball sweatshirt.

"It isn't just my home anymore. This is the headquarters of my organization. The seat of power for the Featherton territory."

Bailey crosses his arms. "You run a gang. Not an *organization*."

When Gabriel sits down opposite him, he doesn't lean back or relax—a snake poised to strike. "Wanting legitimacy isn't an evil plan."

"Legitimacy? For Feathertons? That's what you want?"

A single blinking nod from Gabriel, and then the two of them just watch each other. The silence between them stretches a little too long. *We're both thinking of it, aren't we? The last time I was here. The Christmas party. The kiss.*

The moment is broken when Cecilia Vu, a tiny Asian girl with shoulder-length bleached-white hair, sweeps into the room with a flourish of authority. Stops in her tracks when she sees Bailey. "What are you doing here?"

"I…I'm…" Bailey stammers. He pops up from his sprawl. Stands. *Oh shit, what's the story?* Gabriel made Cecilia his second in command, something Peyton grumbled about at first, before he realized the position involved a lot more than pillaging and clubbing things to death. Bailey waves his hands toward where Gabriel still studies him. "Well…"

"Bailey will be living here in the compound for a time."

"Here? With you?" Her nose wrinkles in disapproval. "I don't think that's a good idea, Gabriel." Even in high school, scary smart Cecilia had been a fierce devotee of all things Gabriel Featherton. Because of her genius levels of smart, and because she acted totally stuck up about it, Cecilia and Bailey didn't interact much back then. But they traveled in the same nerdy circles, didn't hate each other or anything. Cecilia's eyes shoot daggers at him now.

Gabriel gets to his feet with a lot more grace than Bailey's nervous flailing. "I didn't ask your opinion, Cecilia." His eyes don't leave his examination of Bailey. "He's living here. With me." And Gabriel stands close enough that their arms brush together, right in Bailey's personal space.

Cecilia's furious eyes go right to that point of contact. "For how long? People are sensitive about where they stand in the organization, and suddenly having a new person—with no explanation—he will be an *issue*. They'll wonder what his role is in Feathertons."

"He doesn't need a role. He's here as a personal friend of mine."

"He's also standing right here," Bailey mutters. "Look Cecilia, if you think I'm after your job, don't worry. I'm one hundred percent *not*." Then, he points a finger at Gabriel. "I'm not working for you, and I'm not dying my hair. Besides…" He makes a hand rolling gesture that really doesn't mean anything at all on its own. But he doesn't have anything else to add. There is no "besides," unless he says, *"Besides, I'm going to be either dead or feral in a few weeks time."*

Cecilia's eyes trail up and down Bailey and disgust curls her lip. "If you're done here, Gabriel, we have a lot we need to go over today." She turns and paces away to a marble topped antique bureau, takes a metal clipboard from it. "I'll wait for you in the study." After a pause, Bailey hears a door slam.

Aaaand we are back to the stare off. Finally, Gabriel says, "Let me show you where you'll be staying." He leads Bailey to a bedroom. Guest room, maybe? The room has a dark wood desk, an antique wardrobe, a four-poster bed. Bedding, carpeting, and drapes, all the same formal, spotless white as downstairs. "Are you sure you want to keep me here? Don't you have someplace less…clean?"

Gabriel blinks. "What are you talking about?"

What the hell? "Are you going to lock me inside or…" Bailey tries to read the plans off Gabriel's face. "Are you putting together a cage or something? Am I supposed to wait here until you get the basement ready?"

Gabriel's pale eyes scan the empty walls and blank desk. "I'm not going to lock you in, Bailey. You aren't my prisoner." His pale eyes travel the stark room. "Although I can see how this might feel like…" Gabriel turns back toward Bailey. "You like books and…those 3D drawings, pillows…" Gabriel rubs at his bottom lip with his thumb, looking down and talking to himself more than Bailey. "You obviously feel more comfortable with clutter. You filled your bedroom with action figures, puzzles, cameras… I can have someone bring all that here."

"You've been in my room?"

Well, it made sense in a way because Gabriel and Peyton had spent so much time together, and Peyton never had a problem barging into Bailey's room to steal clean clothes, Bailey's laptop, his school supplies, or basically anything else. But it also meant Gabriel *noticed* and *remembered* what Bailey had on his walls or what he had laying around his room. Which had nothing to do with hanging out with Peyton, and they both knew it. Bailey felt his cheeks burn with embarrassment. "Okay. Fine. Have one of your minions bring my stuff to me."

And Gabriel wants to snap back at the *minions* part of that, Bailey can tell. But the walkie-talkie on Gabriel's hip buzzes to life, with Cecilia's pinched voice. "Need you downstairs, Gabriel."

A muscle in Gabriel's cheek twitches. "Make yourself at home."

Make myself at home?

That evening, a boy with lavender hair tosses an overstuffed duffle bag into his room. Someone packed his clothes and shoes, but also his 3D posters of superheroes and spaceships, a stack of spirals from his desk at home, the crocheted green spread from his bed and his stuffed giraffe. Surely, his mother didn't pick all this out. Because she never…she wasn't very good about noticing things. Lila just got tired so easily and had such poor health.

But without Peyton forcing night-watch duties on him…or his father obsessing on the latest news of Super Flu, of the roads, of the lingering functions of government…without Monica Bell stopping by…or the physical presence of his mother to care for and worry about…Bailey's mind keeps turning over and over all the many times he witnessed behavior from his mother that he didn't understand, didn't want to understand. Even before the outbreak.

Lila staring glassy-eyed out the window.

Lila slurring over her words at the dinner table.

Lila asleep in her expensive, striped pool chaise lounge, leaving Peyton to drive Lucy to soccer or Bailey to Ashley's house.

Gabriel accused Monica Bell of trading outside Featherton territory. Trading for… The answer lies just outside the line where Bailey stops his thoughts. *Mom is fine. She's sad about Lucy but fine.*

He tries doing pushups and crunches to wear himself out, tries counting backward in the dark, tries imagining his own room, in his own house with Lucy down the hall in her bedroom. But he *still* can't drift off. *Three days since Don bit me.* He pictures the virus racing through his veins, traveling over his body, nestling into his brain stem. *How much longer do I have?*

He hasn't heard Gabriel come upstairs, so Bailey decides to go look around the house. *I'm not looking for him.* He wanders through the dark wood and white linen rooms. A wall of sliding glass doors open out to a back garden. Like everyone in the post-outbreak world, Gabriel has let the land grow wild. Nettles, pigweed, spiderwort that they used to spray pesticide on had become food. Bailey leans his forehead against the cold glass, closing his eyes.

He hears the rustle of another person in the room. *Gabriel.* And okay, Bailey had gone looking for him. "So leaning against the window with my eyes closed probably makes me look insane."

A huff of air like a laugh. "Can't sleep?"

Bailey turns to see the older boy still dressed in his dark suit from earlier in the day. Bailey can't think of a single reason for dressing like a business douchebag during the apocalypse. Light angles out from the French-doors of the study, and Gabriel's bright hair shimmers in the glow. He tilts his head, looking more intrigued than concerned. "You don't look sick. Yet."

"Yet? God!" Bailey tries for a laugh. "Didn't feel the need to pull the punch on that one?" He buries the heel of each palm into his eyes and rubs. "I guess sensitively approaching the subject wouldn't really match your carefully crafted image as an evil dick, right?"

"You want me to pretend you aren't sick?" Gabriel's eyebrows raise. "Aren't you getting tired of that approach? Pretending?" Gabriel's head cocks to one side, and now the assessment turns mocking. "Like you have with Lila."

Bailey sucks in a breath. Gabriel's words come way too close to things Bailey always avoids, the memories he talks himself out of understanding. "I'm the one pretending? You're keeping me here with you. Letting me sleep in the same house where you sleep." Bailey's voice shakes. "You've seen what they do, when they can't run or hide." And if he pops, Bailey will do all those things...*when* he pops. "Why didn't you just kill me back at The Greens? Why the stalling?" His voice comes out raspy, afraid. *Humiliating*.

"Kill you?" Gabriel grabs Bailey's shoulders like he did back at The Greens, fingers digging down to bone, nails close to piercing his skin. "I brought you here so that those idiots at The Greens *couldn't* kill you."

Bailey shoves him back. "Because you're such a caring, generous guy. Right? Give me a break here, Gabriel. I know you, remember? You're totally evil. And I'm not even talking about your whole post-outbreak overlord thing..." Bailey waves a hand up and down Gabriel's polished appearance. "I'm talking about the guy who could be friends with my psycho brother."

"I'm not Peyton's friend. I'm his boss—"

Bailey points. "There. See? You pretended to be his friend, so you could use him. So you could use his popularity with the other asshole jocks."

Gabriel takes a deep breath, like he has to summon a reservoir of patience. Like Bailey is a child throwing a tantrum. "If you even knew," Gabriel says, voice dripping contempt, "I—"

"And you faked being into Ashley before the outbreak. You tried to break us up just because I rejected you."

Gabriel has the decency to wince at that last one.

"How hardcore rejected and angry do you have to be to enact that plan? Like a total psychopath. What the hell? Is that still the agenda here? You want the front row seat as I pop feral?" Bailey's voice wheezes. His chest feels too tight. "Why are you really keeping me here?"

He can't possibly still want Bailey. Nothing about them remains the same as that night when Gabriel kissed him. It might as well have happened to two completely different people. Bailey's vision gets spotty, and he has to gulp air to suck enough into his lungs.

Gabriel's hands cup his face, force him to focus. "Stop."

"Stop what?" This time he doesn't push Gabriel off. "Okay, yeah, I'm freaking out." Anger. Panic. Anger. As soon as one comes to the surface, the other smothers it. Bailey tries to push Gabriel away, but the other boy just grips him harder. "You'll have to do it eventually. Kill me, right? Just not Peyton. Holy crap, not Peyton—"

"Bailey, stop." Same cold, expressionless Gabriel staring him down. "Take a deep breath," he orders, and Bailey feels he has no choice but to do as Gabriel says. "Now, hold it."

Okay. Bailey lets that air leak from his nose. They stand locked together for a few more slow breaths. *Okay. Okay.* "You can let go of me now."

Gabriel has pulled him into one of the white upholstered chairs as Bailey works to get control of himself again. Bailey leans back trying to relax his body, trying to slow his heart-rate. "Sorry," he says.

Gabriel sits on the edge of a thick acrylic coffee table across from Bailey's chair. "I put you in the room across from mine because I barely sleep and not very deeply. I would wake up the second I heard you leave your room, and I'm absolutely certain that I would be able to get you under control—even if you change in your sleep."

"And you're not afraid of getting infected?"

"No. I'm not." Gabriel peels off his suit jacket, throws it onto the low white couch. He stretches his long arms over his head and yawns. "It won't be a problem for me."

Bailey's so used to Peyton's blustering that he rolls his eyes. "That's stupid. And I don't believe you, anyway. Everyone is scared of the virus."

Gabriel freezes. "I'm not." He rakes a hand through his hair. With it messed from the usual gel-back and without the suit jacket, Gabriel looks more like he did in high school, more youthful than the uptight head of the Feathertons. He sighs, studies the floor for a moment with eyebrows drawn, pensive. Then, he must come to some decision because he lifts his chin and meets Bailey's eyes. "I'm not afraid of getting it, because I've already had it."

What? "You've... You have?"

Gabriel nods.

"Oh. Um... Wow." Bailey finds it hard to meet the other boy's eyes. "And you lived? I mean, like obviously you lived because here you are."

"Yes. Here I am."

"So...when? Like, when were you sick?"

"Early on. I'm unable to remember the first weeks of outbreak, not the whole first month really, because I was in the acute stage, the feral stage, at that point."

A long silence passes while they stare at each other. Bailey wants to ask more questions: *How did you survive? What do you remember? What did you do?* But all his questions feel callous, cruel. "I'm sorry," he says instead. "I can't imagine what you went through. I mean...I guess I won't have to imagine...but I'm really sorry."

"No. Don't be sorry for me." A muscle tightens in Gabriel's pale cheek. "Especially not you."

Bailey swallows. "Um, Okay," he whispers. *God, what happened to him?*

"But don't worry. I can control you. It's not impossible when you take out the fear of infection."

"I still might try to take a chunk out of you."

"I doubt you could." Gabriel rolls his shoulders, cracks his neck. He moves to one of the puffy sofas, stretches out like he plans to nap there.

"Huh." Bailey still feels antsy and kind of pissed at Gabriel's nonchalant confidence. "Well, if it turns out you're not the badass you claim to be, then I guess the worst that could happen is...I kill you." That gets Gabriel's attention again. He rolls his head toward Bailey, icy blue eyes unimpressed. And Bailey does what he always does, and fills the awkward silence with humor. "Just think of the drop in crime if I took *you* out." He means it as a joke, but the words cut way too close to his real feelings about Feathertons.

Gabriel draws himself up, and now, his eyes look cold enough to freeze Bailey in place. For a split second in time, they had become friends. But only for that moment. Now, Gabriel's sneer from earlier comes back. "And all the people I supply with food, with medicine, and with protection? How would they feel if you took me out? Do you think they would agree with you, Bailey?"

17 PEYTON

Peyton cruises the Suzuki up Euclid Street, close to the edges of Olde Town near the Feathertons' compound.

He parks the Marauder in front of Storehouse 7, a squat yellow brick bungalow with lace curtains in the windows. Lieutenants only know the location of the storehouses for their own neighborhoods. If he has a master list, Gabriel keeps it all to himself.

Peyton stands at the end of the sloped driveway. The place looks deserted. *Should have had runners coming and going all morning.* He slides his club from the holster on his bike. *Where's the stock manager?* The Greens goes through stock managers quicker than any other neighborhood because of Peyton's shitty attitude. Gabriel keeps matching him with other jocks from their high school. Craig Spooner and Hector Phelps both begged off after a few months. Colby Mathews got in a fight with some of Colton's people and died. So then, Gabriel assigned Josh Spooner to The Greens, Craig's younger brother. Josh kind of worshiped Peyton, which was fucking annoying. But Josh caught the virus, and Peyton had to put him down. He did it fast, just two or three good bats to the back of Josh's head, but Craig didn't exactly thank Peyton for his service or anything.

"Yo!" Peyton grabs the edge of the garage door and drags it up. The new guy should have come out to meet him. Peyton cups his hands and yells, "Hey, Fuckhead, you're supposed to meet me."

Nothing. "Who the fuck is this guy?" Inside the garage, labeled boxes and bags form narrow rows. In one corner, a scrawny girl in ripped jeans and motorcycle boots leans into a wooden crate. She pulls out an armful of apples and divides them into plastic bags. "Instead of acting like an impatient asshole, you could help me out here, you know."

"No, I fucking couldn't."

When she turns to glare at him, Peyton recognizes the purple haired girl from the pit, the one who tried to give Bailey her orange. Looks like Gabriel decided to try something new.

She recognizes him, too. *Her boss.* "Oh, hey," she says, suddenly friendly. "I didn't realize that was you." She grips a clipboard and pen. "Peyton Tyrone, right? I'm Vanessa. I just got made Supply Chief for The Greens."

When he just stares at her, she flings the clipboard into the apple crate and crosses her arms. "So, I shouldn't have called you an asshole. My bad. But, I didn't expect you to show up like another runner, none of the other lieutenants do."

He shrugs. "I always do the afternoon deliveries myself. And the other lieutenants are a bunch of stuck-up pencil-pushing shitheads."

That makes Vanessa grin and drop her arms. "Hell yes, they are."

He motions toward the apples with his chin. "Leave the apples for someone else. I don't want the cargo trailers slowing me down. I use saddlebags."

"Saddlebags?" Now, she flings the pen in the crate, too. "What the hell for? You don't need that kind of speed right now." The girl shakes her head, and long purple bangs swish over her eyes. "I've reloaded four damn runners already, and they said the roads are totally clear of creatures. Gabriel even had them cleaned of garbage and dead vehicles."

Peyton gives her a flat look. "I don't give a shit what Gabriel did. Clearing the streets doesn't mean the creatures stay away. They don't just stroll down the streets. They hide in the shadows of all the overgrowth." Cruising through deliveries with a cargo trailer sounds almost as boring as counting out apples with her. He wants to push the bike as hard as possible, block out his thoughts with the speed.

"Listen, it will take you fucking forever to make deliveries that way, and who do you think has to load you up every time? Me. That's who. I'll end up walking back to The Greens in the dark. And those fuckers don't mind strolling down the street when it gets dark." But as she gripes about the risk to her life, Vanessa unhooks the trailer hitch and takes the bundled deliveries to stuff inside the Marauder's saddlebags.

"Pack the meds. I'll take those first."

"They already went out. Only groceries left...you know, like *apples*. Which you'll only be able to deliver in two drops at a time using fucking *saddlebags*. I'm telling you, it's gonna take until dark."

"Don't care." After Vanessa packs the bags, Peyton revs the bike and cruises out. Junked cars and broken branches and leaves line the streets. Peyton catches sight of a few other runners in the distance on Broadway and Main, but he cruises alone on the neighborhood streets. People come out of their homes to ask for news, even when they don't take deliveries. With all communication down, the burbs suck.

A gaunt man has Peyton empty his delivery of sugar, flour—and the fucking apples—into a flowered pillowcase.

"I heard patrols won't be coming by. No more rations," the man says, eyes on Peyton's face, measuring his response.

Peyton keeps picturing the M-16 across the soldier's lap from the day before. *Who did he plan to use that on? Sick people? Healthy people?* Peyton shoves the pillowcase back at the man. "Is that a question?"

"I guess it is."

Gabriel briefed them on how to answer questions like this, but Peyton hadn't exactly committed it to memory or anything. "He's got a plan."

"Who's 'he'?"

"Dude, if you're asking who 'he' is, then you don't know shit."

"I don't want a plan. I want rations."

"I'll let 'him' know."

That shuts up the skinny man. Fucker, he knew exactly who Peyton was talking about.

Vanessa silently plugs the saddlebags full of bundles each time he stops back. She predicted right, and the deliveries take until dusk. But by the evening, they work perfectly in sync with each other, rolling the bundles and tucking them into the bags, refueling the Marauder, documenting the drops. On the last pit stop, Peyton helps her drag boxes from inside the house to the garage. Even in the cold fall evening, they both sweat. Vanessa pulls the bangs off her forehead with a purple bandana that matches her hair. Peyton throws his leather jacket over the Marauder's seat.

"We meet at the house on Western tomorrow?" Vanessa asks. "Storehouse 10?"

"Right." Peyton's developed a grudging respect for her work ethic now that she cut out all the "getting to know you" crap.

"Don't suppose you'll give me a lift back?" Vanessa wipes her face with the bandana. She really did help his deliveries go faster, when the other supply chiefs usually left him to pack the saddlebags by himself each pick up. Maybe, he owes her. "Okay. Sure."

The ride back home dries the sweat from their faces. And despite the ever-present smoke, it smells like fall, like school, football games, homecoming parades. Parts of their old lives that have disappeared. *Memory can make you crazy.* Peyton shakes his head to clear it.

When they curve round onto Hickory Hill, Peyton's street, they pass Case jogging through the neighborhood like the outbreak never happened. She even wears her old track team warmup, maroon hoodie and sweatpants. Their eyes meet as he passes, and she turns around, heading back his way.

He didn't promise Vanessa delivery to her front door, and she must not expect it because when he pulls into his own drive, she slides off the seat behind him. As he kills the engine, Case arrives, panting.

Peyton points a finger at her. "It's not safe to go out without a weapon."

Case waves him off, but one of her dimples shows. "I don't remember asking your permission, Tyrone." She knows what he's trying to say. "I stay in the neighborhood. I'm safe enough."

"It's still stupid. Creatures come up from the golf course. I killed one in my back yard just last week." Peyton scowls, making himself get busy rolling the bike into the garage, and then wiping it down.

Vanessa waves a finger in Case's direction, "Hey! I remember you from high school!"

Case's face hardens into the stoic expression she takes whenever someone mentions the past. Peyton gets it—lots of people remember Case's sister Via because she was only a year older than them. By now, people should know better than to ask…it's just too shitty a game to start asking after people like, "Hey whatever happened to…?" The answers are never good.

"I ran distance. The two mile?" Vanessa gestures toward Case's sweatshirt with Memorial High School Bulldogs emblazoned on the front. Case placed in hurdles at State three years in a row. Vanessa shrugs. "Eh, you probably don't remember me. I was a junior when the outbreak started." Vanessa looks back at Peyton again, "Bailey's grade. We were in the fucking honors program together." Vanessa scoffs. She pulls a crumpled cigarette package from her jeans. "Not like that shit matters, right?" She points the cigarette package toward Peyton and his fingers draw one out.

"It matters," says Case. She puts her hands on her head and stretches over to the right, eyes closed. "Colleges are going to switch to full online—"

"That's not true." Vanessa laughs. The laugh turns into a cough filled with cigarette smoke. "My dad was at an academic conference in Boston when martial law started. He was a history professor. I think I would have heard from him if that were even possible."

"The reports on public broadcast say…said…" Case trails of, and the stoicism washes back over her features. Unlike Peyton's father, Case knows when hope twists into absurdity. "Even if all the reports are wrong, this can't last forever," she says.

Smoke curls out from Vanessa's mouth when she laughs. "Right. Yeah, right."

Peyton hands over a long heavy length of iron pipe. It makes a good weapon for a girl because you don't need a lot of upper body strength for a solid hit.

"Cool," Vanessa grins. "Can I keep this?"

"No."

"Fine. Fine." Using the fingers holding her cigarette to wave, Vanessa says goodbye. Her other hand grips the pipe like she means business.

Case lingers in the garage. She pulls her hoodie off to reveal a stretchy tank top and damp skin. Her dark curly hair falls down her back. "Um, hey…" Case looks up at him with big, serious, eyes. "I had no idea my mom was giving Lila pills. I'm so, so sorry. I don't think she gave them to her…before. I don't think she knew about before. I think she didn't realize…" Case squishes the hoodie in her hands to stop her words.

Peyton flicks the cigarette Vanessa gave him on the ground. "She didn't realize Lila was a huge pill head? It doesn't matter. My mom probably started talking about Lucy and Via. She probably did it on purpose to get Monica all worked up and wanting to help her." *He could picture it.* Lila didn't give a shit what Gabriel would do to Monica, to Case. "What's Gabriel wanting from you? You don't look like you're joining up or anything." Peyton reaches out and tugs at her springy hair. Bailey's curls are always an unruly mess, but Case's twisty afro curls resist any attempts to reshape them. The little coils feel good between his fingers, and he takes a long time to pull them free.

Case's eyes close for a long second. "Peyton," she whispers.

Peyton assumed that Gabriel would force Case into Feathertons as payment for her mother trading with Colton, but clearly, that hadn't been his plan. "So what's he having you do?"

"He wants me to contact Colton and ask for more pills, find out where Colton is getting them. I get the feeling he already knows, but just wants me to…make a connection or something."

"A connection with Colton?" Peyton makes a face. "I gotta be honest that…you wouldn't be my first choice for winning over Colton. You know what I mean?"

"Yeah, I know what you mean, white boy, and I agree. Damn, I really, really do agree. But Gabriel doesn't care that much about Colton, it's whoever keeps supplying him with drugs. Someone from the City." She tries to act nonchalant about it, but her hands go back to twisting the hoodie. "Gabriel looked furious."

Peyton shrugs. "He's always furious." They stare at each other a long time, and Peyton wants to say, *"Be careful."* But what good would that do? Gabriel will have her do what he wants, and if she's lucky, she'll stay alive while she does it.

Peyton grabs the tortured hoodie out of her hands and shakes out the misshapen mess she made of it. Sometimes, he wants to protect her. Other times, he gets the same vicious urge he has around Bailey. To crush that weakness, crush her for showing it.

"Put this back on," he tells her. "It's freezing."

She smiles at him, all dimples and glistening eyes. "Didn't ask your advice, Tyrone." But she does pull it back on.

He waits outside and watches her walk across their scraggy front lawns toward her own house. Waits, watching, until she disappears inside.

18 Bailey

Bailey's fingers tick through a line of hanging men's clothes, wool trousers and jackets, button-down dress shirts, the tags click by, showing brand and price. In his life before the outbreak, he wouldn't have bothered looking at any of these clothes. But of course, now, they're free.

The weather has turned too cold for any of the t-shirts and frayed jeans packed in his duffle bag. After the second day in the same gray hoodie, Gabriel started pushing his own sweaters and jackets onto Bailey. But he has four inches of height on Bailey, broader shoulders and longer arms. Bailey looks like an idiot kid wearing his big brother's hand-me-downs.

Bailey catches the older boy frowning at him. "What? Quit staring at me, I get that enough from all your flunkeys." At least, Gabriel doesn't smirk when Bailey catches him at it. For days now, Bailey has felt like the butt of some secret joke.

The constant circle of Feathertons demanding Gabriel's attention and input watch Bailey from the corners of their eyes, sneak knowing glances at each other. At first, Bailey understood their curiosity. Bailey lives in the huge house with Gabriel. They can see that Bailey's curly hair hasn't changed from its natural ashy blond. Bailey doesn't have any duties, no obvious reason to hold their leader's attention, even when Gabriel never lets him out of sight. But those knowing glances aren't curious. *What is Gabriel telling them about him?* Despite the leers and smothered grins, his people all straighten up in Gabriel's presence. Bailey couldn't think of any way to complain about it that didn't sound like tattling, so he ignored it.

"Take whatever you want." He comes up behind Bailey, reaches around and pulls one pair of trousers free. Dark gray, fitted, suit slacks similar to those Gabriel wears. Bailey has only ever worn a suit when his mom forced them all to take family photos or the handful of times they attended church.

"No," Bailey wrinkles his nose. "That's not really…" Gabriel doesn't step back after he hands them over. Bailey feels Gabriel's breath against the back of his neck. "Um…I'd rather wear stuff like I've got on." Bailey motions toward his faded jeans and t-shirt and his ever-present gray hoodie with a mustard stain on the left arm and ragged cuffs. Bailey pokes his fingers through the holes in the front pocket and wiggles them.

A snorting laugh, "Alright." Gabriel swipes one arm toward an area behind the current rack. "Sweatshirts and jeans are stacked on the wall."

Bailey has to wind his way through overstuffed racks and boxes and shelves to make his way there. He finds jeans and a new, thicker, hoodie, and he peels out of his own worn clothes, trying not to feel self-conscious as Gabriel watches. "So…did you move all of Saks here?"

Gabriel's lips curl into a smirk. "Well, I moved quite a bit of Saks here…but not all of it."

"Alriiiight," Bailey drawls out the word. Zips and buttons his new jeans. "But why? This stuff is what people wanted before the virus. I mean, give anyone months of the air-conditioning and heat flickering on and off, or having to boil a pot of drinking water on a backyard campfire, and…you know, priorities change."

"These things are useful as rewards. Treats. You still want these things, don't you?" Gabriel picks up a bottle of cologne, pries the lid off and sniffs it. "You don't need them. They aren't *necessary*, but you still want these things. Don't you?"

Yeah. He does. But he doesn't want to want them.

"You'll need a coat, too. It's getting cold." Gabriel sets the cologne down and turns, rummages through a box. "Here." He wriggles free a dark green leather bomber jacket and tosses it to Bailey.

It's supple, thick, and way more upscale than anything Bailey ever bought himself. He clutches the leather bomber and frowns. "You sure I'll need this?" His eyes meet Gabriel's. "Come on… How much longer can I possibly have?"

In the pause between them, a doorbell chimes. The Feathertons never leave Gabriel alone for long. Bailey starts to pick his way out of the piled jeans and mountains of designer sweatshirts. "Someday, you'll have to show me how you do that," he says. When he turns, he cracks a smile at the confusion that flashes in Gabriel's eyes. "You went right into mob boss mode. How do you always wipe all your emotions away? Anyone can tell what I'm thinking and feeling just by looking at me."

"Anyone can see your emotions because you care. It's a good thing to show. People like that. I like that… And I'm *not* a mob boss."

"If you say so." But, Bailey's face warms. *Did he just say he likes that?* He ends up flustered enough that he trips on a perfectly straight line of shoe boxes. Really cool. Good job.

On the front step of the storehouse, Cecilia stands next to a skinny, nervous Asian kid with dark hair striped in fire engine red bands. The boy looks familiar to Bailey, the way all Gabriel's people do. He looks around their age, probably went to their high school in another life, and had plans for a future that never happened. He sees

Bailey and waves. Cecilia looks like she wants to rip the boy's head off. "I've got this, Lawrence. Go back to your deliveries."

Oh, right. Lawrence Vu, Cecilia's younger brother. No wonder he looked familiar. He played on the freshmen boys' tennis team. Bailey took the team yearbook photo, and he remembers Lawrence and another kid wouldn't stop grabbing their dicks and flashing gang hand signs they probably looked up on the internet. Like anyone would believe two nerdy suburban tennis players belonged to a gang.

But now, Lawrence's bright striped hair-dye and steel-toe black boots mark him as part of Feathertons. *Huh…I guess Lawrence is living his dream.*

"What did I do?" Lawrence whines. "You told me to come with you. You said I was going to be meeting with Gabriel." Poor kid doesn't recognize his sister working up a major case of "woman scorned" syndrome. With each passing day, she hates Bailey a little more—like she thinks Bailey is doing a slow play for her job as Gabriel's lead henchman.

Cecilia ignores her brother so that she can fully devote herself to glaring at Bailey. "I guess we'll have to reschedule because it was supposed to be a confidential meeting. As you can see, someone else is here with him, so it wouldn't be confidential."

"But—"

"Go *away*, Lawrence!" Cecilia takes a long time closing the door behind her as Gabriel waits, his eyebrows still raised from her outburst.

Bailey tries to act busy, stuffing his arms into the green leather bomber. With the hoodie underneath, he's warmer than he's been since the weather changed. Hey, if Gabriel wants to give him a coat, then Bailey will take it. Catching a cold on top of the virus would put a huge dent in his ability to recover.

"We should meet about…the situation developing in Quail Creek." Cecilia pitches her voice low, but it still has a little bit of stage whisper to it. Like she wants Bailey to feel left out, to know that the Feathertons' secrets can't include him.

Okay, fine. He's not a Featherton, so he doesn't get to overhear whatever secret stuff is going down in a completely different neighborhood from where he lives…*or lived.* Bailey pulls the hoodie up, shoves his hands in the bomber's pockets and interrupts, "Gabriel, do you need me to leave?" When Gabriel raises a hand to shush him, Bailey rolls his eyes.

"I've spoken already to our new informant, Cecilia. There's no need to review with Lawrence or with you."

Informant? Bailey coughs out a laugh at the spy talk. "Seriously, I can *leave* if you need to like…discuss secret informants and the sale of shampoo or whatever in Quail Creek."

"No. Stay." Gabriel crosses his arms and lets a coldness slide into his eyes. "Anything else, Cecilia?"

Unlike Bailey, she does a really good job of mimicking Gabriel's trick of washing all her emotions away like a robot. "The group we scouted earlier has arrived. I followed your orders and let them all walk the last miles until they reached the signs marking Featherton territory. They're waiting for you now."

"There are signs?" Bailey asks. "For real? You put up signs?"

"Fine. We'll be right there." Gabriel holds the door open for her. Despite the polite gesture, she recognizes the dismissal and stomps down the front stairs. Only Bailey walks or rides with Gabriel these days, and Gabriel shoos everyone else away from the two of them. "That leather jacket looks good on you. Zip it up."

Bailey fastens the green bomber coat over his hoodie. "Sure thing, *Peyton.*" He holds out his arms. "All bundled up now, okay?"

Gabriel waits for Cecilia to get ahead before he starts to follow with Bailey in tow. Despite making sure Bailey stayed protected from the weather, Gabriel only wears his suit coat, with a thin sweater underneath. Gabriel puts his hands in his pockets, bows his head against the wind.

Bailey tugs on the strings to his new hoodie. "Soooo… When you got sick…" He flicks his eyes over Gabriel strolling beside him, acting untroubled by the start of Bailey's question. "Did you have to go to a camp?"

"No. My parents…My father, really…knew that the camps would be nothing but a joke. The patrols only rounded people up to get them away from those uninfected, not cure or care for them. My father thought he could care for me just as well at home. So, when the change happened, he kept me there."

Bailey and Gabriel walk in silence then. *But where are your parents now?* Bailey wants to ask, but he thinks he knows the answer. Of course, he knows the answer. He clears his throat. "But what will you say when I pop? People are going to be afraid and angry when they know you didn't just put me down."

"You'll be a test case…I'll show that I'm able to contain you. I know I can do it. You'll be an example."

"An example," Bailey repeats. "Of wha—Oh my God…you want to make your own quarantine camp."

"Not a camp. A hospital of sorts. I won't tie down the sick and starve them. We could make iron cages. They wouldn't be left to the elements or threatened. And if we feed them live food, running water, then they won't attack people."

"Until they recover." Bailey can't hide the excitement from his voice. Then, a more sober, "*If* they recover." As they've come closer to the mansion, more people mill about, kids with clown-colored hair, neon and bright in the smoky fall air. "But, Gabriel, that sounds…good." And Bailey likes the idea of something positive coming from whatever will happen to him when the virus takes control. Also, Gabriel's plan answers a lot of questions Bailey had about why Gabriel bothered with him, with jeopardizing everything he's created by exposing it to the virus. It makes more sense than…something connected to that kiss at the Christmas party. Besides, Bailey does not need to have a whole gay crisis going on during the apocalypse. A *possible* gay crisis. *Moving on…*

"Okay, well, that's planned out then. But what are you telling them now? Just so I don't blow the whole thing open too soon, I think you better fill me in on the cover story. Why am I living in your house and constantly with you?"

Gabriel stops to face him. "Bailey…haven't you figured that out?"

"Um, no."

"I moved you into my house, I spend all my time with you, I've given you clothes…clearly, I've told them you're here for sex." Gabriel shakes his head, exasperated. "I thought it would be the best excuse."

"For sex? Sex!" Bailey's mouth drops open a little, but he gets control of himself fairly quickly. "Yeah, okay," he squeaks. "I guess that works."

Although he clamped down on his annoyance, Bailey's cheeks still burn bright pink. Like, okay…awkward and embarrassing conversation. But maybe only Bailey finds it awkward and embarrassing because Gabriel stalks a little closer. "You know, it would help appearances, if you didn't act so hostile toward me all the time."

"I'm not acting hostile!"

"Not acting, or not hostile?" Gabriel smirks at him because Bailey really hasn't had enough smirking in his direction.

"Oh my God! Neither one. I did act hostile. *At first.* But I haven't been hostile…lately."

"Well, you also don't act like someone having regular consensual sex." His head dips closer for a second, and then Gabriel's smirk twists into something bitter, and he shakes his head. "I'd appreciate it if you didn't intentionally project that I'm holding you prisoner here."

Bailey takes a step back, "I don't *project* that." But, maybe he does. He has felt sort of like a prisoner. None of that is Gabriel's fault, though. Okay, maybe Bailey has acted like a jerk since he's been here. "No. You're right." Bailey taps over the bite on his collarbone. "It's just a lot to deal with. But you don't deserve to get the brunt of it."

Gabriel nods his acceptance, and Bailey pulls the hoodie down lower over his eyes as they continue walking. Now that he knows the cover story, *"You're here for sex,"* he doesn't want to catch anyone's eye.

In front of Gabriel's house, a small mass of people wait on the sprawling trampled lawn. They look tired and dirty and remind Bailey of pictures of migrant farmers during the Dust Bowl, weathered to old age from sorrow. They scarf down packaged sandwiches and chug bottles of soda and juice. In the world before the outbreak, it would look like a company's family picnic. Except that the children cling to the adults instead of playing. The adults watch the house, the street, each other with a little too much fear in their eyes. And a layer of dust and soot cover everyone's clothing, a lot of it stained the dark reddish brown that Bailey knows so well.

***

The Land Rover sits parked on the edge of his driveway, and Gabriel leans against it. His expensive pressed clothing, gleaming hair, flawless skin all promise comfort and civilization. Bailey always thought Gabriel wore expensive suits because of vanity, but now, he sees something else in the eyes of the displaced people. He has turned himself into the symbol of all he can offer.

When everything settles down, Gabriel strolls into the middle of the group, and maybe because he assumes it from them, they give him their full attention. "My name is Gabriel Featherton, and this is my territory," he starts. "If you want to leave—if you have somewhere else to go—you can eat and drink as much as you like, and we'll give you weapons and send you back on the road." An impressive offer, unheard of generosity in the post outbreak world. Gabriel pulls them toward him with it. A good piece of manipulation... *If he can spare that much, then he must have more than enough.* And telling them that they can leave makes them want to stay.

"But, if you want to stay here...with us...then I will give you shelter and food and calm that you haven't known since the first month of outbreak." The words sound like a sales pitch, but said in his usual impersonal manner, it doesn't betray any sense of tricks or gimmicks. When Gabriel pauses, the refugees off the road don't dare breathe. "If you decide to stay, I will give you homes and belongings and a chance to make a life here. You will be a part of a community again."

Bailey stands mesmerized, watching the weary crowd turn from people without hope to people who believe in Gabriel's promises. People who found the strength to move forward through hell and chaos dissolve into crying gratitude at their first taste of relief. A dirt and blood covered girl kneels in front of him, throws her arms around his legs.

Gabriel puts one pale hand on her head. "Feathertons can become your community. This can be over for you, if you want to stay."

19 PEYTON

When Peyton can't sleep, he sits at the kitchen table and fiddles with the volume dial on the ham radio. *If it happened...if Bailey popped, Gabriel would come himself. He wouldn't radio it.* He tries distracting himself by listening for creature sightings. Killing as many of them as he can might take a chip out of his anger. Those nights, he gets on the Marauder. He races through the abandoned business districts, past strip malls, circles Memorial High, the football stadium...all the pieces of a safer life he led before the virus.

He takes a bottle of Jack Daniels from the garage of a storage house. Vanessa sees, but says nothing, and just crosses it off her intake list. She doesn't know that Gabriel keeps meticulous records of that shit, reviews everything, trusts no one. Gabriel will know Peyton took it. He won't do anything about it, but he'll also know that Vanessa covered for him. He'll know that she let Peyton steal. Peyton really should warn her.

He's started to appreciate Vanessa's dark-humored chatter throughout the day. "I found a website saying the virus had most likely peaked and numbers would decline. Then, I saw that shit posted in June. Whole fucking news site is just dead. Probably someone popped right in the office that same day and ate the whole staff." She smashes her cheeks and mimics the scream emoji before dissolving into laughter. "That on the decline crap was so wrong. By July, the death toll had passed ninety-nine percent."

Vanessa also invents elaborate scenes that account for the sudden drop in helicopter patrols in the first months and their current absence. "Hear me out...the pilot pops and, like, leaps out, trying to get away from the people. Right? But his body is still strapped into the seat..."

She speculates who she might kill first if she were to spontaneously pop at different points of a typical day. "Like, back when I was a runner there were so many good choices! Like, Mrs. Carty. That old bitch is, like, a thousand years old. But she'll be one of, like, the last people on the planet. Then, who's she going to yell at?" She hunches over and raises a fist, imitating the old woman, "There better not be a broken egg in there, girl. Set it down gently and back away. And when I say gently, I mean gently, you purple-haired freak!" She perfectly mimics the hacking cough old Mrs. Carty ends every sentence with.

Peyton catches himself laughing along, forgetting about his brother. But not for long, Bailey stays at the front of every thought he has, every day. When he steals the whiskey, they share it in Vanessa's kitchen. Peyton never sees a parent or a sibling or anyone else living at the home besides Vanessa. He doesn't ask—the post-outbreak version of polite.

After that night, he slides back into his role as lieutenant and sends runners out, doesn't do it himself. Having to make conversation with news-hungry neighbors sounds beyond rage-inducing. He'd rather have a whole neighborhood filled with Mrs. Carty, people who want their stuff and nothing else. No talking.

"Are the patrols gone?"

"Will they come back?"

"How will we get rations?"

Peyton has no idea how Gabriel wants those questions answered. He needs to go into Olde Town and find out. And he needs to man-up and see his brother. If Bailey's sick...if he's dying...not finding out won't make it less true.

Because he avoided going to lieutenant meetings or Olde Town headquarters, The Greens misses out on Featherton trades from the opened roads and the stream of refugees going west. Eventually, word gets back that Pierce Heights and Quail Creek have fruit and frozen food, avocados and almonds. President of the Watch Lyle Hutton and his wife Jenny bang on the door of Peyton's house, and hand over a list of demands from around the neighborhood: children's shoes, charcoal, antibiotic cream, powdered milk, matches…a list that anyone could have filled in a Walmart or a Target in his life before the outbreak.

They all sit down at the kitchen table, and his dad makes coffee. Lila stays at the window, staring out at fucking nothing. Pulling her away, distracting her from the pointless vigil for Lucy, was always Bailey's job. *Bailey.* His brother's name keeps bouncing round in his head, driving him nuts. "I'll find out what's in the next shipment and put claims down," Peyton says. He should go today, put orders in. Maybe, he could avoid the Featherton mansion altogether and just ask Cecilia. He doesn't know her that well, except for the fact that she acts way more interested in kissing Gabriel's ass than getting out on the streets and doing the physical stuff. Peyton gets so tired of the politics.

He keeps his black boots near the back door, and he gets up to retrieve them, shuffles back to the table to put them on. The weight of his too-long blue hair falls over his face. It reeks of cigarette smoke and the whiskey from the night before.

Mason brings out the coffee. "The shipments should be regular now that the government opened the roads again," Mason offers in his booming voice. Jenny and Lyle accept their steaming mugs with all the fake protests people once used to refuse extravagant gifts. Jenny closes her eyes when she takes a sip.

"Oh, and coffee, Pey. Tell Gabriel we need more coffee." Mason flips his hand toward Jenny, showing off.

Peyton shakes his hair back. "I already said I'd put an order in."

Jenny and Mason chat the way they might have in their previous lives—like two neighbors who run into each other at the country club or the Starbucks. They talk about the roads opening like they won't ever close again. *Disgusting.* They all hang on to all these little rules and customs of the past. *None of that shit matters anymore. Why do they want to pretend anything will ever be the same?*

Killing, taking, surviving, that's what matters.

Lyle Hutton scowls and stares into his cup. Not a fool, not like his wife. "I don't see the patrols too often anymore," Lyle says.

Peyton's father and Jenny Hutton both quiet.

"Didn't see one at all this week." Lyle looks up from his cup to fix his stare on Peyton. "What's Gabriel going to do when the roads close back up? What's he going to do when there's nothing left to raid?"

"Gabriel has a plan for everything, every possible outcome." Peyton doesn't know those plans, but he does know Gabriel. And knows that he lives for planning and forming contingencies to stay as many steps ahead of everyone else as possible. "He's seen this coming for a long time." And the truth washes over Peyton. "He saw this coming right from the start of martial law."

"You trust him, then?" Lyle asks.

"I do." Peyton wants to shake off Lyle and Jenny, go about his day, tick off another span of hours avoiding the wait for Bailey's infection to show.

"But, you're his lieutenant here in The Greens. And you've been keeping to yourself, angry and…people say they see you drunk. You reek of it now," Lyle tells him.

Is that the real reason you came down here? So, it's not only a problem with the deliveries? Peyton squints, a snarl starting to curl his lip. "Go report me to Gabriel if you—"

Lyle holds up a palm. "I know that we can't judge anything by what the world was like before. You were a good kid, a leader, even before the Super Flu."

Peyton stares back at him, tries to morph his face to one of Gabriel's blank expressions. He can't do it. His hands ball to fists and his teeth grind. He wants out of the room and out of this fucking conversation with Lyle Hutton.

"People here need you to—"

"I don't care what they need, I don't answer to them." Peyton stands and grabs his leather jacket from the couch. "I answer to Gabriel."

His father rises to his feet, comes up beside him. He places a hand on Peyton's shoulder. Mason's touch turns Peyton's stomach.

"I think what Lyle is trying to say here, Peyton—"

Peyton slaps Mason's hand away. "I don't give a shit what he's trying to say. Unlike you, *I've* got a job to get to."

hope

20 Bailey

Bailey's leg keeps knocking against the wide mahogany desk they share in Gabriel's study. "You're giving me some seriously pointed looks there," Bailey says. He points a fat yellow highlighter toward Gabriel's face.

"Stop fidgeting."

"Sorry!" The Featherton leader gave him a bunch of simple bookkeeping jobs to do, called it "rent" when Bailey complained. And, yeah, fair enough. Bailey does owe him. So he makes lists of inventory from empty houses in the neighborhoods. *Empty the way the Clement's house now sits empty.* But seriously, Bailey's done nothing but tally up apples for the last hour. Freakin' apples! "So, maybe instead of hash marks, the runners could write actual numbers. Then, I wouldn't have to literally count a bunch of tiny lines. I'm going cross-eyed over here." He drums the highlighter on the desktop.

Another pointed look.

"Sorry!"

A long, put-upon sigh. And Gabriel bends his head back over a layered map and mess of paper. His dark crimson hair hangs over his eyes, broken loose from his usual slicked back style to dangle down nearly to the desk, one long finger traces supply routes toward storage houses. Numbered, renumbered, switched around and hidden, those houses hold food, medicine, fuel... Those maps, detailing what-and-where, have more value than anything else in their new world.

Gabriel always keeps them locked in a homemade safe under a floorboard. Bailey thinks he might be the only person besides Gabriel to know this. And Cecilia Vu, of course. Gabriel definitely trusts her with all the important information and his hiding places. *Cecilia. God.* No wonder she acts like such a bitch to him—she obviously considers Bailey a gold-digging whore, screwing her boss so he can live in the Featherton mansion and wear designer clothes. *Ha!*

Nice guys like Bailey might as well have "Friend Zone" tattooed on their foreheads. How does anyone believe that he, *Bailey Tyrone,* managed to attract the attention of the gorgeous, evil overlord running all of Feathertons? Bailey bites at the end of the highlighter, then taps it against his teeth.

Wait, gorgeous? No! God! He cannot start thinking of Gabriel Featherton as—*in any way*—attractive. No. Nope. His leg starts to jiggle again. *Maybe this is the start of my brain going rogue?* Mental confusion, emotional turmoil, those are symptoms…it's only been a week, so it's still kind of early… *Oh my god…*

Gabriel's hand slams down on Bailey's leg, fingers curling into the flesh of Bailey's thigh, locking the two of them together. "Maybe you should work out or—"

Bailey misses whatever suggestions Gabriel makes, too focused on the weight of Gabriel's hand on him. He shakes his head. "No, it's fine. I'm fine," he says around the highlighter.

Gabriel removes the hand on Bailey's thigh to yank the marker from his mouth and tosses it across the room. "You're bored. I can find something else…"

"No. I'm good! You don't need to keep finding things to keep me busy. I'm not a kid." *God, probably Gabriel wonders what he ever saw in me…as a friend…as a potential friend.* "I'm not going to, like, color on the walls or anything if you aren't watching me 24/7. Heh—"

"That's not why I'm watching you."

Right. *Exactly.* Bailey stands to crack his back. He paces around the room and then collapses onto one of the plush linen sofas.

"Alright?"

"What? Oh, I'm fine." Bailey ruffles his hair back and takes a deep breath. "Just…thinking… Hey, do you play the clarinet?"

"The clarinet?"

"I wasn't snooping, but there's a clarinet case and a folded music stand in the closet of my room. And a bunch of practice books, too."

"And you weren't snooping?"

Bailey's eyes bug. "Okay, so your voice just dropped the temperature in the room by a thousand degrees." He jams his hands in the front pocket of his brand new designer hoodie. "You gave me a bunch of clothes, and I saw it in the closet. Sorry."

Gabriel stares down at the map again. He smooths it flat and shifts a heavy glass paperweight to hold it. "I played clarinet as a child."

"For real?" *Don't laugh!* "Uh… Were you any good?"

"I was a child. I'm sure I was quite bad at it." Gabriel tucks the hanging strands of crimson hair behind an ear and then carefully places one hand over the other.

"Huh. I got to tell you…that's really hard to picture. And not just the clarinet, the you being bad at it part…" Bailey slouches lower into the couch, reaches out a foot to tap against the edge of the desk with his shoe. "You're seriously the most controlled person I've ever met. It looks stifling and exhausting to live with that much rigid discipline."

Gabriel's shoulders straighten, like Bailey's words affect him, like Bailey's opinion affects him.

Bailey lowers his foot, not really in the mood to torment Gabriel further with his annoying habits. "Anyway...I want you to know..." The words stagger out of him. They're hard to say. "At the start of everything, the outbreak, martial law, I thought what you and Peyton were doing was just making everything worse. I thought you were acting like...thugs." He scratches at his mop of hair, tries not to make eye contact because, *what the hell did he just say?* "Well, Peyton still is kind of a thug, I guess."

"Are you getting to a point here, Bailey. Because your brother has already told me many, many times that you disapprove—"

"No, wait!" Bailey throws a hand out to stop him. "I said I thought that in the beginning, and yeah, for a long time after the beginning, too. But, I don't think that *now*. What you said about wanting to help the sick, and the way you were with those people yesterday..." He's talking way too fast and scratching his head again like a total spaz, so he makes himself take one of those calming breaths that his speech teacher told him to do. "Listen, I'm not dying my hair some crazy color and joining up or anything. I'm not interested in acting as one of your followers. But I can do more than this. To help. To help *you*." Bailey pulls himself up. "I *want* to... So, give me something real to do."

Gabriel bites at his cheek, like he's trying to stifle a smile, even though Bailey doesn't bother to hide his own. "Yeah, yeah. You won me over...a little." Bailey holds up his fingers to show an inch of space. "I'm this much won over."

And that actually gets a laugh out of the mighty Featherton boss. "Then, I'll take that much. For now."

21 PEYTON

After the shit with Lyle Hutton, Peyton pushes aside the headache and sweat of his hangover. Vanessa offers him a beer at the storehouse, but he waves it off. He wants all his wits about him for what will come next that day—checking in on Bailey. And, as usual, Gabriel manages to predict Peyton's mind better than Peyton himself. On the bottom of Peyton's delivery list, written in Gabriel's curlicue script:

"Bailey's doing well."

Vanessa flips pages on her inventory, studies it extra hard. *She must have seen what Gabriel wrote.* Peyton smudges out Gabriel's writing with the heel of his hand.

"I have a big order from The Greens," he tells Vanessa. He hands her the list that Jenny and Lyle Sutton gave him. Vanessa's expression gets darker and darker as she reads.

"We don't have any of this. Can you bring them—?"

Fucking great. "No! I need to bring *this* stuff. The head of my Neighborhood Watch came by this morning to complain. I need this *exact* stuff."

Vanessa taps the paper against her chin. "Hmmm… You could get everything from the Pierce Heights' stores. You know Derek Sams? He might spot you some of it. If you tell him you'll trade later."

"Derek hates me," Peyton grumbles. "I gave him a bunch of shit in high school, and he's holding a grudge or something." Come to think of it, none of the other four Featherton lieutenants like him either. He hasn't spent a lot of time trying to make friends in the post-outbreak world. The two girls, Cecilia Vu, who heads Olde Town, and Angelica Loeza, lieutenant of Quail Creek, he doesn't even know that well. The Pierce Height's lieutenant, that show-off fuck Derek Sams, had always reminded him of Mason, so Peyton regularly messed with him back in high school. That left Jadyn Clegg, who manages all the unincorporated streets, the little pockets of people who resisted Gabriel's attempts to relocate them into one of the major neighborhoods he supplies and guards. "I think I remember Jadyn being okay. He was friends with Bailey." Fuck all this. He just wants the Huttons and the rest of The Greens off his shit. He rubs the back of his neck, "What do you think?"

"Well…" Vanesa keeps giving him these little half smiles and twisting her purple hair around her fingers when she talks to him. Flirting? She does that now as she bites her bottom lip. "You could ask Clegg, but the unincorporated streets don't have many people left. I doubt he has even half this stuff."

Her flirting starts to really get on his nerves. "So, fucking focus on the problem here and tell me who I can go to."

Vanessa's girlish grin drops away, and her eyes narrow. She looks pissed now. "Why don't you ask your brother? He's got Gabriel's attention front and center. You could get everything you want from Olde Town. Why are you even messing around trying to trade with the other lieutenants?"

Front and center…what the fuck does that mean? "What do you know about Bailey?"

Vanessa takes a step back. "I just know he's…*you know*. He and Gabriel are…together. Right?"

Together? It takes a full minute of Peyton staring at Vanessa with his brain a stupid blank to understand. Together. Like *that?*

No fucking way.

Peyton thought that maybe, when he finally got the balls to check on his younger brother, he might find Bailey with dyed hair and steel toed boots. But this? *It's a cover story. It's gotta be.*

Gabriel likes guys—that makes sense. Even back in high school, Peyton never saw him with girls. And Peyton really doesn't give a shit how Gabriel gets off. But Bailey had that long-time girlfriend, Ashley.

Yeah. It's a bluff. But it's a fucking annoying bluff. Peyton has given Gabriel everything since Lila overdosed and the outbreak started…but not *this*. Bailey belongs to Peyton. "They aren't together." He doesn't care if he wrecks the cover Gabriel made. "Bailey's not gay."

"Well, according to what—"

"No," Peyton says and points a finger in her face. "He's not. I know Bailey. I know him better than anyone. A lot fucking better than Gabriel."

"Okay!" Vanessa holds her clipboard up like a shield, but Peyton lunges forward and grabs one arm. He must look half crazed because Vanessa freaks. "Let go! Let go! Let go!" Looks like their tentative friendship has come to an end.

Peyton shakes her. "Call Derek Sams and get my stuff." Peyton rips the satellite phone off her hip and shoves it into her chest. "Do it. Right fucking now."

Vanessa nods and starts pressing buttons on the bulky satellite phone, her eyes wide and wet looking.

"And stop spreading lies about my brother."

22 Bailey

"Dude, stop hovering." Bailey sits at Gabriel's huge desk. "I'm fine."

"You didn't eat breakfast." Gabriel pulls the pen out of Bailey mouth and presses a protein shake into his hand. "Stop calling me dude."

"Yeah, yeah. Sorry to not show you the proper respect, great leader…" Bailey takes a huge gulp of the shake, thumps it down and goes right back to chewing the pen. "So, what am I looking at here?" Gabriel gave him a stack of scribbled on maps showing the United States, then the Midwest, then the state, then the suburbs, and zeroing in on his territory. As Bailey reads each page, some of Gabriel's scribbles look pretty ominous. Like he tried to sketch out

what the rest of the country might look like based on stories—
gruesome, scary stories—told by the people trickling into his territory.

Gabriel's long fingers trace along the roads and highways that
lead toward the middle of the country. "Most people don't have the
skills to make it on their own, living on the land or living rough. If
we bring them into Featherton territory, we can capitalize on skills
they *do* have, skills that only matter in a society."

The final map shows all the twisting, curling streets of the
neighborhoods in Featherton territory with, as Bailey suspected, the
storage houses all labeled. Not only that, all the occupied and
unoccupied houses, with descriptions of each, and notations
regarding the lots they sat on. "I have thirty-four new families who
need places to live." Gabriel hands Bailey a stack of index cards with
names, ages, skills, and other information about the dusty and
haggard people he'd seen gathered in Gabriel's yard. "Can you find
them neighborhoods where they might fit? Places where they will get
along with the other neighbors. You know what I mean, find them
appropriate houses, split evenly between neighborhoods, with good
yards, the right belongings."

Yeah, he can do this. Bailey nods. He holds the cards in his hands,
aware that each card represents a life, a new beginning for someone
who has gone through a hell he can't even imagine. "Three daughters
under the age of ten," he reads. "Parents dead but arrived with an
aunt." *They need a house near other kids, near a playground.* "Hang on. I
just filed an inventory for a house in Pierce Heights." He jumps from
the chair and starts picking through the folders. "Ah ha! Look!"
Bailey slaps a piece of paper on the desk. "Retired couple that kept
bedrooms for their granddaughters." The old couple both died in
the first week of outbreak, but the granddaughters weren't visiting.
"Where is the family staying now? On compound?"

"In the old YMCA building, here in Olde Town. Most of the
incoming people sleep for several days after coming off the road."

Bailey reads the inventory list and nods along to both Gabriel's words and the ones on the page. He yanks the pen from the corner of his mouth, taps it on the inventory sheet. "There's clothes and everything in that house. Do you think someone can go check the sizes on what's in the closets? Clothes and shoes?" He turns to eye the file cabinets he was organizing. "Actually, if the sizes in the house don't match, I can move some stuff around..." Bailey notices Gabriel staring, and he stops chattering. "What?"

"You're good at this. The girls' rooms and the clothes. I wouldn't have thought of that."

Bailey never accepts compliments very well. Peyton trained him to expect a snide follow-up or a literal punch to the gut after any praise. "Well, yeah. It's about taking care of people. That's kind of my specialty. I mean..." Bailey shrugs. "Since the outbreak. I'd rather help people who need it than beat them to a pulp when they get sick."

Gabriel hands over another stack of notecards, "Write down everything you need, and I'll have Cecilia take over the logistics of making it happen."

"Yikes." Bailey jams the pen back in his mouth. Ink has started to leak a little from the plastic, and he can taste it. *Gross.* He pulls the little trashcan near him closer and spits the pen into it. "Leave out the part about my involvement when you tell Cecilia. *That* won't go over too well." Bailey wipes his mouth on the sleeve of his hoodie.

"She doesn't like you. Why? I don't remember the two of you ever interacting in high school. Did something happen that I'm not aware of?"

"Uh, seriously?" Bailey concentrates on shuffling the index cards. That *"for sex"* explanation of his presence definitely does not need to be said out loud. And anyway, how clueless can Gabriel be about this? His fingers start the nervous tapping again. "Come on...you can't think of any reason that she might not like me?"

Gabriel's blank face shows a quick tightening of his mouth and an almost imperceptible narrowing of his eyes. He's not such a pro at hiding all his emotions when he gets even a little off balance. And he knows Bailey's making fun of him.

"Well, I'll just let you figure it out in your own time then, buddy." Bailey smacks a fist against Gabriel's arm. He holds the index cards up and shakes it. "I'll get started on this."

23 PEYTON

Peyton leans on the doorframe of Gabriel's guest room, watching his little brother punch numbers into a calculator. Bailey's made a huge mess of the once spartan room. Stacks of paper cover the desk and dresser top. Bailey's clothes and books pile on the floor. That dumb stuffed giraffe. And Bailey cross-legged in the middle of the bed, a configuration of sticky notes and folders spiraling around him. Relief twists so hard inside Peyton that he wants to puke.

"Okay, so I think I have most of this figured out," Bailey says.

"What figured out?"

His brother's curly head pops up, and the wide gray eyes grow even wider. "Oh. Peyton." Then, a wrinkle creases his forehead. "Why are you here? Did Gabriel make you come?"

"No, he didn't make me come. I wanted to see how you were." Bailey wears a new pair of jeans and a dark green sweater that Peyton's never seen before. Expensive looking. So Gabriel doesn't keep him in a cage or anything. That's good. Peyton gestures to the mess in the room. "What the hell are you doing? You should be resting."

Bailey starts to gather all the sticky notes and folders. "It's nothing. Just some stuff for…"

Peyton grabs the folders out of Bailey's hands and opens a few. Paper rains down from between them. Maps. Lists of furniture and clothes and other shit not worth looting.

"Peyton, I had those organized. Give it back."

"He's making you work for Feathertons?" Somehow, this offends Peyton more than if he had found out Gabriel kept Bailey tied down in a locked room.

Peyton himself might mock Bailey for his principles and general unwillingness to participate in everything their new life demands, *but that's different.* He likes when Bailey fights him on morals and all the other bullshit he believes in. He needs Bailey to draw those lines for him, even when he crosses them.

Bailey jumps up from gathering the flying papers and notes. "God! Relax! He's not forcing me into Feathertons or anything. I'm trying to help out on this one project. I'm helping relocate the asylum seekers into houses…homes. I'm trying to put together things they need and…help them."

Peyton's eyes narrow. "Why?"

His brother sighs, tossing all the paper and folders onto the bed, destroying whatever order he had created for them. "I don't know, Peyton. Maybe, I want to do something useful around here while I still can."

"Working for Gabriel doesn't make you useful."

"That's not what I mean." Bailey drops back onto the bed, grabs one of the pillows and squeezes it against himself like it's a fucking teddy bear. Like it's that stuffed giraffe he's kept since before he could talk or walk. "Why are you here? Did you really just want to see me?" Bailey's mouth twists. "I know you, Peyton. You aren't here because you miss me or anything. What. Do. You. Want?"

Say something. "Um… Mom and Dad said to say hi. They wanted me to see how you were doing."

Bailey's eyebrows shoot upwards. "Really?"

Again, Peyton can't think of a response. He wants to tell him, *"No, of course, not really. Bailey, you total dumbass."* They both grew up in that house, but Bailey still hasn't figured out that their parents don't care about anything but themselves. Lila doesn't even seem to notice Bailey's absence, and Mason spends all his time down at the Huttons trying to suck up to Neighborhood Watch. Finally, Peyton settles on a noncommittal shrug in place of a response.

Bailey's face falls. "Is Mom sitting at the window again?"

"Always."

"Make sure she eats and takes a shower. She forgets about everything except—"

"Don't say it."

"Everything *except* waiting for Lucy. It's just been really hard for her, Pey. You should be more... Ugh. Fine. Let's drop it."

"Fuck Lila. Fuck Mason." Peyton looks Bailey over again, searching for changes. Has he lost weight? Does he act stressed? Seem tired? But his memories of his brother go too deep, and he only sees the things about Bailey that he has always seen. The shaggy curls that hang over his eyes, the freckle on his lower lip, the jittery hands and bitten nails. "Don't get so involved in whatever this crap is that Gabriel has you doing. You should be eating and staying hydrated, staying healthy."

Bailey tosses the pillow aside and sighs. "I am not stupid, Peyton. I am doing all that."

"Good." Peyton stays in the doorway, ready to leave, but wanting to stay. "So..."

"So..." Bailey stands, goes to the window to look out. "God! What else? Spit it out, Pey."

Peyton raps a knuckle against the door. "You know what people are saying about the two of you, right? What Gabriel's been telling them?"

137

When Bailey turns around, his face has flushed red. "Yep. What's the big deal? So, what?" His voice comes out so raspy that Peyton strains to hear. Bailey's hands twist into the hem of the expensive-looking sweater, and his eyes meet Peyton's for only a second, then skitter away.

Oh…okay.

Peyton waits him out, waits for Bailey's eyes to meet his again. Then, he'll leave. The next time, his gaze sticks, and they give each other a long look.

Peyton raps his knuckle on the door again. "So, nothing," he says.

24 Bailey

So, now Bailey has to deal with his brother visiting each day. They don't talk, not really, but Bailey lets himself get looked over. *Yep. Still alive.* Then, Peyton leaves. *Thank God.*

After Peyton goes, Bailey comes downstairs to meet Gabriel in the study.

He slams the door. "Not awkward at all! Thank you so much, Gabriel for the thoroughly embarrassing cover story."

"I've offered before to intervene. Have you decided you want me to?" Gabriel leans back into his chair, hands dragging from their work at the heavy desk to land on his thighs.

"Um…no. And you're giving me some serious supervillain vibes right now. So, yeah. No thanks." Gabriel keeps a chair near his own, so they can sit side by side to go over the relocation plans. Totally practical. Not at all cozy. Or anything. Bailey slides into his seat and takes out his collection of sticky notes and maps. "Man, I expected this job to taper off, but it's only getting harder."

"Yes, it is…" Gabriel twirls a fountain pen between his fingers. The cap looks warped, chewed on. One of Bailey's pens. *Hopefully, Gabriel doesn't notice.*

"So, it's not just me? It seems like a lot of people keep getting added to my pile needing houses. You might need to add a new neighborhood. Well, seven more houses would be good."

"I'll get some ready."

Bailey has a clear as day memory of student council, of Gabriel marking through a list of duties for the spring fundraiser—that they never had the chance to hold. At the time, he'd thought Gabriel relished every second of taking charge of those plans, bossing everyone around. But maybe, Gabriel had really cared about raising money for… Bailey can't even remember the cause they'd wanted to help fund because he'd only focused on how Gabriel got the job over him.

"I should have been nicer to you," Bailey blurts out. "Back in school, before all this started." He motions toward the maps, the sticky notes, the lists.

Gabriel looks up from his own lists. "Why do you say that?"

An old-fashioned wooden clock chimes softly from across the room. Bailey takes a steadying breath and meets Gabriel's pale gaze. "Because I misjudged you."

"I…no I don't think you did, Bailey."

What? He lets the clock finish chiming out. *Is it 5 billion o'clock or something?* "So," Bailey says, his voice coming out a little high, a little unsteady. "Are you warning me off you now?" The papers under Bailey's fingers tremble but not because of him this time. Gabriel's hands are shaking.

"I…" He does that blank look again, the cold Featherton leader slamming into place. "I can get you more than seven houses if I annex Piney Woods neighborhood into Pierce Heights. It would be easy to plow out a road between the two here." Gabriel's finger taps at a flat green park separating the two.

Okay…back to business. *See if I put myself out there again.* What did Bailey expect? That Gabriel would have been pining away for him all this time? Bailey's face heats up, but he focuses on his job, shuffling through his lists for information on the empty houses in Piney Woods. "Do you think we'll fill it?"

Gabriel shoves his shaking hands in his pockets. "I think I will. There are more people than I expected to make it this far."

"It must be terrible back that way. Back toward the East Coast." Bailey smooths the curling map down, traces the route so many refugees come from.

They work together for another hour. Then, Gabriel sends a little squad of runners out to Piney Woods to get more details for Bailey's rehousing plans. Once the runners come back with new lists and a gruesome story about stumbling into a nest of dead creatures, Cecilia pulls Gabriel away for other duties.

"This shouldn't take long, Bailey," Gabriel says. "But stay in here until I return."

In case I pop and start killing everyone. "Sure thing," Bailey answers. With Gabriel out of the study, Bailey replays the "warning me off" question in his head, alternating between hoping it sounded casual and teasing, when he knows it probably did not, and wondering how he wanted Gabriel to answer. *Do I like him? He kind of scares me sometimes, but do I like him?*

25 PEYTON

Peyton has no clue what happened to Gabriel's original neighbors, if they all died or if the Featherton boss moved them out. But, once he had the manpower, Gabriel built a tall privacy fence around the entirety of Olde Town and claimed the entire historic neighborhood as his base of operations. He locked it up tight with a guard tower and tall gate. Because he's a lieutenant and Gabriel's "friend," Peyton can usually cruise right in on the Marauder, drive right up to the mansion and park on the curved front drive. Not today, though. Some kind of standoff looks like it's going down at the compound entrance.

Great. Peyton just wants to do his morning check in—make sure Bailey looks okay, that Gabriel is feeding him and shit. Now this.

Feathertons form a long, deep, and forbidding line at the front of the entrance. At least thirty teenagers with crazy neon hair and clubs. They bar the way of a tight cluster of government types from coming inside, older guys in military camo. With guns.

In front of the Feathertons' ranks, Peyton recognizes Shane Liu, the former National Guardsman. His dark buzz cut now bleached and dyed a metallic silver. He gives Peyton a tight nod as a greeting.

So far, none of the five soldiers has drawn on the teens.

"What the fuck is going on?" Peyton yells toward the whole mess. He parks the Marauder and unhooks his club. Not much use against a gun, but Peyton only has the one weapon.

Shane stands up straighter, practically salutes. "Gabriel's orders, no government soldiers allowed inside."

"And that stopped them?" Peyton scoffs. Then a heartbeat later, he wonders if soldiers showing up at the compound has anything to do with his brother. Did they find out that Gabriel offered protection to someone with the virus? Peyton's grip tightens on his club.

"Just calm down, son," says one of the military men. "We're just here for protection, not to storm your little clubhouse."

Shane crosses his arms. "Yeah, and there are a lot more of us than there are of you. Don't forget that part."

A female voice comes from behind the cluster of soldiers. "Peyton Tyrone," the blonde woman says as she steps forward. She looks familiar…maybe. Long nails tap at a tablet in her hands, and she wears a skirt suit and heels. Seriously? This prissy bitch holds the leash on five armed soldiers? Peyton can't hold back his snort of laughter.

The blonde has those same ice blue eyes as Gabriel. "Something amusing?" Gabriel's dangerously calm, inflectionless pissed-off voice, too.

"Okay, so you know who I am. Big deal. Lots of people know who I am."

Peyton and Gabriel never exactly swapped stories of their childhoods or families, but Peyton always got the impression that he had a handful of blood relations in the City. This girl? Clearly one of those. Just look at her. *Snotty bitch.*

"Yeah, something is really amusing," he says. He lets his eyes roam over her body, checks her out. Then smirks. "I think it's pretty amusing when people get all dressed to impress, when that crap doesn't really matter anymore."

"People like me and my brother, you mean?"

Brother?

He sees it now, the high cheekbones and sharp lips, the same almond shape to their pale eyes. "I don't care who you are. Get out of my way and go home, or leave the soldiers behind and come inside. I really don't give a shit either way."

Shane takes a step forward.

Then, the camo guys tense up, start inspecting Peyton's grip on the club, his demeanor. Like he might pose a threat.

The blonde doesn't seem bothered in the slightest, though. She flicks a hand toward Peyton's blue-tipped hair. "Aren't you his second in command of this operation?"

"There is no second in command."

"No. I guess there wouldn't be. My brother has always been selfish about his things. But you were there from the start, weren't you? His best friend here in the suburbs and all that. And now, he's claimed everything for himself." Her eyes flicker over his face.

This again. She doesn't know how little Peyton cares about all Gabriel has claimed. "Yeah, other people have tried this shit before you. Trying to get me to make a move against him."

"So, you're loyal." Her voice hovers between a whisper and a laugh. "The good little soldier."

"I'm not the good little anything," Peyton says. "Now, get out of my way."

She doesn't even flinch, but Shane takes a step between them. "Go on in," he tells Peyton with his flat security-man expression. Then to the girl, Shane says, "If you want to talk to the big boss, then you'll come back without the armed escort."

For a second, the blonde's eyes flash with something more than detached amusement. "He can't keep me out of my parents' home. He doesn't have the right."

Peyton laughs, loud and mocking. "Looks like he doesn't need the right. You want to go to the house, then you need to do what he says."

It takes her a long, deep breath to pull back from the rage Peyton sees on her face and body, something Peyton has seen Gabriel do. And a part of Peyton can respect that. He has always had such a hard time pulling back from the edge himself. Like Gabriel, she looks uptight and pretentious—but, also like Gabriel, Peyton can see the ruthless fighter inside her. Peyton decides that awards her a moment of his consideration. "Listen, Gabriel's sister…your home doesn't look the same, and I seriously doubt he saved anything." Peyton tries to sound sincere. Maybe, this girl gave a shit about her parents. Gabriel didn't seem too torn up over whatever happened to them. "Listen, if your pride can't take the hit, then don't bother… Fuck Gabriel."

Shane moves out a hand in an ushering gesture. "Okay, that's it, Peyton. Let's go."

The men surrounding the blonde make a bunch of noises like they would really like to stay and teach the punk kids a lesson. One of them even says it out loud, and Shane flips him off.

Gabriel's sister has one lingering look for Peyton before she turns and walks away.

Six feet inside the fenced perimeter, Gabriel stands beside a furious looking Cecilia Vu. The Featherton boss also has his arms crossed and a cold sneer but not for Peyton. The expression directed at the gate entrance and the sound of the Hummers pulling away.

Cecilia Vu steps up to Peyton. "I can't believe you. I don't know why Gabriel even keeps you around."

Peyton ignores her. He *always* ignores her, usually just to piss her off. But to Peyton's surprise, this time Gabriel also doesn't acknowledge her.

"Bailey is at the house." Gabriel sounds unbothered by the "Fuck Gabriel" comment outside the gate and greets Peyton with a placid familiarity that hasn't existed between them since before the outbreak. "Try not to give him a hard time."

guilt

26 Bailey

Another afternoon of matching houses and people, of arranging a storehouse for the Piney Woods addition to the Pierce Heights neighborhood. Bailey feels good about this work, like he's making a difference, and that matters to him just in case he doesn't...well, *just in case.*

A staccato of knocks, and Cecilia pushes open the study's double doors. Glittery white hair tucked behind her ears, the expression of having smelled something bad when her eyes spot Bailey working side by side with her boss.

Oh my God, can she stop with the passive/aggressive sneering for once? "I'm not stealing all the Featherton secrets in here, Cecilia. I'm doing an actual job." Bailey shakes a handful of notecards at her. "See—I'm working!" Although, to tell the truth, before she popped her head in, he and Gabriel had spent more time snickering at Bailey's homemade map than getting anything done. But hey, Bailey's trees did kind of look like penises when you saw them from a certain angle. It was funny, okay? And making Gabriel break his "I am Aloof and Superior" act always felt worth it to Bailey.

But in front of his Olde Town Lieutenant, Gabriel drops back into his usual blank facade. "What did you need, Cecilia?"

"A...government official is here." Cecilia's stiff posture must be nerves, something she picked up from Gabriel. "I only just got the call from the front gate." She gives Gabriel an eye-widening expression loaded with meaning that goes over Bailey's head.

"Huh? 'Government Official?'" Bailey makes air quotes. "Official *what?*"

"This doesn't involve you," Cecilia snaps. "This is sensitive information about the running of Feathertons."

Gabriel stands. "And she's come without her guards this time?" His suit jacket hangs over the back of the chair, and he puts it on, smoothing out the creases.

Bailey touches Gabriel's wrist. "Who is it, Gabriel?"

"My sister."

"That I met at the party? Bad Twin Renée?"

Cecilia looks imploringly at Gabriel. "Talking about this in front of him isn't wise."

Bailey tips his head back and groans. "*Who* am I going to tell, Cecilia? I don't know anyone besides Feathertons anyway. My own brother is a lieutenant!"

Gabriel holds up a hand. Like he expects Bailey to stop defending himself and fall silent at his command. And for a second, it works. Until Bailey realizes it worked. "No, I'm not going to—"

But Gabriel, that total prick, talks over him. "Stay in here," he orders, and shuts Bailey inside the study. Again.

"Asshole!" Bailey gets up to defy him but then hears the front door open, and the corridor outside the study fills with voices, so he hesitates. Back in high school, Peyton thought he had Gabriel all figured out. Maybe Peyton still thinks this. Bailey's brother acted as Gabriel's faithful sidekick both before and after the outbreak. And Gabriel turned to Peyton first with all his plans for Feathertons. Still, Peyton never once mentioned anything about Gabriel having a sister, and Bailey doesn't credit that to Peyton acting discreet. *Peyton didn't know because Gabriel didn't want it known.*

Bailey waits at the study doors then presses one ear against the crack between them. It all sounds civil enough. Featherton guards' low gruff voices, and Gabriel answering back in a calm and even manner. But then, the laugh of a woman, a laugh that has nothing to do with amusement and everything to do with ridicule and spite. Not Cecilia's style. It's Renée, the sister. Bailey can't tell what they say, but some order comes from Gabriel's voice, and the heavy footsteps of steel-toed boots leave.

The lighter tapping of high heels on the dark wood floor comes closer.

Without thinking, Bailey dives back toward the expansive mahogany desk and swipes the paperweights away. He curls the maps and papers in on each other. But he can't stash it anywhere because of the bulk and mess of the roll, and he doesn't want to reveal the floor safe. *Crap!*

The study doors sweep open.

Sweat beads on Cecilia's forehead, her face tight and pale. When she sees the bundle of top-secret maps in Bailey's arms, she gasps before slapping a hand over her mouth. Gabriel comes in behind her.

"Oh, no," Renée coos. "I've interrupted something important. What a good little worker-bee you must be to be entrusted with all the top-secret information." She wears an outfit similar to the one she had on at the party. Black dress, black pumps. Her blonde hair curls around her shoulders.

"Renée, why are you here?" Gabriel snaps. "What do you want?"

She doesn't look back at him, her light blue eyes, anemic and menacing, just like her brother's. "I'm here to tell you to stay out of our way." She strolls around the room like she's shopping antiques, pauses at the annoying wooden clock. "We won't let your feud with Jaxon Colton get in the way of what we need in the City."

Gabriel jams his hands in his pants' pockets as he watches her move around his study. Bailey remembers him doing that earlier when they shook. But his voice sounds calm enough. "If you or Colton want to use our roads, then you'll give us a cut of whatever you transport." Bailey gets the feeling that Gabriel's artful slouch is as fake as his calm—that his sister's presence grates against his nerves worse than Peyton does with Bailey.

"For how much longer, little brother? Both Colton and I are getting tired of this game." Her slow perusal reaches Bailey. His grip on the maps tightens. "Oh…I remember you. You're the little brother. The one with all the moral objections to creature cracking." She laughs at him. Sort of…

Renée gives Bailey the creeps. Like all the worst of Gabriel, all the coldest and oiliest traits Bailey has witnessed in him, distilled into a hot blonde.

"Yeah? I'm sure you find it easier to live in the apocalypse without any of my pesky morals," Bailey deadpans. "I remember you pretty much admitting that murdering all those sick people was your idea." He steps to the side as she advances on him. He needs to defend the maps, they contain the location of every storehouse, every home under Featherton protection. But Bailey also wants to stay clear of the long fingernails she used on him before.

Gabriel comes forward and snaps a hand around her arm, keeping her from advancing further. Renée looks down at the hand more fascinated than angry that Gabriel has dared try and stop her.

In the pause between siblings, Cecilia rushes forward and takes the roll of papers from Bailey's arms. She shuts them into an ornately carved wooden cabinet on the wall by the fireplace and locks them inside with a little skeleton key waiting in the old-fashioned lock. As she slips the key into the front pocket of her tight black jeans, Cecilia's chin lifts. Bailey has learned to dislike that look of smug triumph on Cecilia's face. But in this exact moment, he wants to high-five her.

All of Renée's attention leaves Bailey, and the ice-chip eyes move to settle on Cecilia's defiant face.

Gabriel lets go of his sister's arm, wipes his hand on his pant leg, like touching Renée's skin makes him sick. He lets Renée close in on where Cecilia stands. He doesn't seem too worried about that tiny iron key in her pocket, or at least, not too worried about Renée taking it from Cecilia. He has a lot of faith in his second-in-command. He even lets Renée reach out and flicks a piece of Cecilia's glimmering white hair.

"This girl seems much better suited to you than the last one, Gabriel. She's obviously way less trusting than that idiot teenager you screwed in our City penthouse."

Cecilia blinks and her eyes dodge to Bailey.

"Did he tell you about her?" Renée purrs near Cecilia's ear. "She went to that boring high school my brother insisted on attending. Pretty long brown hair...Stacey or Casey...timid little thing."

Pretty long brown hair? There's only one girl from Memorial that Gabriel ever showed interest in.

Ashley.

Renée would love to get any kind of rise she can out of Cecilia. But, none of her words can hurt the person she directs them toward. Not like they cut at Bailey. Renée can't see him, can't see his face with her back to him, but all the pain she so gleefully aims at Cecilia devastates Bailey. His muscles turn to stone.

Ashley. They spent the night together in a City penthouse? When?

In the weeks before the outbreak, she canceled on Bailey several times, acted strange about it...guilty. Bailey remembers seeing Ashley and Gabriel together at the end of the school hallway, the lunchroom, near Ashley's car. As soon as Gabriel spotted Bailey, the older boy would whisper in Ashley's ear, eyes on Bailey, and then walk away. *He doesn't really want her,* Bailey always told himself. The words are out before he can stop them, "You dick. You total dick."

He'd thought Gabriel wanted to prove a point with Ashley—prove that she and Bailey didn't have the solid relationship Bailey claimed they did on the night of the Christmas party…when he'd pushed Gabriel away. But this went deeper than flirting between classes. Gabriel had taken Ashley to his penthouse and seduced her…*fucked* her. The girl Bailey loved, who he grew up with and thought he would marry.

Gabriel retreats into his standard armor of blankness, but his pale skin blanches whiter than usual, and his lips look bloodless.

Renée must think Bailey has jumped in to defend Cecilia. "Let's hope he treats this one better than that other conquest," she says. "He was so determined to impress her, to get laid, but it didn't mean anything. He didn't care at all about her. He didn't even care if she lived or died."

Bailey freezes. "What?"

Cecilia gasps. Renée managed to rattle her after all. But, Gabriel's Olde Town lieutenant's loyalty runs deep. "I don't believe you. Gabriel would never—"

"But he *did*. He knew he had the virus. He and my father had already made their plan to let him wait it out here at home. Too bad he never bothered to tell his girlfriend." Renée shakes her head, she looks at her brother and pouts. "I'm guessing she didn't make it?" Her words sound hazy and far away to Bailey, like someone saying them in the next room.

"He knew he had the virus."

Gabriel hauls Renée away from Cecilia, away from the cabinet with all his maps and plans locked inside.

"Too bad he never bothered to tell his girlfriend."

Bailey struggles to make sense of what happens after that. Everything in the room disconnects from him, and none of it matters.

The commotion of an argument.

Renée turning on her brother.

Gabriel forcing her out of the room.

Cecilia following them, snapping orders at Bailey.

None of it touches him. Bailey finds himself standing alone in the study. Legs too wobbly to stand, he slaps a hand down on the desk to stay upright. The sound of a door opening and closing.

Gabriel stands in front of him.

"You killed her."

"I didn't—" Gabriel wipes at his mouth. "Bailey, I'm sorry—"

"You knew you were sick. She's *dead* because of you... And you're *sorry?*" Bailey doubles over. *God—I'm going to be sick.* He's going to vomit right here on Gabriel's expensive rug in his pretentious study. "You think you can apologize for *killing* her, like when I chew on your pens or interrupt your work." He manages to straighten himself up again, steady himself. "Like she didn't matter. Like she wasn't a *person?*" His voice breaks.

"I knew, but I also didn't know, hadn't accepted—"

Bailey sucks in a long shaking breath, like he's coming up for air from a deep dive. "I don't want to hear it." He pushes past Gabriel to leave. Then stops.

And Bailey slams his fist into Gabriel's back. Into his kidneys where it really hurts. Peyton has punched Bailey there plenty of times, so he knows. "Fuck you. You should have died instead of her. You're fucking evil, you're..."

Now, Gabriel leans against the desk, one arm draped over his stomach in pain. Like Bailey nailed the kidney punch, got exactly the right spot to make the pain shoot through to the gut. *Good.*

"Just fuck you, Gabriel."

27 PEYTON

Cecilia Vu opens the door to the Featherton mansion to let Peyton inside. "Ugh, it's you." Even though they both wear similar clothing—black steel-toe boots, black jeans, heavy sweaters—she gives him a once over and wrinkles her nose. "You reek of burial pit."

"Yeah, fuck you, too." Peyton kicks the door closed behind him. Unzips his leather jacket, fans it open so that the dirt and dried blood flake from his arms and back. "You got no idea what's outside the Olde Town perimeter fence."

Cecilia shoots a worried look in the direction of the study. "Yes, Peyton, I actually do. You're the one with no idea of the big picture that—"

"Who gives a shit about—"

"Not so loud!" She looks over her shoulder, then whispers, "Just go upstairs to your brother and leave Gabriel alone. He's…in a mood."

"Yeah? How can you even tell? He's a dick, even when he's supposedly happy."

"You don't know him as well as you think you do, Peyton." Cecilia hesitates on the threshold. "And Bailey doesn't really know him, either. If he did, then he would respect Gabriel more." She slams open the front door, walks out without shutting it.

Peyton kicks it closed again. "Jealous much?" he grumbles.

A loud crash comes from behind the French doors. Something made of glass and very breakable just got thrown into a wall. Huh. Peyton has seen Gabriel lose control plenty of times, get angry and explode just like Peyton sometimes does. And although he and Gabriel never had the kind of friendship where they talked about their feelings or their lives, things feel different between them now.

Because of Bailey, Peyton wants Gabriel and Feathertons to succeed in a way he didn't care about before. Peyton jiggles a knob on one of the study doors as warning and finds Gabriel pacing the length of the study. Looking fucking irate. And kind of freaked out. Behind him, lodged inside the face of an antique wall clock is the heavy glass paperweight from his desk.

"Nice throw," Peyton says.

Gabriel's spins round. "What are you doing here? Did Bailey call you here?"

"Dude, how is he even going to call me? No one I know has gotten a cell signal in the last two months." Peyton throws himself onto a white linen couch, props his dirty boots on a low glass coffee table, and studies his former friend, now his boss. "Is there a problem I should know about?"

Gabriel puts his hands on the back of his neck. "No, of course not." His eyes squeeze shut. "Everything is just the same as always."

"Not even with your sister? That was quite the scene yesterday, with a military guard at the gate." Peyton watches as Gabriel slumps against the desk. His hair has broken from the usual slicked-back style and hangs over his face. His shirt is untucked and wrinkled. *Something* went wrong.

"She doesn't seem too fond of you. I see why you've never mentioned her."

Gabriel kicks at the papers on the floor. "*I've* never mentioned *her* because she's irrelevant."

"Irrelevant how? What is she even doing here?"

"She's irrelevant to anything happening here, to Feathertons. And to you. Just…go upstairs to Bailey." Gabriel swipes a hand on his forehead. "I'm sure he wants to see you."

"Fine with me," Peyton says and drags himself out of the couch cushions. "But you better keep your shit together enough to protect my brother. If you fuck that up, Gabriel…" Peyton crunches over the mess of fallen papers and detritus of Gabriel's meltdown. He moves to stand in front of Gabriel, one of the most powerful leaders in the post outbreak world. That doesn't matter to Peyton. "You fuck up Bailey's chance for survival, and I will fucking end you."

Gabriel doesn't move from his slouch against the desk, but the colorless eyes meet Peyton's. Whatever crap had him raging enough to throw that paperweight, he's managed to stuff down deep and lock back inside. "You don't tell me what to do, Peyton. I tell you." Gabriel straightens up, stiff, poised. Back to normal. "Bailey is under my protection, living in my house. Anyone who dares to cross me on this will regret it."

Peyton nods. "Good. "

Gabriel goes back behind the desk, places his fingers on the swept-clean surface, and looks down as if he can still see whatever list or note had once been there. "I need you to do something for me," Gabriel says.

Peyton crosses his arms. "What?"

"I want you to follow Case out to Quail Creek. She's doing the fuel car switch for us." No one can just stockpile or loot fuel because it goes bad in a month. So, the City, the suburbs, everyone needs access to a steady supply. But the refinery in Cushing is part of Colton's territory. "You can be her backup," Gabriel says.

"You can trust Case."

"Can I? Her mother must have gone to a lot of trouble to meet Colton's runners. Unless they came right into The Greens."

What the hell is that supposed to mean? "No one came into The Greens. If they got in our territory, then they must have parked just beyond the perimeter fence."

"Why don't you *know*?"

Fuck Gabriel. Peyton seals his lips tight enough to keep the words inside. Whatever had Gabriel so angry earlier didn't get buried quite deep enough. "What do you want me to do?"

"Follow her. Then report back to me."

***

Even before Gabriel ordered him to, Peyton considered following Case. The tanker switch will take place at an abandoned toll station near the mall in Quail Creek. Colton's ignorant as fuck crew will switch out an empty fuel truck for a full one—the price that Colton pays to travel over the stretch of road between the refinery in Cushing to the City barriers. Peyton rides out separately on the Marauder to meet Case in the truck. When he gets there, she's shaking out her hands the way she used to loosen her muscles before a basketball game.

"These guys don't like you, Peyton." She reaches up, flicks a piece of blue hair from his eyes. "Go hide."

He hates to say it, but she's right. Whoever Colton sends will probably have heard of Gabriel's blue-haired lieutenant. "Yeah, I guess I've beaten down enough of them." Peyton rolls his bike to the side of the road, behind an abandoned Greyhound bus. He wishes he had a better weapon than the club. It will have to do.

Colton's fuel truck, a white and silver Peterbilt exactly like their own, appears around the bend. He sent two guys, stringy-haired hicks in boot-cut jeans and flannel shirts. *Hopefully, these country fucks aren't racist.* But, they greet Case with friendly, familiar body language. The switch happens fast—the two hicks hop into the empty tanker and pull out. Case starts up the full truck to make like she's leaving, too, but then, she just waits.

Peyton walks out from behind the bus. "What now?"

Case leans out the driver-side window. "The connection for the drugs should be coming next. I'm supposed to wait here."

"Leave, and I'll meet them."

"Gabriel said—"

155

"Just go. I'm pretty sure I know what he was thinking. Go and tell Gabriel that I met with them in your place."

Relief and worry battle it out in Case's dark eyes before she nods. "I'll tell him." She throws the truck into drive and takes the exit back into Featheron territory.

Peyton leans against the toll booth, out of the dust blowing across the road, certain he knows what's coming. When a string of khaki Hummers curves down the highway, Peyton grits his teeth so hard his jaw aches. Why have Case do this? Why not just ask Peyton from the start?

He thinks I'm a fuckup. He's right. I am. Everything made sense in the beginning, fighting the creatures who spread Super Flu, looting whatever he needed, wanted. Gabriel should have never made him a lieutenant, and Peyton should have never accepted the job.

He still holds the chained bat in one hand as he steps forward to meet the first Hummer. It gets all the way to the Toll Plaza before Peyton sees the familiar haughty face through the windshield. When the Hummer stops and Gabriel's blonde sister gets out, he can't help the laughter creeping up his throat. "*You.* Fucking, of course."

"I was hoping we would see each other again."

Peyton shakes his head. "Not me." Peyton won't quite wipe the smile off his face. *This girl.* "You might as well give me whatever you planned to bribe Case with."

The blonde smiles. This time she doesn't look like a shark when she does it. She shrugs. "Sure, why not?" The wind whips her golden hair around her face when she returns to the Hummer and pulls out a battered duffle. Peyton unzips it partway to see inside. Boxes of pills, ampules, and needles. He whistles. "This is some high-end loot. Case didn't say she would be getting all this, just finding out about doing trades in the future." Peyton zips the duffle shut again and meets those eerily familiar eyes.

"And then, you showed up, football hero."

"I'm not here for your brother, I'm here because Case is my friend. I don't want her getting in the middle of a grudge between you and your brother."

"I'm sure that even if he didn't send you, you'll be reporting back to him." She tilts her chin up, widens her stance. This girl might look willowy, gorgeous, like a model, but she's still Gabriel's sister. He should remember to see past the beautiful face to that brutal core inside. "And it's way bigger than a grudge. I don't want my brother snatching up everything into his own empire to rule. That's how he's always been, wanting to own whatever he sees, wanting to slap his name on it and make it his." She opens her arms, a gesture meant to encompass far more than the ruins of the toll station. "You've seen it yourself, haven't you? Doesn't that bother you?"

Sometimes, yeah, it does. Peyton tries to steel his face, but he pictures his brother's messy curls bent over Featherton notes. Bailey's stuffed giraffe resting on the guest bed in Gabriel's house.

The blonde climbs back into the Hummer, and Peyton can't help himself… "What's your name anyway?"

Another smile that looks real, not scheming, not mocking. "Renée."

Oh, he knows that flavor of smile. *She likes me.* Peyton hoists the duffle over his shoulder, "I'll see you around…Renée."

28 Bailey

Bailey still works on the housing assignment, but he stays in his room to do it. No side-by-side work in the study. Boiling anger and searing grief make it difficult to even consider facing Gabriel. In Bailey's head, Peyton's voice calls him weak, calls him gutless.

Oh my God. Stop! Turns out, he doesn't even need to live with his brother to feel his constant overbearing presence. When Bailey hears

Cecilia's voice, he creeps down the stairs to meet with her, and together, they rearrange the contents of all the unoccupied houses. Without Gabriel present, he and Cecilia get along fine. She still scrunches her nose when she sees him, making Bailey want to sniff under his arms. She rolls her eyes at his jokes, but she hears him out on the rehousing plans. Still, after so much togetherness with the Featherton boss, it feels weird to spend the day alone. And the next day, too.

Maybe Gabriel feels weird, too. On the third day, he opens Bailey's bedroom door without knocking, like he owns the place. Well...he does *actually* own the place. But, still...Bailey hadn't even gotten up yet. Because with the rehousing work finished, he doesn't have a reason to get up.

"I want you at the lieutenants' meeting this afternoon." Imperious stance, disinterested tone. Over the past week, Bailey had gotten used to something a little warmer, a little more invested, from Gabriel.

Bailey considers ignoring him, tries to summon some idea of how Peyton would handle this. But Peyton is so... *Peyton.* "Why?"

Gabriel leans back against the wall, but he doesn't relax. *Nice imitation of nonchalance there. You aren't fooling me.* "You will sit in for The Greens in place of your brother."

Bailey throws off his blanket and sits up. He only wears boxers, and Gabriel stands over him dressed in his usual rich-guy casual. "And he suggested that? Peyton's never wanted me mixed up in all *this.*" And Bailey packs an impressive level of scorn into that last word.

A muscle twitches in Gabriel's jaw. A tell that Bailey's words hit right where he wanted them. "You will sit in for your brother because I say that you will." Gabriel turns, grasps the door handle. "Also, I want this door open whenever you're in here."

"What the...? *Why?*" Unlike Gabriel, Bailey doesn't have an ice-cold image to maintain. *Thank God.* He grabs a pair of sweats from the floor and stumbles into them. "Is this some kind of punishment? No privacy until I agree to be your friend again?"

"If you're going to act like a child, then I'm—"

"You *killed* my girlfriend!"

Gabriel blanches, and Bailey's words hang in the air between them.

"You know, I finally figured out why you want to help me. Not as Exhibit A for your hospital idea, that was just an excuse. You're only offering to take care of me because you feel guilty." Despite Gabriel's controlled detachment and Bailey's fury, they've moved closer to each other. Bailey imagines shoving the other boy hard against the door frame, cracking his skull. "You killed her, and now, you think saving me is some way to atone for that." He stabs a finger against Gabriel's chest. "Well, it won't." And fucking hell, he might imagine fighting Gabriel, making him hurt like he hurt Bailey...but standing this close, he also can't shake the remembrance of the kiss or the easiness that built between them over the last week. His fists clench, and Gabriel's eyes flick toward them.

"No," Gabriel says. "It's not guilt."

"No? Because it looks a lot like guilt from where I'm standing."

Gabriel says nothing. Instead, he gives Bailey a long look, eyes running over his bare chest, really checking him out without any of the usual filters on. The pale blue of his eyes darkens.

Bailey hops back a step. The anger still churns inside him, but he can't deny that something beyond that rage also exists. A heavy awareness that began for Bailey with the kiss ten months earlier at the Christmas party. And, right now, he really wants to burn it out from inside of him, forget he ever felt it in the first place.

That same connection seems to affect Gabriel as well. He takes a deep breath, like he has to force himself to not lash out. "I'll expect you downstairs this afternoon."

***

For the meeting, the neighborhood lieutenants sit at Gabriel's long dark wood dining table. Like the rest of the mansion, the dining room's decor is white and wood and minimalist. A wall of glass looks out on a frosted strip of lawn, sooty smoke billowing in the gray sky. Bailey tried to time his entrance so that he wouldn't have to talk to anyone alone. The cover story, that Gabriel keeps him there like some kind of concubine, makes him itch with self-consciousness. *God. How is this my life?* Gabriel doesn't sit at the table, although no one takes the head chair.

All the lieutenants went to Memorial High School, and Gabriel knew each one of them before martial law. Like Peyton, they all followed him long before Super Flu and Feathertons.

Bailey sits in the chair closest to Angelica Loeza, the head of Quail Creek Neighborhoods. She came from the senior class, same as Gabriel, as Peyton. Once a straight A student with a volleyball scholarship lined up for the next year, she now supports three younger brothers and two sets of grandparents from her position with Feathertons. She dyed her long dark silky hair with maroon and silver streaks, their old school colors. Bailey can understand why Gabriel recruited her. Angelica is smart and reliable. She knows how to play for a team.

Cecilia Vu represents Olde Town neighborhoods, which includes Gabriel's compound. True to form, she shoots daggers at Bailey now that Gabriel is in the room with them.

Across from Bailey, Derek Sams makes a big show of shuffling a stack of papers that look like ledgers. Derek manages Pierce Heights.

Like Bailey, he'd been a junior and an officer in Student Council. Derek used to remind Bailey of an overweight terrier. Short, stocky with an aggressive attitude and a mop of blond hair. In his new life as a gang lieutenant, he dyed his hair a shiny jet black, which Bailey considers cheating on the "dye your hair" commandment. As soon as he notices Bailey, he turns to where Gabriel stands at the head of the table. "Good move replacing that psycho Peyton with the little brother."

Gabriel doesn't move or respond in any way, so Bailey speaks up, "I'm not replacing Peyton." It bothers him that Derek calls Peyton a psycho like that in front of Gabriel—technically their boss. Bailey might have agreed with Derek, might have said the same thing. But not right here, not right now.

"No? Gabriel, buddy, you gotta do something about Peyton. I keep telling you." Derek waits for a reaction from Gabriel that doesn't come. He then tries to shrug off the awkward one-sidedness of the conversation by turning to Bailey. "I keep telling him that Peyton needs to be replaced. He's a good fighter, but the guy's a mess and always has been."

Bailey swallows everything he wants to say. Instead, he follows Gabriel's lead and pretends to look right through Derek at the other people in the room.

The last person to arrive, Jadyn Clegg, sports a springy mess of bright green curls. Clegg runs all the unincorporated streets within the big neighborhoods. Also a junior, he and Bailey had been casual friends in high school. But everyone likes Jadyn, he's much more of a politician-type than Derek Sams. He slaps Bailey on the shoulder when he first walks in the room. "Good to see you, man!"

Bailey mumbles something and tries not to turn red. Gabriel's cavalier, *"I've told them you're here for sex"* playing on repeat in his mind. Bailey keeps his head down, trains his eyes on the table in front of him. *God this is so fucking embarrassing.* And infuriating, too. He pretty much hates Gabriel with a burning passion—and everyone in the room assumes he's lusting after him.

Because the lieutenants meet every week, they don't do the usual back and forth tally of people missing or sick that Bailey has become used to. They wait in silence for Gabriel to speak, to sit down, to do whatever he does at these meetings.

When the pause becomes uncomfortable, Bailey decides to get over himself and looks up to find Gabriel pacing back and forth behind the white silk chairs, his mouth tight and eyes glittering and hard. He has his hands in his pants pockets as if on a stroll, but the whole room becomes awash in tension. Angelica and Jadyn keep giving each other knowing glances. Cecilia stares down in front of her, as if fascinated by the high gloss finish on the long table. Only Bailey and Derek Sams watch Gabriel.

"Are we getting started or what?" Derek grouses. "I've got a ton of shit to unload today." He slouches forward, takes in the other neighborhood lieutenants with disdain. "You guys have no idea what I have to take care of with Piney Woods getting added to Pierce Heights." A gripe, but also kind of a brag. *Oh, look at all the work I have to do because I have a more important job than you.*

Bailey really has to question Gabriel's judgment in picking Derek. *Derek, the insufferable ass.* In high school, Gabriel treated his cobalt blue Lexus and designer clothes with a nonchalance that annoyed Bailey. He let Peyton drive it! No one should trust thrill-loving Peyton with their automobile. But Gabriel had shrugged off any concern like—no big deal if the transmission blew, or the car got banged up, or totaled—he could always get a new one.

But Derek went a step beyond this careless disregard and loved flaunting his wealth. Reminding everyone that his family had a vacation home in Aspen, that the maid would clean up the mess, that the cook could whip them up a snack. And even more annoying, Derek made constant reference to the BMW he drove. As in, "Let me pull my *Beemer* around to the front," and "I'm headed out to my *Beemer* for lunch," or "Want a ride home? The *Beemer* is parked right out front." Bailey and Peyton loved to mock him behind his back...

Peyton may have mocked him to his face also. A lot of people had hated Peyton. Bailey suspects that even the people who regularly invited his brother to parties or cheered him on in football games mostly couldn't stand him.

Derek leans back in his chair, addressing them all, "My territory is way more work than any of you have to deal with, trust me on this."

Right. It never fails to amaze Bailey that even in the apocalypse, jerks like Derek Sams still manage to annoy him. "The Greens is the same size as Pierce Heights," Bailey cuts in. "And it's filling with more people every day. Gabriel has even started moving displaced people into the back streets near the golf course."

Derek scoffs at that. "I have the bigger storehouses, though. I also have the most runners coming in and out. And the largest security force...it's..."

Gabriel's pacing stops at Derek's side, and the Pierce Heights lieutenant stutters to a halt. "No, go on, Derek," Gabriel says, voice gentle. Polite sounding. "Tell me about your storehouses and your runners and your people." Gabriel places one hand on the back of Derek's chair.

"You know what I mean, though." Derek shuffles his stack of papers again. "I'm just saying—"

In a flash, one long fingered hand entwines in Derek's black locks and slams Derek's face to the table. Wet squelching and the hard thwack of bone on wood. Blood pours from Derek's nose when Gabriel's hand yanks him back up and hammers him down again.

Bailey gasps, even though no one else in the room reacts in fear or even disgust. He finds himself on his feet rounding the table. "That's enough! Gabriel, stop it!"

Jadyn, closest to Derek, also stands. But Jadyn doesn't try to stop Gabriel. He steps back, blocks Bailey's approach.

Everyone else stays sitting, frozen. Like Peyton, these lieutenants have held their positions from the beginning of martial law. Like Peyton, they've all taken part in the violence and brutality that has built Feathertons. But Bailey isn't like Peyton or the rest of them, and Jadyn has to grab at him to keep him from interfering.

Gabriel's hand tightens again in Derek's hair, but Derek fights him now. His words garbled because of his smashed face, he screams curses and flails his arms.

Derek jolts from the chair and tries to break free of Gabriel's grip. But Gabriel has a head of height on him, longer limbs and sharper fighting moves. Derek kicks and throws his fists in a frenzied attack, until Gabriel uses both arms to lock the other boy's head in place against his chest. Derek goes slack, panting sodden gasps.

"I want you to remember." Gabriel's dulcet, silvery voice shows the pleasure he just took from the fight. "*Remember* that those are *my* storehouses and *my* people, Derek. Those are *my* homes and *my* streets where I *let* you live, where I *let* your mother and your little sister live." With his hand still gripping Derek's hair, Gabriel hefts him off his feet and back into the dining chair.

"Take your seat, Bailey," Gabriel says without looking away from Derek Sam's limp body.

"Wha...What?"

Gabriel shoots a look at Bailey with his eyes ferocious.

Is Gabriel the crazy person here, or am I? "You've got to be kidding me."

Jadyn nudges Bailey back. "Go on, Bailey. Show's over."

"I wasn't... God! I wasn't trying to get a better fucking view."

Derek's nose and lip have become mush. But he wipes his face on his shirt...ready to move on. *Everyone* looks ready to move on.

Bailey settles back in his chair.

Gabriel stays standing, now stationary at the head of the table instead of prowling along behind all of them. "The government patrols have officially ended."

He raises a hand at the noises they all make at his announcement. "We've already emptied the warehouses. We are going to have to make a schedule and start distributing rations out to the people in our neighborhoods."

"How soon will you start delivery?" Bailey blurts out.

Gabriel cocks his head toward Bailey, looks pleased by the question. "Friday."

"That's actually..." Bailey trails off. *Good. It's good.* But he won't give Gabriel the satisfaction of hearing him say it. Bailey ruffles his hands through his hair. "You know, Feathertons doing this one decent thing...okay, several decent things lately...doesn't make all of you heroes."

Bailey watches the pleased look slip from Gabriel's face.

Cecilia raises her pen like a dagger, points down the table at Bailey. "No one asked for your approval."

"I didn't say—"

"Enough." Gabriel nods at Cecilia, and she's up and opening the door to the dining room. She lets in a collection of vagabond-looking runners, kids Gabriel swept up to join him, a few Bailey even knows. "I agree with Derek that you need help with management. The neighborhoods have gotten too big for a single lieutenant to oversee everything. I assigned each of you a team of assistants. They will report directly to Cecilia and myself."

Angelica Loeza raises her hand before she speaks. "Gabriel, I can just use my brothers for—"

"No, Angelica." Gabriel's tone, his eyes, turn to ice. Long pale fingers drum against the table, then flick toward the group of runners. "Your brothers will be working with me in Olde Town. They'll be living here in the compound, too, starting today."

Angelica starts to tremble. "If there's something… Is this about…?"

Gabriel's hand smacks the table. One of the new assistants jumps. "I'm doing something to help you, something that is kind. I'm relieving you of the burden of trying to feed and manage three teen and preteen boys."

Tears run down Angelica's round cheeks, snot pools on her upper lip. "Please. Gabriel, please…"

"Gabriel, you can't break up her family like that."

Gabriel's hand shoots out and clamps onto Bailey's arm. The order to stay silent is clear.

"Angelica, I'm not going to punish you for stealing. You need your job, so I'm not even taking away your position as lieutenant. But I can't let you sell to the people in your neighborhood without turning over your trades to our stores."

"Oh, hell." Bailey rubs a hand over his face. The possessive, controlling leader of the Feathertons just beat a lieutenant's face against the table for a handful of misspoken words. Bailey slumps back into his chair. Gabriel went easy on her, his judgment has been kind.

Gabriel waves a hand, and the meeting ends.

One of the new assistants is a kid Bailey knows, Spencer Clarkson. They'd worked on yearbook together. The two of them share an awkward hello. "It's good to see you, Spencer." Bailey remembered him as a cheerful freshmen who worked hard on staff. He's lost weight since then, grown more somber, dyed his pale hair a cotton-candy pink.

"You're taking over for Peyton?" Spencer asks.

"Not yet," says Gabriel, as always, hovering nearby.

Bailey takes a deep breath and then releases it. *Not ever, asshole.*

Spencer nods along. "Then, I guess it's your brother I'm reporting to. I'm going to be an assistant for The Greens."

"Good luck," Bailey tells him. "If anyone understands how miserable it is to be Peyton's assistant, it's me."

29 PEYTON

Peyton balances a plastic crate of potatoes on one shoulder, while fishing in his back pocket with his free hand. "Fucking finally," he says around a cigarette as his fingers draw out the silver lighter. It has the name *Janice* engraved on the side, and he'd snagged it from a big stucco house with Mediterranean tiles. Real fancy shit. He had to put down everyone in that house. They'd all turned. Peyton thinks he might have pummeled what was left of Janice into the orange tiles right before he found the lighter. He tries to light the cigarette with his free hand. "Shit. Help me out here, kid."

"Oh! Sorry, here. Sorry." The new kid takes the lighter from Peyton and flicks it a bunch of times before he gets a flame. He holds it out.

"Where are the potatoes?" Vanessa hollers from the driveway. They're back at Storehouse 7, the yellow bungalow. Only now it's called Storehouse 11. They all get emptied, refilled, renamed, every few days because "security" or whatever. Peyton just goes where Gabriel tells him to go. "Yo, potatoes?" Vanessa shouts. "I've got three runners, like ready to go! Like, now!"

Peyton sucks in a lung full of smoke and hefts the crate to the new kid. "Jesus, bring her the fucking crate before she breaks my eardrums." The kid wobbles like he might go down from the weight of the potatoes, but manages to stagger out of the garage without dropping anything.

"Who the hell are you?" Vanessa screeches. "Peyton, who the hell is this?"

Peyton squints against the blue stream of cigarette smoke blown back in his eyes. The kid handed him a note that Peyton read a few lines from. He thinks he got the gist of it. "My new helper." He passes the cigarette to Vanessa to keep her mouth busy. "And stop fucking shouting all the time."

All three of them hunch over when a gust of wind blows in from the north. Vanessa takes a hard drag off the cigarette, burns it nearly down to the filter. Greedy bitch. "Helper?" She looks the new kid over as her face sours. "Does he have a name?" She flicks the still smoldering butt to the ground and stomps on it.

"Spencer Clarkson," the kid says and goes to shake her hand, like the three of them are business colleagues or some bullshit. He has puffy pink hair and glasses. The pink doesn't look intentional, more like his pale hair won't hold color.

Vanessa smirks at the outstretched hand. "Yeah. I don't care." And Peyton laughs.

After that, Spencer acts nervous around them, moving to the other side of the garage when they load up the runners. He disappears for long stretches into the stacks of boxes and crates to swap out the trades they made. As long as Spencer Clarkson stays out of his way, Peyton doesn't even think about him.

Vanessa, however, won't stop baiting the kid and then lashing out when nerdy Spencer falls for her traps. "So, you're like, second-in-command here, then?" she asks in a voice so sweet that Peyton can't believe it came from her. Stock managers do inventory and lieutenants manage the runners. Completely separate branches in Feathertons, but Peyton knows Vanessa likes to think of herself as his second.

"Second-in-command? Yes…I suppose? Until Peyton is replaced at least?"

Vanessa throws down her clipboard. "What did you just say? Peyton did you just hear that?" She gives Spencer a shove. The poor kid just takes it, looking bewildered. "You think that Gabriel is going to make *you* lieutenant over Peyton? Gabriel and Peyton are *best friends*."

"No, we aren't, Vanessa." Peyton snags the clipboard up and shoves it toward her. This little nerdy kid somehow reminds him of Bailey. *Something in the way he stands around, wanting Peyton to show him the ropes.* The comparison creates a tendril of compassion in Peyton for Spencer. A tendril as thin and pale as one of Spencer's pink strands of hair though, so the kid better not expect too much. "Okay, that's enough." Already, Peyton's sick of dealing with the fucking tension between these two. "Show him how to assign the inventory and shut the fuck up," he tells Vanessa.

Spencer scrambles to follow Peyton's command, and Vanessa tosses the clipboard at the kid's head.

"Where did you hear that from anyway?" she asks. "Who told you Peyton was getting replaced?"

Spencer has his face buried in the clipboard, but he doesn't seem brave enough to ignore her completely. He mumbles something, and she leans in closer to him.

Peyton rolls his eyes. "You're freaking him out, Vanessa. *And,* I don't give a shit where he heard it. I don't even care if it's true."

"No! I want to know where he thinks he heard that!"

Spencer flinches away from her. "Um...Gabriel said it? He's training Bailey to take over for The Greens?" Under the sheen of his glasses, Spencer's eyes jitter between Vanessa and Peyton. He settles on Peyton as the safer point to look at. "I think it's sort of undecided? I hope I'm not the first to...I'm really not sure?"

"*Gabriel* told you that?" Vanessa shifts from anger to incredulity. "Like, I'm so sure. Like, Gabriel really said that. That Bailey would be taking over." She turns to Peyton.

Anyone who knows Peyton, anyone a part of the Featherton machine, has long stopped asking when Bailey will join up. Peyton always cuts them off by breaking the news that Bailey calls them thugs, refers to Gabriel as a crime boss. If Spencer heard right, then Gabriel really believes that Bailey has a chance of coming through the Super Flu infection. *Yeah. Good. That's really good.*

But taking over as a Featherton lieutenant? *Bailey?* As far back as Peyton can remember, Bailey has always wallowed in the self-righteousness of tattling. Even though their parents didn't care. Lila and Mason looked the other way when Peyton got caught cheating on a test, vandalizing shit in the neighborhood, or beating up other kids, but Bailey never did. Bailey always delivered the lectures that should have come from a parent.

Peyton shakes his head. *Gabriel must think he knows Bailey better than I do. But he's wrong.* "Bailey was born with that do-gooder stick up his ass, he will *never* join up with Feathertons." There's no holding back Peyton's wide grin, his sudden bark of laughter. "And that must really eat Gabriel up. It must make him crazy." Peyton slaps Spencer on the back and sends him stumbling back a step. "Good one, kid."

***

Spencer lives in Olde Town in one of the houses in the Featherton compound. So, they split up after work. But, it's become routine for Peyton to give Vanessa a ride. He doesn't mind really, as long as she keeps her mouth shut on subjects that piss him off. They get on the final long stretch toward The Greens when in the distance he sees a staggering rabble of dark shapes. He slows the bike down to a crawl.

"Are they creatures?" Vanessa shouts from in back of him.

"Nah. Not out in the open like that." The light slants behind them, and they look like...*people*...actual people. A group of about forty of them walking on the frontage road. Vanessa lets go of Peyton's waist and points as the figures swell from dark shapes to life-sized people.

"Refugees."

"Yeah, you're right." Now that he rolls closer, Peyton sees that the people carry bundles of belongings, some ride bicycles, others push or pull wagons. All of them headed toward The Greens.

Vanessa grips him tighter, just as wary of this destitute group as she acts around the feral sick. Her mouth close to his ear, she whispers, "Can you slow down, like just a little, okay?" Maybe Vanessa knows some of the dirty, blank faces turned their way.

"Sure. Yeah." Peyton thinks he might recognize some of them, despite the dirty torn clothing, matted hair, flesh sunken from bones.

That woman with a little girl tied in a sling on her back taught Spanish in his middle school.

The little boy gripping her hand while he pants, open mouthed and shaking beside her, Peyton remembers seeing the boy splash around in the country club swimming pool.

A teenager with sunburnt arms.

Peyton's heart doesn't even pick up as he surveys them. *Stop looking,* he tells himself.

No soccer kids.

No Lucy.

Because she didn't survive. She couldn't have survived. Screw this constant searching, getting up his hopes like a chump.

Inside the gates, people gather to see which of their missing neighbors have returned. Not many. A lot of the gawkers hope to see their kids who had been away because of sports or field trips…college. But, most of the people coming off the road didn't live in The Greens before the pandemic. Drummer and Denny Sawyer use clipboards to wave people off Augusta Drive toward Glen Mills. "Come on, folks—not much farther. We got brand new homes for you. Running water. Food." Drummer throws one long leg over the seat of his Yamaha. His springy orange dreads vibrate with the motorcycle's engine as the bike crawls forward. "Stay with me now!"

Denny must have just touched up his hair because red dye drips down his neck like blood. "Who does this little girl belong to?" He shouts in cupped hands to amplify his voice, but no one stops. "Yo, people! Someone claim this girl here!" Round dark eyes stare out from a thin face, transfixed on the red snaking sweat coming from Denny's choppy hair. "You got parents, kid?"

Skeleton legs poke out the hem of the girl's long sweater, sleeves rolled above tiny hands. She looks about eight or ten, but she doesn't answer Denny, not even to nod or shake her head.

"Is that um…" Vanessa points over Peyton's shoulder as Lila breaks from the bunched up neighbors. His mother still wears her pajamas and her hair looks greasy and matted. She kneels in front of Denny and the little girl, takes one of the girl's small hands between her own.

Peyton brakes and stamps the kickstand down. "Jesus, what now?" He leaves Vanessa behind on his Marauder, and the small crowd of neighbors part before him.

"Mom, get up."

Lila ignores him and smiles at the shell-shocked face of the little girl. "Are you all alone, sweetie?" The girl's eyes finally leave the dripping red dye job on Denny. Maybe she sees Lila, or maybe the little girl sees right through Peyton's mom, but she doesn't say anything. Lila looks up at Denny, imploring. "She can come with me."

"Sounds good," Denny answers, at the same time that Peyton says, "No."

Lila stands and pulls the little girl to her side, smashes the blank face against her dirty bathrobe. "She needs a home, Peyton."

The neighbors love the show, and Lila and Peyton's little scene starts to get attention. "Hey, it's fine with me if your mom takes the kid." Denny turns the clipboard toward Peyton, offering it as if he wants The Greens' lieutenant to double check his work. But, Peyton slaps it away. "The girl must have gotten counted in with some other family," Denny says. "I got no idea where she goes." He leans in to Peyton. "Gabriel is gonna get pissed about how this looks." Denny makes a meaningful scan of the watchful crowd.

Peyton clenches his jaw. Fucking awesome. Gabriel hates when Feathertons don't appear perfectly in control. "Yeah, okay." He focuses on his mother's glassy-eyed happiness as she combs her fingers into the little girl's dark lank hair.

"What's your name, precious girl?" Lila asks. And of course, she gets no answer. Whatever happened to the kid before she made it to The Greens must have messed her up good. "Well. That's okay," Lila murmurs. "How about for now…we'll just call you Lucy."

30 Bailey

Bailey stews on everything from the meeting. *With his door open.* Gabriel's *"not yet"* keeps ringing in his head. If Bailey survives the virus, will Gabriel demand he become a lieutenant? Has Gabriel finally revealed the price of his protection?

Well, Bailey won't do it. No. Absolutely, not. He didn't mind helping traumatized people find new homes and a new life, but he will never accept a role as lieutenant. Not after witnessing the violence of the meeting, the way everyone in the room accepted Gabriel mangling Derek Sams' face, the ruthless dismantling of Angelica's family. Even if it means that Gabriel backs out of his promise to protect Bailey, the Featherton's leader needs to understand that he will *never* become one of them.

Bailey pads down the wide curved stairs to the bottom floor. This late in the day, the mansion has emptied of the usual workers and their vibrant hair. Sunset floods the white walls and furnishings with color. Rose. Peach. Sand. A deceptive warm glow in a frigid house.

"Gabriel?" Bailey pushes open the study doors. "Gabriel?" Inside, he finds him using a rolled newspaper and some twigs to start a fire in the hearth. Gabriel glances over his shoulder but doesn't say anything. He goes back to tucking the kindling into a neat triangular shape at the base of a stack of firewood.

"What are you doing? I mean...I can see what you're doing but..." Gabriel really, *really,* does not strike him as the outdoorsy type. As the fire begins to catch and spread across the first log, the heat draws Bailey closer. He hadn't even realized how cold he'd gotten. "That's going to feel good once it gets going." Bailey holds his hands out toward the fireplace. Then tilts his head toward Gabriel. "How do you even know how to do that?"

"My father." Gabriel stands, brushing his hands together. "We had a hunting cabin in Kentucky."

They watch each other, looking for cracks. Waiting to see what might leak out between them. Bailey drops his arms and steps back. "What happened to him?" Maybe, it's a shitty thing to ask. Because Bailey can *guess* what happened. Most of the homes that he relocated people to had at least one room that needed the flooring pulled out or a wall repaired. He'd seen his brother come home from neighborhood welfare checks, holding a blood and gore smeared club, wearing a scorn-laden smirk. *"Just more assholes trying to hide someone infected. Never works."*

"It's exactly what you're thinking, Bailey. I killed him."

In their post outbreak world, people have had to club their own siblings to death, have watched their parents rip each other apart, have awakened from the feral stage shaking, sick, and starved in a house filled with the corpses of their own family. *This had happened to Gabriel.*

"I never know what to say when I hear that stuff. I can't imagine what that was like." Bailey accused Gabriel of feeling guilty about Ashley, but maybe, Ashley only made up a small part of that guilt. "I'm really sorry. Even with…" A deep breath. "I guess when people say they wouldn't wish something on their worst enemy…well, that's like this, right?" Bailey looks away for a second.

"But doesn't change what happened with Ashley." Gabriel's pale forehead wrinkles before he adds, "That I was the cause of her death."

The fire snaps and part of the elaborate twig structure collapses, but the lower logs have caught and are now beginning to lick upward. Bailey crosses his arms, squeezes his eyes shut. He didn't come down here for *this*. He only wanted tell Gabriel that he would not be taking Peyton's spot at The Greens. But, he can't stop *wanting to know*. How? Why? The words just won't come, and they hurt way too much to force out.

Thank God, Gabriel doesn't wait for him to ask. "I didn't know for sure that I'd been infected. It wasn't a bite, like you. I hit someone, and their blood…" He holds a hand over his eyes. Like he can block out the memories by blocking out his sight. "I put it out of my mind. That's the only way I can explain it. It just wasn't real to me." Gabriel drops his hand and straightens his shoulders like a man readying to accept judgment.

Bailey drops into the couch, lets his head fall back, so he can look at the ceiling instead of maintaining the intense eye contact. "I don't get… Why Ashley? Why the affair?"

The pause takes so long that Bailey scoots up again to watch Gabriel squat in front of the wide hearth. He pokes one of the sticks further into the hot orange heart of the ever-growing fire. "Do you really need me to answer that?"

It all comes back to that night. The Christmas party. The kiss. "You went after her because of me."

Gabriel turns to give him a sharp look. "What I did isn't your fault. You know that, right?"

Bailey rubs fists into his eyes. "Okay. Yeah." He drops his hands back to his lap, tries to gather his thoughts. *Just ask.* "Do you even *like* girls?"

"I thought…" Gabriel pushes up from the floor to stand. Long red strands fall forward over pale cheekbones. "You're loyal, trustworthy. Not like her." The words come out like Gabriel reads this part of the story from a script… No. From a *plan*. "You would have never left her unless—"

"So you seduced her. And she died. All because I rejected you at a stupid Christmas party." Bailey shoots back up to face him. "You piece of shit. You total—"

Gabriel's eyes lock onto Bailey's. "Ashley came to me. She's the one who pushed. She was never worthy of—"

Bailey shoves him backward. "Shut up." Gabriel takes the shove as if he expected it. But, Bailey's the one trembling and off balance, "You didn't even know her."

"I wasn't trying to know her. I was trying to prove a point. *To you.* And I was *right,* wasn't I?" He thrusts a finger at Bailey's face.

Bailey remembers a sweet bubbly girl who decorated his locker on his birthday, who cried during romantic movies, and who loved cherry-flavored Slurpees, singing in the car, anything in the color pink. The Ashley who spent the night in Gabriel Featherton's City penthouse? That girl is a stranger.

Like he can read Bailey's thoughts, Gabriel's lip curls. "Maybe, it was something she'd done before?"

"And you're *still* trying to prove your point? Only now, you want to drive a wedge between me and my grief for my girlfriend." *To hell with Gabriel.* Bailey stood by and let Peyton pulverize the virus driven creature that Ashley's body had become, but he won't let Gabriel tear down all his memories of the sweet girl he grew up with and loved. "You did all that just because you're spoiled and always have to get everything you want. Well, you don't get to have *me*, not back then, not even if I survive."

The mask disappears again, leaving Gabriel with a genuine look of astonishment at Bailey's words. His lips part, but Bailey won't let him speak.

"No. I don't want to hear it. I don't want you to ever say Ashley's name to me again." No matter what happened between Gabriel and Ashley, the memories he has of her belong to him alone. *Not Gabriel.* "I didn't even come down here to talk about this. I came to tell you that I'm not *ever* going to take Peyton's position as lieutenant in Feathertons. If I survive the virus, if you're only hiding and helping me because you think I'll join up afterward, well that's not going to happen."

There. More rejection. Gabriel can choke on it, that asshole. Bailey won't turn into one of Gabriel's devoted followers, no matter how much the mighty leader of Feathertons promises. Brushing past him, Bailey wants out of the room and out of the conversation. But Gabriel grips his arm.

"You think I'm spoiled? That I get whatever I want?" Gabriel's grip turns to iron, and he shakes Bailey hard enough that his teeth clash together. "I don't have *any* of the things I want."

"Let go of me!" Bailey tries to yank his arm back. When that doesn't work, he takes a swing at the other boy.

Gabriel catches Bailey's fist in his own like a damn ninja. "I want order and safety that doesn't first need threats or violence. But I keep getting forced to use both. I want to build something without my sister trying to destroy it. But she won't leave me alone." Gabriel pulls him closer. "I want this virus eradicated...but it keeps spreading." His hand opens, and Bailey's arm drops. "And I want you. I've *always* wanted you...but you hate me."

Bailey closes his eyes, shakes his head. When his eyes open again, they focus on the fire, which has now engulfed every log in the hearth. Gabriel moves away, and from behind Bailey, the study door snicks closed.

the upward turn

The next day, more displaced people come from the East. They line the roads as Peyton and Vanessa cruise by them, headed toward the The Greens. Ragged, hollow-eyed people who rubberneck as he steers the Marauder past them.

"You think any of these new people are infected?" he shouts back to Vanessa. "We should take a quick ride along the golf course. Check out who's popped—"

Vanessa smacks his arm. "Jeez, *asshole*. Everyone can hear you, " she shrieks.

Ahead of them, a scrawny teenage boy stands in the middle of the road, ogles them as they approach. He has patchy hair, like someone ripped chunks of it from his scalp, and scarred, gray skin. No fingernails. A missing ear.

"Oh, my God," Vanessa breathes near Peyton's face. "I think I know him…that's Martin Miller."

Peyton brakes before they get much closer. He raises one arm in the air, snaps his fingers. "Start acting like a person, numb-nuts, or I'm bashing in your skull!"

The boy blinks and raises a hand back. "I'm good," he rasps, and shuffles toward the side of the road. The shoes he wears look like cheap dress shoes. Dried, dark blood cakes his calves and new red blood rims his ankles.

179

Peyton waits until the kid gets all the way over before twisting the throttle to come closer. He brakes again. Vanessa was right—it's Martin Miller. "How long you been awake?" Peyton asks him.

"I…I don't know. We've been walking since last night—"

"No, how long since you recovered?" He reaches down, pats the club strapped onto his bike.

The boy's hands start shaking. "Not sure. About a week?" He's got some teeth missing, too. His eyes keep darting to where Peyton's hand caresses the hilt of his club. "I'm just trying to get home." Martin's face crumples, and he starts to cry.

"For fuck's sake…" Peyton pulls the throttle again, and he and Vanessa speed off. She calls him an asshole as he bends forward and guns the bike toward home. They lean hard into the turn as they enter the gate.

"Slow the fuck down," Vanessa yells from behind him.

He slows the fuck down, and blue hair sweeps over his eyes. Too many people fill the entrance. Augusta splits around the burning pit, and one fork of it leads back to Hickory Hill and Peyton's home. He has to crawl the Marauder through the throng of waiting neighbors past them. *Their faces.* He hates the hope in their eyes almost worse than the desperation on the faces of the refugees. Peyton drags one boot on the street to keep the bike up, has to break completely when Raquel Miller stands dumbly in his way.

"Oh, my God, Raquel." Vanessa slides off the bike. "Your brother is on the road. He's alive." Raquel had also survived the virus, but whatever happened to her at the quarantine camp messed with her brain. She stares, enthralled by the loud motor and shiny blackness of Peyton's motorcycle. So, Vanessa has to tug her out of the way. "Let's find your mom, okay?" Vanessa curls an arm around Raquel's waist but just gets a vacant smile for her efforts.

"Move her. I need to get past." Peyton wants to get as far away as possible from all the families who get to marvel at the miracle of survival. The Millers, Raquel and Martin's parents, will be one of those.

"I don't see the Millers, like, anywhere. I think they forgot about Raquel… Can you believe we saw Martin? He was in Dallas at a speech tournament. I was supposed to be there. But, I…I slept in…" Vanessa jams one fist against her mouth. "I blew it off. I…" Her knees buckle. She doubles over, hands moving to steady herself, gripping her thighs.

"Are you going to get sick, or do you want a ride home?"

"Don't you get it, Peyton? I thought they all died." Vanessa stands up again, sucking in air, hands on her head. Raquel imitates her, patting herself on the head. "I thought they all died, and then I thought maybe I was supposed to die, too."

"Pull yourself the fuck together."

"I slept in, ya know? I missed the bus," she keeps saying. "I slept in that morning, and then the outbreak happened."

"Yeah…great story, Vanessa." Peyton revs the bike higher. "Get Raquel out of my way, so I can go home." *Where's Lila?* He expected she'd be here searching every face. He sure as hell wants to get out of this crowd before *that* happens. Peyton spots his dad standing on a grassy spot near the front gate. Mason has his head thrown back laughing. One hand running down Jenny Hutton's arm, just the backs of his fingers trailing down from her shoulder toward her wrist. A move Peyton remembers seeing him make on Pauline Featherton.

"I need to think about myself for once, Pey."

"Yourself?"

"You see how difficult it is…"

After his father spilled to him about the affair, Peyton had gone to confront Pauline Featherton, to confront *Gabriel.* Did he know about his mom and Mason? *He had to have known.* Gabriel knew everything. Had he expected Peyton to just let Mason leave? To let his father get in a car, or on a plane, and leave the mess of their family behind him? To hell with that. No one was leaving their house, their family, unless Peyton *let* them leave. He'd pulled the borrowed blue Lexus up to the stately home in Olde Town, tires half onto their perfect lawn, crushing the flowers that lined the drive, churning up dark mud.

When Gabriel opened the door, he looked hungover, dark circles under his eyes, posture drooping, skin more gray than its usual bloodless white. Whatever he'd done the night before must have turned into one hell of a party. Peyton had never seen Gabriel look so bad. He tossed Gabriel the keys to his Lexus, but Gabriel didn't even try to catch them. They just thumped against his diaphragm and clanked onto the marble entryway floor.

Peyton tried to shoulder his way inside. "Where's your mother? I want to talk to her."

But Gabriel sprang to life and blocked his path. "She's not here."

Peyton imagined Gabriel's willowy, glamorous mom waiting in some ritzy hotel for Mason to arrive. Or was she at the airport? "Where are they meeting?"

Gabriel let out a low breathy laugh. "Oh, you finally noticed? Or did Mason have to tell you?" His laughter dissolved into coughing. "You didn't figure it out at all, did you? He had to tell you, didn't he? Are you really that stupid? They were so obvious that I thought even you would—"

Peyton lunged. "I'm going to fucking kill you."

But Gabriel moved faster. Even hungover, he had no problem leveling Peyton with a quick jab to the mouth. Peyton went sprawling backward onto the glossy floor. Blood streamed from where his teeth had pierced his lip. He swiped it away, ran his tongue between his bottom teeth and the fleshy gash, and tried to scrabble up from the marble entryway.

Gabriel crouched over him, fists clenching and releasing in a flash of rhythm, his expression crazed. *What the hell?* Something was wrong. No time to decipher. Gabriel has problems, but Peyton has his own. Peyton rubbed again at his bleeding mouth. "What…shit… Gabriel, what am I going to do? If he leaves, I'll be the only one taking care of Bailey and Lucy. They don't have a clue about Lila, or about just how much of an asshole my dad really is." How much more of Lila's dysfunction could Peyton keep from Bailey and Lucy? If his selfish dick of a father left, how much longer would his pill-hound mother stay afloat? "I'm barely holding shit together with my mom as it is. If he leaves…" Peyton pushed himself to his feet. "Aw, fuck." His back had hit that marble floor fucking hard. "Lucy and Bailey don't deserve this."

Gabriel uncoiled from his crouch, but slowly as if it cost him a lot to get control back. His hands shook and sweat beaded on his upper lip. "Then, you have to keep going, for Bailey…and Lucy. I'll help you, I can give you money for Lila's rehab. I'll switch it to you today, right now. You just keep your mother's shit together through this. Can you do that?"

"I don't know, man."

"You have to. Peyton, you *have* to."

***

Once he's free of the crowd, Peyton speeds home. He expects to see his mother sitting in the window, but no Lila. Not necessarily a good sign. How many times has Peyton found her in bed, the drugs leaving her zoned out, or snoring and dead to the world. "Mom?"

"Peyton, stop shouting. I'm right here." His mother and the creepy little girl sit together at the kitchen table in front of a spread of food that makes Peyton's stomach grumble. Pancakes and eggs. Peanut butter sandwiches. Chocolate chip cookies with milk.

"Does Dad know you made all that?" Peyton scoops up a handful of the scrambled egg and stuffs it into his mouth.

"That's for Lucy!" Lila uses a spoon to tuck the remaining eggs back into a neat pile. "Don't you want anything, baby?" She cuts the stack of pancakes with a fork, pierces a chunk and holds it in front of the little girl's face. But the kid doesn't even look down at it.

"Are those Lucy's clothes?" The pink flowered t-shirt and red soccer shorts look familiar, except the dark haired little girl swims in the loose fabric. Lila might have cleaned her up, but she also made it easier to see the bruises and cuts covering the little girls arms and legs. "She looks bad...really bad. Maybe she forgot how to eat?"

"I didn't think of that. But I think you're right, she just forgot. Of course, she did." His mother gathers the little girl in her arms, and onto her lap. "That's why you're so quiet. You just forgot."

"Mom, you know that isn't really—"

"Shhh, Peyton. Lucy needs to rest. She needs her rest to get better." The girl's limbs stay stiff like a doll's arms and legs. Her gaze locked to the nothing space in front of her. "Mommy's here..." Lila croons. "Mommy's here..."

32 Bailey

Bailey feels...off. An itch in the back of his throat. A slight pressure inside his ears. A restless feeling in the muscles of his arms. *I'm just bored, letting paranoia get to me.* Because he's back to having nothing to do...except wonder about the virus progressing through his body. *Is this how it starts? If only...* Wait... He sits up. There *is* someone he can ask.

Downstairs, a group of Featherton runners and supply chiefs bide their time in the vaulted-ceiling entryway. *If even one person gives him one of those smirky, knowing smiles...* Each of them wait their turn to meet with Gabriel.

Cecilia stands guard at the study doors with her ever-present clipboard. She doesn't even glance toward Bailey, but her lips tighten. *Yeah, okay.* Bailey never had to wait before, but no problem. He'll just…put himself on the docket—so to speak—along with everyone else waiting to see the boss. All the brightly colored heads turn his direction. Conversation dies. *Well, of course it does. They all think I'm screwing the boss.* Not awkward at all.

"Um, Cecilia…" *She's not even going to look at me, is she? She's going to make me ask.* Bailey points at the clipboard. "Can I—"

"Gabriel has a very tight schedule right now." Cecilia's eyes don't move from the list of names she holds.

Bailey crosses his arms. "No problem. I can wait."

"Fine. Then go to the back of the line." Cecilia drums at the clipboard with her pen, trying to stare him down. They both know that as soon as Gabriel sees Bailey in line, he will drop everything else. Bailey glares back at her.

A girl with a green pixie cut gets in the way of their standoff. "Hey, Bailey." She has a squeaky voice, and combined with the hair and her freckled face, she reminds Bailey of a leprechaun. Gabriel has got to do something about this crazy hair-dye situation—can't he give them all sweatshirts or jackets instead?

"Hi," he says. "Nice hair."

"Oh my God, for real? It was supposed to be blue, but the color came out weird on me." She thrusts a hand toward him. "I'm Sophie, I moved into The Greens with my little brother. So, we're going to be neighbors. I mean…when you move back. I mean if…"

If? His heart speeds up as his right hand, the one not gripping Sophie's, goes to the scabbed-over flesh of the bite he hides beneath his hoodie. "Why wouldn't I move back? Of course, I'll move back." He tries to pull his hand away, but Sophie doesn't let go.

"Oh, you are?" She giggles. "That's good to know." She dips her chin and looks up at him through mascara-thick lashes. "I wasn't sure because of some rumors I heard?"

"Rumors?" He feels a little lightheaded now. Did Case tell anyone about his infection? Her parents? His parents? Bailey's stomach clenches.

Sophie leans in to whisper in his ear. "That you and Gabriel...well...you know."

"Oh...ha!" *Right—those rumors.* "Yeah... Well, actually..." His hand feels sweaty and clammy against hers. *God, how long have I held Sophie's hand now?* Her fingers lock with his, and she draws them toward her chest, sending him stumbling against her.

She does the chin dip and blinking thing again. "I didn't know if you remembered me."

Remember her?

The study door opens, and a group of kids with neon rainbow hair emerge, followed by Gabriel's naturally bright head. Ice blue eyes go right to where Sophie cradles Bailey's hand against her chest, and Gabriel adopts that familiar frozen arrogance.

Bailey yanks his hand free.

"Cecilia!" Gabriel holds the study door open. He doesn't wait for her to answer. "Handle the rest of my appointments." He doesn't tear his eyes from Bailey.

Cecilia slaps the clipboard against one palm. "Gabriel is that a good idea? Why don't I send Bailey—"

"I said handle them!"

Cecilia snaps to attention. "Everyone outside now!" She grabs Sophie's shoulders, pivots the girl away from Bailey.

Gabriel rewards his Olde Town lieutenant with a slow, pleased, smile. It drops away when he looks at Bailey again. "Come inside."

"Yeah. Okay." The door slams shut behind him. "You didn't have to make such a big dramatic moment out of it. Everyone out there probably assumes that we're totally going to bone each other."

Gabriel knocks past him toward the desk. "Sorry to embarrass you."

"I'm not—" Gabriel clears the papers from his desk in sharp choppy movements, throws the pens into a drawer. If Bailey learned anything, it's that a jealous Gabriel means a dangerous Gabriel. Bailey might not remember Sophie, but he won't stand by while Gabriel unravels some elaborate revenge plot against her. "The girl with the green hair thought we knew each other, that's all. So don't get all…" He can't think of a word that works for both "be a dick" and "murder."

"She was on yearbook with you."

"Really?"

"And she joined Photography Club once she realized *you* were in it."

Bailey looks at the closed study door as if he can see through it to the spot where green pixie-cut Sophie had clutched his hand. Now, he feels terrible that he didn't let her down easy, that he didn't say anything about rumors she had heard, that yes, he and Gabriel…

"You're interested in her? Some stupid freshman who had a crush on you, who has done nothing but cower since this virus destroyed everything?"

"I just felt bad that I didn't remember her. And…so what if she *cowered*? She's a kid who got relocated into a house in my neighborhood. She probably wanted to know that she had a friend nearby. Jesus Christ—Calm down!"

Gabriel wipes at his forehead, smooths a hand over the red hair he keeps gelled back behind his ears. "Yes. Of course. I apologize."

Bailey looks away, examines the wall. What happened to that noisy antique clock? All that chiming must have finally gotten on

Gabriel's last nerve. *Okay, quit stalling and just say it.* "Listen…What you said earlier, Gabriel, you were wrong." Bailey twists his hands in the hem of his shirt. "I don't hate you. I thought about it and…" He turns back around to find Gabriel studying him. "Actually, I get how you didn't really believe you'd been infected. That part…I understand." Because how could he expect Gabriel to react any different than the rest of the world had? "I mean, the virus was raging out of control in the hospitals, and my mom let Lucy go to a soccer tournament. My dad played golf with friends, had lunch in the country club dining room." He shakes his head, and a bark of laughter escapes his chest. Laughter that feels like a sob. "That last day, before martial law, I'd planned to go to a movie, to sit in a dark theater with a hundred strangers. So that part, *just that part*, I think I can forgive."

Gabriel's eyes squeeze shut. The frozen expression melts. "Thank you, Bailey. I don't deserve it, but thank you."

Bailey moves closer, and they both lean against the heavy desk, look at the empty spot where the clock used to hang. "Anyway. I wanted to tell you that, but I also need to ask you something. I'm kind of freaking out. I don't feel sick…" He bites at his lower lip and releases it. "But I don't feel completely right either. You know what I mean? Sort of achy, and my head is heavy."

"Heavy?"

An insistent knock interrupts them. Cecilia Vu throws open the door. "Sorry, Gabriel. I don't mean to interrupt. But, this can't wait." She steps aside to let Case Bell in behind her.

Case's wild hair ripples out and down her back, full and wind-puffed like the lion's mane. And she's sucking air like after a run. "I had to come. I know you told me to keep my distance for now but—"

Gabriel springs up and meets Case in the middle of the room. He points Cecilia back into the hallway. "Wait outside."

Case's cheeks and neck flush red. "I made another trade with Colton's people." She stops to catch her breath. "And one of them pulled me over—a kid named Beau who says he's working for you. He has a message for—"

"Trade?" Bailey stands. "What's going on?" Case must notice him for the first time. Her eyes scan his face and body. She shrinks back when he comes closer. *She's afraid of me.*

Gabriel's voice whips between them, "What message?"

"Beau said that Colton is going to do an attack on Featherton territory. He…he made a bunch of creatures…" Case swallows. "The people coming off the road—"

Spit fills Bailey's mouth, and he gags. "That's fucking *sick*. It's evil!" He thinks back to the party in Pierce Heights, to all those people thrown into the empty swimming pool. Fast, vicious…new. "Oh my *God!*"

Gabriel's hands cradle Case's face, shutting out Bailey's freak-out and everything else. "I need you to explain everything Beau told you, Case. Where will the attack happen?"

"Right. Okay." Gabriel's trick to calm her down worked. "They've got a bunch of caged trucks like from the party. They're going to dump them right behind the refugees. Off the highway near The Greens."

My family. Bailey turns to Gabriel. His voice raspy and faint. "Please." He doesn't know exactly what he asks for, what he wants. But, it still flips a switch in Gabriel. The Featherton leader throws the study doors open. He pushes Case toward the two guards. "Get the trucks!" he yells. "Get *everyone!*"

Bailey moves toward the door, but Gabriel shoots out his right arm to block him. He and Bailey lock eyes. "I know. The Greens is your home. But, it makes more sense for you to wait here." Before Bailey can protest, "*Your head feels heavy,*" Gabriel reminds him. "I'll bring this situation under control. I'll check on your family. Then, I'll come back."

Outside, the trucks in Gabriel's fleet roar to life, the smell of exhaust filling the street.

Doors slam.

Horns blare.

Tires squeal against the pavement. Then…silence.

33 PEYTØN

"This shit again." Peyton steers the bike onto the uneven shoulder, away from the people trudging down the middle of the street. The bike oscillates and swerves.

Vanessa's voice rattles when she yells, "Will it kill us to like…wait for them—"

The motorcycle lurches back to the blacktop.

"Oh, thank you, Jesus!" Vanessa declares with a tinge of irony.

Peyton turns back to her. "Feel free to hop off and walk."

Up ahead, a woman holds hands with a little girl, then grabs her up as the bike whizzes by them. "You nearly hit them—Watch where you're going!" Vanessa head-butts his shoulder. "Slow down asshole, you are going to kill someone!"

When Peyton darts around the opening gate, Vanessa's fingernails dig into his sides. "That's it. Let me off!"

A gust of dense smoke engulfs the bike and obscures the street. They both close their eyes and mouths, turn away, and hold their breath.

"Shit, someone popped, and I missed it?" Peyton circles upwind of the burning pit. When they come out of the black fog, they find the usual crush of neighbors waiting to see who comes in off the road.

Lyle Hutton takes a step in front of them. He raises a hand, signaling for them to stop. Peyton grits his teeth but still cuts the engine. Lyle's face has a streak of soot on one cheek. "We had a problem this morning. One of the new people, a woman, popped. The husband tried to talk her down."

Peyton laughs, and it makes both Lyle and Vanessa wince. "He did? What a dumbass. Why do people always talk to them? It just freaks them out. You gotta kill 'em before they know you're a threat."

Exhausted perspiration soaks Lyle's button-down. Big half-moon stains under each pit. "Well, there was some trouble."

Peyton pops the kickstand down. "What kind of trouble?" He can't help but scan the crowd, searching out his mother and father. *But why should I care if either of them got jumped? I shouldn't! Selfish fucks.*

Vanessa slides off the bike but keeps a hand locked onto his leather jacket. "The refugees are coming in." She raises up on tiptoes, squints against the ashy smoke. The crowd has grown. Gawkers curious to find out who survived the road—Rubberneckers anxious to find out who went into the pit.

Lyle clears his throat. "Well, the husband must have spooked her, and she lunged at him." He wipes the sweat from his forehead, leaving behind another long ribbon of soot.

"See?" Peyton curls his lip.

"Yep." Lyle nods along with Peyton's judgement. "The neighbors heard him screaming, but by the time they got to him, she'd ripped out his throat. One of your people was on patrol. Tall kid, I didn't catch his name."

The smoke rolls back from the street like an ocean wave. Two boys with Featherton-dyed hair, thick boots, and leather jackets like Peyton's drag a rolled tarp behind them. From the end of the tarp, neon-orange dreadlocks drag on the ground.

"Oh, Hell… Drummer." Vanessa's face loses color. She looks like she's about to pass out, turns and grips the handlebars of the Marauder to steady herself.

"How the fuck did some creature get the drop on Drummer?" Heads turn, the faceless neighbors shrink away from Peyton. "I must have done a hundred raids with him. He's quick and—"

Lyle holds up his hand again. Peyton might have to break it if he tries that move a third time. "The kid jumped right in. I'll give him that. But he must have missed the spot." Lyle waves a hand behind his head. "Cervical junction…brain stem… She grabbed him and…well…" Lyle shakes his head. "He got bit. The old lady bit him…infected him."

And now, Peyton can see that the front of Lyle's shirt has other stains as well. Rust-brown, dried-stiff blood stains. *What did you do?* With the heel of his boot, Peyton scrapes open the back snap to the harness securing his club. His fingers dance along the taped grip.

Lyle Hutton puts both palms up now. "Your guy gave himself up. He knew…in a matter of weeks, he'd be just like that woman. This kid—Drummer you said?" Lyle just shakes his head. "Peyton, you know it had to—"

"You should have *waited.*" It comes out like a snarl. "He was a Featherton. He—"

Vanessa rams Peyton aside, her knuckles white, her arm cocks back to punch Lyle. Fist hovers in the air, but Lyle doesn't notice, because he's focused on something beyond them. "Holy—"

One high scream rises above all the other noise of people coming together, the reunion of neighbors, the clamor for news from beyond the suburbs, and the argued speculation of *how much longer…how much worse…* Peyton feels everything closing in. The neighborhood gate stands open at the mouth of the street, every smoke darkened silhouette turned toward it.

Behind Peyton, that one scream becomes a chorus of screaming billowing through the crowd. *Someone popped.* Peyton swivels, left hand sweeping the club free from its harness, body launching off the bike, muscles tense. *Ready.*

A frenzied stampede moves from the gate and passes the pit. A woman collapses under the force of the charge. A man tumbles into the glowing coals of the burning pit. As the horde separates, Peyton gets his first look at what everyone runs from.

Creatures. Blood and drool drip from their open mouths. Hands frozen into the rigid claws. Eyes bulging white with animal terror. They dart through the crowd howling, senseless. Newly turned and fast, all of them.

One leaps toward Peyton. A flash of teeth, fingers, eyes rolled back like a shark. Peyton can't get the club up fast enough, so he has to dodge. The thing flies past him. It tackles Vanessa to the ground instead. Peyton has his club up and on it, batting the thing's head down, stomping the brainstem, but not quick enough. Blood pulses from Vanessa's neck, her hands scrabbling there, trying to piece the flesh back together. *She's a goner.* He stands over her, wonders if he should just club her, end it quicker than—Someone to the right of Peyton screams, and he pivots away. And he launches into action.

Another. Another. The club in Peyton's grip crashes and sticks, crashes and sticks, like a living part of him. He loves this—his body fully engaged and mind blank with the effort of the fight. Fighting is real. Fighting matters. So much better than the scraping, tedious struggle of eking out a life in the post-outbreak world. Fuck that bullshit. The pull in his shoulders and back become a continuous burn. Feels good.

Under his boots, the ground turns so slick with blood and brains that he keeps a wide stance, digging in his heels to wrench the club from where he buried it deep in clinging flesh and bone. *Another. Over there!* Figures dart in front of him, and he strikes without thought, straight from the core of his animal body. Most of the creatures are weak and small, one good blow from overhead, and they go down. But they move fucking fast, faster than any he fought before this. Peyton kicks out, knocks the latest snapping one to the ground. He has only a second to gauge his distance from any of the others. *I'm clear.* Crash and stick! He glides both hands down the slick wood and pulls. Then comes the wet squelch, and the chains rip free from the creature's skull. *Another? Another?*

Peyton swings the club around him, spinning. *How many was that?* He should have counted. He should count them now. Adrenaline races up and down his spine. He raises his dripping, gore-coated club in the air. "You all see that?" he shouts to everyone and no one. *"I'm fucking unstoppable!"*

defiance

34 Bailey

My mom, my dad, Peyton… Bailey doesn't want anyone to die, not his neighbors, not the runners assigned to the winding streets of The Greens. Losing anyone else in his family makes him lightheaded with panic. Lucy's disappearance never tortured him the way it did his mother…or Peyton. For Bailey, the uncertainty of never knowing gave him hope. *Maybe, she survived?* He would rather stay in that wishful space, rather than face the certainty of never again seeing someone he loves.

In the alcove outside the study, he finds Cecilia waiting for him. Bailey tilts his head to the side, he'd thought Gabriel left him alone in the mansion. "You're still here? Just hanging out around the study doors?" *She probably eavesdropped on Gabriel's goodbye.* Heard his promise to take care of Bailey's family, to come back.

And she doesn't look too happy about it, hands on her hips, that smug tilt to her chin. "It makes sense for me to stay here." Her sharp voice bounces through the vaulted marble foyer. "I can run things. I'm *valuable*. But, why doesn't Gabriel want you here, too?"

He tries to move around her, but she slides to block his way. He's so sick of her taking out all her jealousy on him. They got along fine for two days. Then, one hint of preferential treatment, and she turns back into Gabriel's condescending second-in-command. "Are you really that useless at fighting?" She looks him up and down with a smirk on her face. "Not like your brother."

"Wow... Really?" For a second, he wants to tell her the truth, that Gabriel left him behind because Bailey is infected—that his blood, his saliva, his snot, all of it is deadly. "I'll be sure to pass on how much you admire my brother's skill at killing frightened and cowering sick people."

"Your brother is a pig. And the creatures don't cower once they get—"

"Yeah, I'm aware of what's happening right now in The Greens. *Where my family lives.* Thanks." He knocks past her. The rubber bottoms of his shoes squeak on the floor as he heads for the stairs. But she follows him and darts in front of him again.

"He's protecting you," she says, voice dripping with accusation. "He should have made you go. It isn't fair."

"Are you kidding me? Since when is Gabriel fair in his decisions. Like when he clobbered Derek Sams or broke apart Angelica's family?"

"That's different. Sometimes, tough decisions have to be made, Bailey. You don't know how hard he's worked, how tirelessly, to make Feathertons."

"Because he's obsessed with power!" But once he says it, Bailey realizes that he doesn't believe that anymore. He sighs and turns away. "I'm going to my room." He's suddenly exhausted. That weird feeling in his head from earlier still present. Like he needs to pop his ears. Like he needs to lie down.

"It isn't *your* room. This is Gabriel's house. You aren't even a Featherton. You have no business even being here."

Bailey's not about to repeat the embarrassing cover story about his "business being here." He won't throw it in her face like that just to hurt her. But, he also won't take any more of her endless crap. "Why don't you stop acting like a jealous girlfriend, Cecilia?" He rests a hand on the carved wooden bannister, looks down at her. "Gabriel is *gay*." He makes a sweeping gesture to take in the mansion, *Featherton Headquarters* in all its minimalist luxury. White linen, Italian marble, expensive track lighting. "He was never going to be more with you than *this*."

Cecilia's mouth drops open, and she flushes all the way up her neck to the perfectly maintained pearlescent roots of her hair. "I hate you," she seethes.

"Right back at ya!" Bailey calls over his shoulder then continues trudging toward his room. He topples face-first onto the bed. He should feel sorry for Cecilia, caught up in an obsession with a boy who will never want her back. But God, she makes him crazy with the way she fawns over Gabriel and tries to come between...

Oh no. Bailey groans into the mattress. *There's nothing to come between.*

Outside, he hears the trucks thunder back into the compound. *That was quick. Quick is good, right?* He leaps back up and rushes to the window. But those aren't the Featherton trucks returning. Instead, a flatbed and a hauler truck idle in the street. One has a metal cage in back, like the government patrols used. The men driving the trucks, and those riding in the truck-bed all wear denim and flannel jackets, cowboy boots, ball caps, and none have the bright-colored hair of Feathertons.

These are Colton's men.

Bailey has a moment of frozen confusion watching them unload and approach the house. Six men without clubs. Carrying guns.

He sprints to the staircase. "Cecilia!"

35 PEYTØN

Something smacks hard into Peyton from behind, slams him to the ground. *I missed one.* Air rushes from his lungs, and his weapon rolls free. Peyton's hands and chin scrape against the pavement.

It's on him.

On his back. Fingers grasp Peyton's hair, twist his neck. How many times has he witnessed this part? The creatures always tear into the throat or face first.

No.

Peyton bucks and manages to knock the thing off. He flips over. Gets both arms up in front of this face, fists clenched. The creature falls back. Then…*stands?* Peyton's eyes focus.

Gabriel. The low hanging sun makes Peyton squint, while relief and lingering terror war inside him.

"That's enough!" Gabriel barks. He says other words, too, that Peyton can't quite take in. All of it gets delivered like the short, hard commands Gabriel used to give back in the beginning—when they still looted and fought side by side. But Peyton can only hear his own breath gasping, his own heart pounding in his chest.

"What the hell? You fucking tackled me." Peyton's skull thuds against the pavement. The smell of blood and gore—still wet and congealed—overpowers him, and Peyton lets his eyes close for just a moment. *Fuck*, he thought…he thought…

***

Brightly-colored hair floods Augusta Drive. Gabriel taking over the chaotic scene. They scrape the dead creatures from the streets, drag them to the pit. Twenty of them. Small. All newly popped and still clear eyed. Blood still thin, skin still pink.

"Jesus, Peyton. They were just kids." Gabriel paces in a tight circle, rubbing one hand against his forehead.

Peyton finds his club, snatches it up, and bangs it on the street to clear the looped chains of blood and muck. "They weren't *kids*, Gabriel. I wouldn't kill kids."

Gabriel spreads his arms. "Look around you!"

And Peyton sees the blood and brains in wide smears leading to the burning pit. The neighbors and the other Feathertons scrape at the carnage with shovels, spray the blood away with hoses. But they flinch away from looking at Peyton. His sweat-damp body, his still dripping club. "They weren't kids. They were creatures. Kids never make it, and everyone knows it." *I did what I had to do.* "Where'd they come from anyway? Who did this to them?"

Gabriel's arms drop to his sides. "Colton. Colton did this. He— I never thought he would go this far…" He starts pacing again. Rubs at his lower lip with his thumb. "Why? Why now—?" Then, the Feathertons leader digs his hands into his red hair. "God, I'm so stupid!" He looks and sounds rattled worse than Peyton has ever seen him. "This wasn't an attack, it was a *diversion.*"

"A diversion from—?"

Gabriel grabs Peyton's bloody leather jacket and hauls him closer. Face to face. "Go to the compound. To my house. That's where they'll go next."

"No, man. Let go. I need to find my parents."

Peyton feels Gabriel's hand clench. He looks down and sees a grip so tight that the taller boy's fingers have turned a deathly white. "No. The house. Bailey is there. I don't know what they'll do if they find—" Gabriel waves over a mass of Feathertons. "Get a truck! I'm taking a group back to the compound—*now!*"

"You said you would protect him." Peyton's entire body heats up with anger and renewed strength. "You were supposed to take care of him." He steps close, hand tightening around his club.

"Peyton, you idiot, fighting me isn't going to help. There are guards at the compound gate, but I don't know if that will stop them. Not now that I've seen this."

"If anything happens to my brother…I'm coming back for you." Peyton points at him.

"Fine," Gabriel says. "I'm right behind you. Just *go!*"

36 Bailey

"Cecilia!" Bailey cranes his neck to look down from the upper stair landing. He can't see her. "Cecilia?" Did she hear the trucks pull up? Below him, a thunderous crack. "Cecilia, *hide!*"

The front door lock explodes through the wood frame, the busted metal pieces skittering across the marble floor. Bailey sinks down, taking cover behind the heavy bannister. His heart jackrabbits in his chest while the men stomp around the first floor. A high pitched shriek from the study. They found Cecilia.

"What are you— What the hell do you think—?"

A slap.

Bailey cringes, tries to see around the thick carved balusters shielding him. No one in the hall. *Cecilia?* Bailey's fingernails dig into his palms. *What did they do to her?* At least, they haven't used the guns. *Please don't use the guns.*

Paper fluttering. Furniture scraping against the wood floor. The thud of something upended. Bailey creeps across the landing for a better view of the entryway.

Another scream. Higher pitched and frightened. One of the men drags Cecilia out of the study, his huge chapped red hand seizing her by the neck. Cecilia's toes dancing from the marble entry to the glossed wood of the hall.

"Where's your boss?" His voice low, deep, nothing like one of the teenagers who Gabriel employs.

At least Cecilia doesn't look cowed by him, her chin jutting, hands balled into fists. She even makes a try at kicking him between the legs.

The redneck steps out of her reach. "Where's the storehouse?" The man wears a green ballcap that hides his face from Bailey's view above him. Bailey cocks his head to get a better look, but still can't see him well with the damn hat in the way.

Ballcap rams Cecilia against the wall. "You'll tell us now or after I hurt you, but you're gonna tell us." She sags for a second until the man's forearm pins her under the chin and scrapes her up to standing. Then a little higher, so she dangles just above the floor. Ballcap smacks his free hand on the wall near Cecilia's head and leans into her. "Where's the storehouse? Where's the boss?"

From inside the study comes the wincing smash of objects breaking, the low vibrations of wall demolition. *They're looking for Gabriel's maps. Ha! Good luck, fuckers.* Gabriel keeps a thin metal pick on him that opens the floor safe. Without that pick, no one can distinguish the safe from the rest of the hardwood floor. Now Gabriel's quarantine renovations make sense. Evil twin sister probably told them about the maps, about the locked armoire in the study. But she doesn't know the floor safe exists.

"He went to check...the attack—" Cecilia claws at the man's hairy arm against her windpipe. "Let...go!" she gasps.

Ballcap spits on the floor. "Pretty boy went himself? Ha, I don't think so."

Bailey touches the bannister with his fingertips and guides himself up. He keeps his eyes glued on the scene below—at Cecilia sputtering against the grip on her throat. He eases himself up onto the bannister to crouch in a perch.

He doesn't have his brother's fighting abilities, but he can't live with himself if he lets these men hurt Cecilia. He *has* to try to help her.

Bailey sees his chance.

Muscles tensing, he pushes off with his hands and feet. Soars upward and in a stomach-plunging arc, comes down feet first fast crashing into Ballcap. It hurts like hell—and he hopes the man also feels the pain. The snap and crunch of bones breaking cascades across Bailey's senses. Bailey scrambles to stand, but his right knee gives out. The man doesn't move. And there's a lot of blood.

"Run!" he wheezes in Cecilia's direction.

Bailey wills his right leg into action. It throbs and sends jolts of pain throughout his body. He bolts after Cecilia toward the back of the house. *The glass doors to the patio!* He rounds the hall into the main room.

Cecilia! A flannel shirted redneck has his arms around her waist. Bailey skids to a stop. She'd looked so strong before, but she's thrashing and terrified now.

"Just let her—"

The punch comes from a different man, a volcanic slam against Bailey's temple that drops him to his knees. The room wavers around him. Cecilia screams again. "Just let her go…" Bailey's right eye throbs. *Get up.* His hands sink down to the floor. *Get up!*

Shouting from behind him. The others found the body of the man Bailey dropped onto. "He's dead!" one of them yells. Then, another fist to Bailey's head, and darkness closes over him like deep water.

***

When he comes to, Bailey's stomach rolls, and his throat and lungs burn. Scratchy twine binds his wrists behind his back, and his fingers have gone numb. Someone wrapped a cloth reeking of body odor and blood over his face. The material flattens his nose and knots across his mouth. And now that he's awake, he has to focus on breathing then trying not to panic. He can't see anything, but the deafening engine rumble and rattling metal floor tell the whole story. They threw him in the bed of the caged truck. He should pay attention to the turns they take, the voices, the things they say. But he feels sick and cold and suffocated... *Calm down, you dumbass. Think!*

Now, he notices that other bodies jostle against him. Groans. Crying. *Wait. I remember crying.* He'd woken up at different points, when the men shoved other people inside the cage with him. Bailey works his bound hands underneath him and up, arms and shoulders aching, joints straining and bruised. Once he gets his arms in front, he rubs his face to work the knot out of his mouth. At last, he spits it free. "Cecilia?" he whispers, waits.

Nothing.

Panic starts to build inside him, and nausea comes back in a hard wave. "Cecilia?" he hisses a little louder than before.

This time a sob answers him. "Bailey? Are you—I thought you were—" Another sob.

His wrists are bound with twine, but he fishes his hands between the bodies packed inside the pen. Someone kicks his arm in warning. Someone else gasps in fear. Then, his seeking hands find a smaller, narrow palm.

Cecilia. Her thin fingers twist through his own. "I thought you were dead," Cecilia says. He squeezes her hand in response, as hard as he can. He tries to give her more than just the reassurance that, yes, he's alive. He tries to tell her he plans to stay alive. *And so should she.* Since the bite, Bailey's gotten a lot of practice reassuring himself.

Stay alive with me, Cecilia.

37 PEYTON

Peyton opens the throttle, pushing the motorcycle as fast and hard as possible. Smoky wind stings his eyes, but he gets that numb clarity he always had in football games. Everything clicks together, sharp and unshakable, as he rips past strip malls falling in on themselves, parking lots and sidewalks becoming cracked chunks of cement, green areas turned to jungle and spilling over. He crests the hill to Olde Town's gate, as winded as if he ran the whole way. Sweat and ash coat his neck. With only four bars left on the fuel gauge, Peyton slows the bike. The gate tower looks deserted, and the wide gate doors stand open. No one shouts a greeting or warning. *Where are the guards?* Peyton guides the bike past the tower and into the compound.

He cups his hands and yells through them, "Hey!"

Since the roads opened up, Gabriel has recruited too many new kids. Peyton can't keep track of all the names or who works where. "Hey! Where the hell is everyone?" Only the most loyal Feathertons get promoted to the guard positions, men and women who would never abandon their posts. *Something has gone wrong.* The thought begins to form when he sees one of them—a kid spread eagle on the street. Lime green hair, steel-toe work boots, and a gray North High hoodie with blood soaking through. Peyton nudges the hem up with the toe of his boot.

Bullet hole.

After the many gruesome deaths Peyton has encountered or caused, seeing the near pristine corpse of a boy his age takes a moment to process. He cuts the engine to the bike but rolls it closer. Next to the boy's hand, a walkie-talkie crackles, and Gabriel's voice demands the kid let Peyton inside.

"Jake, do you copy?"

Nope, Jake does not fucking copy. Peyton scoops the walkie-talkie off the ground, his heart pounding. Between the encroaching darkness and the blinding sunset on the horizon, he can't see shit. Anyone could have eyes on him, and Jake's body in the middle of the street a trap. Peyton depresses the call button, "Jake's dead."

"Peyton?" A chirp of static on the other end, and Gabriel sounds breathless. "They also shot one of our runners—just off the I-35 exit near your neighborhood—Killed him." Stress continues to shake through his voice. "Go to the house," Gabriel says. "Bailey's at the house."

"Shit." Peyton hurls the walkie-talkie down onto Jake's body and guns the engine. The Marauder jumps to life under him and tears out for the mansion.

The gate guard isn't the only casualty. He blows past four more. The dead bodies of kids, curled in on themselves, dark lumps. Closer to the mansion, Peyton steers through a crazy obstacle course of scattered crates, shovels, crowbars, motorcycles like his, cargo trailers with the lids and doors curled open...*looted*. He keeps his eyes on the ever-darkening houses, the shadowed trees, the massed bushes, leery of attack.

The mansion is lit up, front door hanging crooked and broken. *Am I too late?* Peyton's right hand clenches the throttle. He accelerates so hard that he catches air on the curved drive. Hard enough that the bike lays over and shoots out from under him. Peyton scrambles toward it, intent on unfastening his club. He wants it in his hand, even if it won't match up to any weapon he may face inside.

It doesn't matter. He won't let his brother die alone. Peyton can't stay in this fucked up world without him. This is the truth he's battled against since the moment he saw Don tackle Bailey to the floor. He has nothing left to live for if his brother doesn't make it through the virus, if he finds Bailey dead inside that house. He unfastens the club from its holster, throws his shoulders back, and heads up the walk.

When he pushes the door aside, its hinges groan and snap. "Bailey!" If any of them stayed behind, then he just announced himself—gave up the advantage of surprise. His boot skids in a wet trail of blood on the marble floor. *Fucking...* "*Bailey!*" Let whoever attacked the mansion find him. Let them laugh at his club. Let them gun him down. He just wants Bailey to know his brother came for him.

But he doesn't face laughter or guns. The house is empty. Peyton crouches near a puddle of fresh blood. Footsteps track in and out of the puddle, the wide smear of a body getting dragged out the door. Someone took a pummeling right under the stairway and then got hauled out the front. His fingers touch the edge of the puddle. If this belongs to Bailey...*I will kill them.* He will beat them to death.

Outside, the harsh growl of engines, the slam of car doors. Movement surrounds Peyton as he stays frozen near the red spill. Then, Gabriel stands beside him. "I know this looks bad, but *think,* Peyton."

Gabriel's impersonal tone echoes in Peyton's head. *Think? What good will thinking do?* "If this is my brother's blood..."

"*Think,* Peyton. If they'd killed Bailey, then they would have left his body like the guards."

If they'd killed Bailey... Peyton surges up, his hand a vise on his weapon.

Gabriel steps back, out of range of the club. The inscrutable mask in place. "Don't," he warns.

But Peyton can't help himself. The race to Olde Town, the dead bodies, the blood. Reacting on instinct, Peyton lunges for the other boy.

But Gabriel moves faster, reflexes trained to maximum efficiency. He grabs the arm that swings the club and twists, forcing Peyton down face-first onto the blood-painted floor. Gabriel continues to apply pressure until Peyton's grip on the chained bat loosens. Finally, his hand convulses, and it clatters onto the marble floor.

Gabriel delivers a raspy whisper into Peyton's ear, "I've let a lot go because of Bailey. But, if you hit me, I will retaliate." To emphasize his threat, Gabriel maneuvers his right knee onto Peyton's back. The pressure makes it impossible to breathe. All Peyton can do is nod, yes. Gabriel releases him.

Peyton's right arm feels numb and stunned, so he has to lift himself with his left, takes a staggering step to the wall. Electrified pain shoots down his shoulder to his fingers. "Who did this? Who took my brother?" He's tired as fuck, more exhausted than he remembers ever feeling.

"Not just Bailey. They took Cecilia—they were the only two left in the house." Gabriel's trembling fingers rake through his hair. "I know who did it but—"

"Colton took them. You know it, and I know it. That hillbilly piece of shit, he's going to regret this." The feeling returning to his hand, Peyton scoops his club back off the floor. "I'm getting Bailey back. Right now."

He doesn't make it out the door before Gabriel slides in front of him. "Armed with a club and a fucked up arm? That would be extremely foolish."

"Get out of my way."

But Gabriel only lifts his chin at Peyton's demand. "No. You aren't going after Bailey alone and without a plan. You'll get him killed." Peyton squints up at Gabriel in the half light between the darkened front step and the glowing entryway. "I can't take that chance, Peyton. Not with Bailey."

"He's *my* brother." All Gabriel's flashy-haired minions surround them, watching. "I'm not waiting on some elaborate bullshit plan of yours." Peyton doesn't care right now what Gabriel has told his people or what really happened between Bailey and him. "He's not a Featherton. He doesn't belong to you."

Gabriel's jaw tightens. "Alright," his voice like ice. "You want your brother back. I want this attack on my territory punished. You can trust me to do that, can't you?" He pauses but doesn't wait for Peyton to answer. "Colton's entire operation needs to be eliminated, and that takes planning and weapons. One impulsive reaction from a boy armed with a chained baseball bat isn't going to accomplish anything."

Peyton remembers Gabriel as the new student at Memorial High, someone stuck up and dressed all wrong and lacking interest in football, someone Peyton should have seen as a victim, but somehow hadn't dared to. Instead, Peyton had seen *this*. A cold and calculating appreciation for viciousness like his own. *He's a fucking psychopath.* And Peyton needs a psychopath right now. He lets his club slide from his hand, fall to the ground. "Okay. Okay, we do this your way."

38 Bailey

When they reach their destination, men rip the blindfolds away. Dawn. Overcast sky. Bailey's eyes adjust. Trucks. Fencing. Dogs on chains. The men cut the twine on their wrists. Bailey wants to shake out his prickling hands, but Cecilia locks her fingers with his.

"Bailey, I'm scared."

Bailey looks at her standing there, barefoot. Her black pants torn, unfastened. Her shirt crumpled. *No. No. Please.* Blood stains on her face and neck and even painted across her white hair. *Those assholes.* Cold rage makes his gut ache, his eyes itch with unshed tears. "It's going to be okay," he whispers, the only comfort he can give her, even if it isn't true. Someone shoves him from behind.

"No talking!"

Colton's men wear bandanas on their faces like old-timey bank-robbers. They all carry guns. One of them pokes at Cecilia's back with the barrel of a shotgun, shoves her forward. Behind them, the dogs strain and growl. Someone shouts, *"Move."*

Cecilia stumbles, so Bailey slides next to her and wraps his arm under her shoulders, drags her along. He tries to imagine what Peyton would do in his place. *He'd be strong. He'd be angry.* Not shaking and afraid like Bailey.

Colton's men drag two teenage boys from the cage as well. Burly hillbillies with guns surround them, chain their hands to a thick wire line. They pull the line toward a wood barn attached to a grain elevator. Inside the barn, they hook the wire line to bolts in the cement floor. Blood stained cement. They aren't the first prisoners Colton has locked up in here. When the doors slam shut, Cecilia starts to cry. Bailey tries to give her a hug, but the metal cable and floor bolts keep him in place. Instead, leans in as close as he can. "It's going to be okay, Cecilia."

"What are they going to do to us?"

He doesn't have an answer. "I'm right here. I'm with you, okay?" She's become a different person, not at all the sharp, difficult girl he knew these weeks at Gabriel's house.

One of the boys chained on the line turns toward him. Wide-eyed and afraid but strong looking with broad shoulders and muscled arms. "Who are you?"

Bailey knows better than to say his name out loud here. Not with the chance that anyone puts him together with Peyton. These men would love to take out all the anger they harbor for Featherton's ruthless blue-haired lieutenant. "They took me from Gabriel's house," Bailey says instead. "Featherton territory."

"That's twenty miles from us. We only started getting deliveries from Feathertons." He looks Bailey up and down. "They look different. Not like you."

"I'm not a Featherton. I was just there."

The shorter boy on the end of their line tugs at his chains, trying to break free, but his efforts only result in rattling the entire line. "We didn't even buy from Feathertons. They took me by mistake!" The boy has flame red hair. *Bright enough to get mistaken for a Featherton?*

The barn's walls have shrunken narrow gaps between them, and light stripes in across the empty room. Colton's men leave them for hours in the dark and damp. The barn's plank walls let the cold seep in from outside. Because of the stiff cable, they can't even bunch together for warmth. Colton's people don't seem concerned about their comfort or health, though. Another long stretch of time, and Bailey watches Cecilia's toes and fingers turn blue. Bailey worries she won't survive if Colton ignores them much longer. He twists his body toward a crack in the wallboards.

"Hello?" Bailey shouts into the slit between the planks. Hours earlier, he'd heard yelling and the rumble of engines. But, only snarling and whining from the guard dogs for a long time now. He can't see anything through the crack, just a thin slice of light. "Are you seriously going to leave us here? You must have taken us for something—so get in here and fucking do it!"

"Shut up," hisses the red-haired boy, he's shivering hard enough to send a vibration up through the steel cable.

"You want to freeze to death?" Bailey says. But then, he thinks of all the other ways Colton might kill them. Maybe, the kid has a point, and Bailey should keep quiet and hope their captors forgot about them.

No such luck, though. His shouting must have attracted attention. The barn door slides open, and men flood into the room. One of the guard dogs trail behind them growling. These are the same men who raided the mansion. Colton's stocky barrel-gut body in the center of them. He doesn't wear a ball cap or bandana like his underlings, and his ruddy face fixes into the hard, smug smile of a bully. His eyes go right toward where Bailey and Cecilia lean together. They narrow on Cecilia. He squints and frowns as he focuses on her and swaggers closer.

"What happened to all your fight?" he asks Cecilia. "My boys tell me you're feisty for a little thing." Cecilia doesn't answer, but her shaking makes the chains on her wrists jingle like bells.

"Please, just let us go," she says.

"You're asking now?" One of the men behind Colton laughs. "You don't remember giving me this?" He shows Cecilia four long fingernail scratches on his cheek.

Bailey jerks the line toward him, toppling Cecilia against his side. "Leave her alone. She's scared," he spits out. "What you did to her back at the house..." He won't say it, not with Cecilia right there. But he knows. "Gabriel would never let that happen to *anyone*." He has their attention now. "All of you are trash. Criminals. At least Gabriel—"

Colton's punch knocks Bailey backward, and his upper lip explodes against his teeth. He starts to topple down, but the taut line unrepentantly holds him up. Bailey hawks blood onto the ground. *Don't pass out.* Cecilia needs him. *Stand back up.*

The growling behind the men intensifies, and the redneck with the scratched face steps aside. Colton pulls the snarling dog forward by a heavy leather leash.

No. Not a dog.

A creature, grunting, panting, and angry. A little boy, maybe seven or eight. Lucy's age. They've bound the kid's arms to his sides with the same rough twine they used on Bailey, only tight enough that his childish arms look misshapen and purple. When the boy twists and lunges against his leash, Bailey sees that someone hammered a metal spike into the back of his shoulder.

"What did you do to him?" Bailey's voice comes out reedy and gurgling because of the split lip, the blood still in his mouth. "You're *sick!*" he shouts, but Colton and his men just laugh.

At the end of the lead, an iron pole keeps the boy from lunging back against Colton. He knocks him to the ground with the pole and lets one of his men kick the spike deeper into the little boy's back. The boy howls, revealing a tongue ripped to shreds inside his sagging mouth.

The other two teenagers chained to the wire with Bailey start screaming, kicking out at the creature to keep him back. They force the cable down, scrabbling to get away.

Bailey doesn't shrink from the little boy like the others do. Instead, he twists his body, tries to shield Cecilia. Bailey doesn't need to fear the boy's biting teeth, his drool, his blood. Not like the others. For a split second, his eyes meet the crazed glossy centers of the feral boy's eyes—*how much longer until I look just like that?* Bailey recoils, and he lets the cable line pull him back with the others.

rage

39 PEYTON

Gabriel won't move against Colton until dark. No matter how much Peyton rages, threatens. "He's going to kill them."

"He's not. I'm certain he's keeping Bailey and Cecilia alive. Colton doesn't just kill his prisoners." Gabriel's lips pinch until they go white, holding back whatever else he wants to say—keeping himself in check. He sits at his mahogany desk like always. Colton's guys smashed everything else in the study, but the desk, they'd just flipped over.

Peyton keeps picking up and setting down his club, contained violence in every cell of his body. "How do you know? You have a spy?"

"Yes. Spies. Now, get out, I have to think."

So, Peyton waits out the day prowling the mansion. Runners come and go. A girl with a long turquoise ponytail mops up the blood under the stairs. Shane and the other remaining gate guards take a meeting in the dining room that Gabriel refuses to let Peyton attend. When the guards finally leave, Gabriel waves Peyton inside.

"Sit down."

"No." Peyton puts his hands on his hips. "Just tell me what we're going to do. It's been hours, we should have gone right after them, maybe caught them on the road."

Gabriel rubs his forehead, rakes back his lank hair. He sinks into the chair at the head of his polished dining table. "Colton sent twenty men here, and all of them were armed."

Guns? "No way." Peyton saw the shit-fit people had when patrols took their guns. It was all over the internet. "That's the first thing during martial law—"

"The patrols looked the other way for Colton. Good ol' boy stuff." Gabriel's lips curl, he drums his fingers on the table in front of him. "They wanted him in charge and not a bunch of delinquent teenagers. They underestimated us." The drumming fingers intensifies. "They underestimated *me*." Then, Gabriel jolts up, his chair tips backward, crashes to the floor. "How dare they come into my house and trash it. How dare they take my lieutenant and take *Bailey*… If they hurt him, I'll burn the whole place to the ground with them inside it."

Peyton steps back as Gabriel goes to the wall of windows looking out on his frosted garden. Gabriel with his brother, Gabriel thinking he has some kind of *claim* on Bailey turns Peyton's stomach, but he can see that the Feathertons boss wants revenge as much as Peyton does. *Good.* They'll annihilate Colton and his entire operation.

"So, they're armed. That's still only twenty guys." Peyton smacks a hand on the glass to get Gabriel's attention. "Just here in Olde Town, we have more than four times that. I say we rush the place. I'm not afraid."

"It *will* be something like that. But, we're going to have to wait until dark." Gabriel sighs, smacks his forehead against the glass then straightens and pulls his shoulders back. "Alright." He reaches inside his suit jacket, and with one slow draw pulls out a black handgun.

"What's that?"

"It's a Glock. Have you ever shot a gun?"

"You know I haven't."

"Come on," Gabriel pulls open one of the sliding glass doors. Cold smoke-tinged air rolls inside. Despite the temperature, the sun is shining, and frost covering the mansion's terrace sparkles like glass. Gabriel holds the gun out to Peyton, waves toward the tall white brick fence surrounding the back yard. "You can practice a few times but only a few times. There are seventeen rounds, and I don't have any other ammo."

"Why are you giving this to me? Obviously, you're the one who knows how to use it."

"Because you're the better fighter."

Peyton's head jerks up. He meets Gabriel's eyes, expecting to see anger or jealousy... Maybe satisfaction that all Gabriel's training hadn't gone to waste. But Gabriel just looks sad. With a jolt, Peyton recognizes that this is Bailey's same expression whenever Peyton picks up a club.

"You were made for this world," Gabriel says.

40 Bailey

Their wrists chained, Cecilia and Bailey strain against the thick wire cord heaving back and forth. The feral boy's teeth can't reach them as long as they all stay flat against the wall. But, the two boys chained on the other end of the line keep scrabbling to escape, causing the cable to dip. If one of them gets knocked to the ground, he will take the whole line down. And they will all come in range of the little boy's fingernails and teeth.

"Stop!" Bailey yells, but the other boys don't hear him, too panicked to escape the little creature Colton taunts them with. "You're going to pull us down!"

The more they scream, the more agitated and afraid the creature child becomes. At least Cecilia, as frightened as the other two boys, retains more common sense. "Calm down! You're making it worse." She trips forward, feet leaving ground as the metal line pulls them all left.

When the red haired kid on the end stumbles, Colton's men spit on the ground and guffaw. One of them, a skinny dust-coated hick with blue bandana loose around his red neck, kicks a boot toward Cecilia's leg. "This little girl puts you two to shame!" He strikes again, this time with more purpose, his heel glancing off of her left knee, causing her to crumple against the cable. Cecilia bites her lip, holding back any sound, pain scrunching her face.

"God! Stop it!" Bailey wants to reach out and punch this guy in his face, but his bonds and the metal cable keep him fixed against the wall.

The man doesn't even look at Bailey, instead he laughs and spits. His saliva hits Cecilia's forehead as silent tears run down her cheeks.

"That's enough, Ray. Don't want her clamming up too soon," Colton says. He drags the iron pole back, pulling the little creature away.

A man with dark, bushy hair and a long thick beard, snatches the front of Cecilia's torn shirt and jerks her forward for a closer look. Earlier in the day, Cecilia's button down shirt matched the pristine white of her bleached out hair. Now, both have degraded into tatters of rust colored blood and dirt. "You're pretty," he says. "Is Gabriel Featherton your boyfriend?"

She looks exhausted, doesn't try to fight him off, her head wobbling on her neck. "Go to hell."

The bearded man laughs at her, hauls her closer. Her arms pull taut, hands turn red as the chains strangle them on the cable.

No. Bailey won't let this happen. "Leave her alone. She's not his girlfriend. She's just a girl. Gabriel doesn't have a girlfriend." Bailey swallows hard. "Gabriel doesn't even like girls. He's gay."

A sharp barking laugh, "I might even believe that," Colton says. "I've never seen that stuck-up iceman look once at a woman, and I've thrown enough of them toward him at those government patrol parties."

"Then, you know I'm telling the truth. She's nothing to him."

"But I saw *you* talking to him at one." Colton's eyes rove over Bailey. "You're the only person I've seen him talk to that wasn't connected to business."

The man holding Cecilia drops her, and she flops back against the wall, panting. Bailey has their attention now. He pulls as far away from Cecilia and the other boys as he can.

"He doesn't like girls," Bailey offers, "but he doesn't want any of the other Feathertons to know…so he keeps her around. Let them go. Gabriel doesn't care what happens to random people in his territory, they're just numbers to him."

"And he cares what happens to you? Even though he don't make you dress like some Country Club boy the way he does, didn't even make you change your hair? I'm not sure I'm buying what you're trying to sell me, boy." Colton turns away from him and motions for Ray.

Ignored, the little feral boy had curled into a whimpering ball. When Ray snaps the leash, the boy's eyes flick open, and he dives forward with biting teeth.

"Bring it here," Colton orders.

Bailey and the other prisoners hug themselves to the wall again. The red-haired boy chained on the end of the wire line starts to babble a string of incomprehensible curses followed more clearly by shrieks of, "Keep it away! Keep it off me!" over and over again.

Colton shakes his head. "Relax, son. We don't want you getting ripped up. We want fighters. One way or another…" The light from the open grain elevator door makes a spotlight, and Colton takes a thick pole and pins the little creature in it. The boy has Super Flu's

217

speed and strength, but Colton manages him with practiced ease. He stomps one heavy looking cowboy boot onto the feral boy's back as he quivers, frightened and useless underneath Colton's weight. "Jacob and Cal, come here. It's time."

Then, the bearded man pulls thick leather work gloves from his back pocket and slides into them. He drops to the ground and maneuvers the boy's rabid face into the concrete to hold it steady. Another redneck produces a large syringe tipped with a long thick-gauge needle. He shoves it into the base of the child's skull. The feral boy rasps heavily, almost seeming to relax as the redneck slowly draws cloudy yellow fluid into the clear tube.

The cervical junction. The exact spot where the virus takes control. Bailey flashes back to all the creatures Colton brought as party entertainment. Their arms bound to their sides, much like this boy, and dumped into the empty swimming pool so that Peyton and others could kill them for fun. Fast, angry, strong—Colton hadn't rounded them up from anywhere. *He'd made them himself.*

Two other men raise shotguns, point them as Ray unhooks the line, unlocks the twisted chains, freeing Bailey, Cecilia, and the other two teens.

"You," Ray says to the trembling red-haired kid, seizing him by his bright hair. The soles of the kid's tennis shoes scrape on the concrete floor, as Ray drags him forward. The boy's eyes still fix on the little creature under Colton's boot, so he doesn't realize what Colton intends to do with the syringe. He still thinks the limp little creature boy might attack him.

Ray throws him to the ground at Colton's feet. The kid's entire body quakes in fear at his proximity to the feral boy.

"You scared?" Colton asks.

The boy doesn't respond. His face has gone white as if in shock.

Colton snaps his fingers toward the man with the syringe. "I'll do the honors. Hand it over," he orders. He takes the syringe, and the other man takes over restraining the little creature with the pole.

Colton taps the barrel of the syringe with his fingers, eyes the yellow liquid inside it. "You'll like this," he tells the shivering redhead. "It will make you brave." He stabs the needle into the back of the red-haired boy's neck, the same spot he took it from the creature-child. A small trickle of blood comes out and slides down and soaks into the boy's sweaty t-shirt. Colton depresses the plunger, and the viscous fluid begins pumping into the young kid's skull, directly into his brainstem. The boy flinches, jerks, but does not fight back, too paralyzed by fear.

"He's just a kid!" Bailey shouts. "You'll kill him!"

"Nah, it ain't gonna kill him. Leastwise, not right away." The men holding the guns back away like they expect the kid to change right that moment, but he doesn't move.

Colton turns to face his remaining three captives, like he's deciding between them. "Draw me up another dose, boys." The two men go to work on the squirming creature child again. Once they have another sickening yellow dose, they pass it off to Colton, who brandishes it in front of Bailey, Cecilia, and the other teenaged boy.

Bailey hears the remaining boy start to sob. Cecilia screams as Colton grabs a handful of her bleached hair. "You tell us how to find Featherton's storehouse."

She pants in fast quick breaths, but doesn't say a word. "She doesn't know!" Bailey shouts. "She's a grunt. Gabriel doesn't tell her anything."

Colton lets go of the shaking girl and holds the syringe in front of Bailey. "Then, you tell me."

Bailey pictures the territory map nestled in the floor safe under Gabriel's desk, but he can't recall anything. It doesn't matter. Despite all the times he distanced himself from Peyton and Feathertons,

Bailey would rather die than let Colton run the suburbs. In that moment, Bailey feels as solidly loyal to Gabriel as any of his neon-haired, sworn members.

Colton pulls him forward, holds the syringe over him like a threat. "Tell me what I need to know, and I won't turn you. Whatever that smug prick had you doing, you could do that for us."

Every word of that, Bailey finds hilarious. Even if he wanted to, he can't hide the laughter foaming up inside him. "No, thanks." His laughter unnerves everyone. Colton, his men, Cecilia all look at him like he's crazy. Bailey can't see the other boy they captured, but the sobbing stopped. *Jesus, is this it? Am I losing it?*

Colton, red-faced, obviously thinks the joke's on him, and he doesn't like it. "What's so funny?"

God… One moment, Bailey's gasping for breath, and the next all humor disappears. He looks Colton in the eye. "Go fuck yourself."

⑪ PEYTØN

Just before sundown, they gather a hundred of the best fighters and athletes in the territory. Not just Feathertons, but neighborhood people who the lieutenants can vouch for. They use spray dye to mark their hair, so no one gets confused in the upcoming brawl. Peyton catches a glimpse of Case's fluffy hair getting turned a metallic purple. He doesn't even realize he's crossed the street, gotten into her face, until he's already shouting. "The fuck are you doing here? Go home. Now."

"No way. You need me there." She flips the mass of sopping purple hair over one shoulder, staining her shirt and the skin on her neck.

"I don't want you there."

"I don't care." A hose gets passed around to rinse out the dye, but she waves it away and grabs a towel instead. "You *need* me there," she says again, and dammit, he fucking does. He needs everyone because he can't think straight worrying about being too late.

"Fine. Stay." He pats the gun tucked into the waist of his jeans, but it's hidden under his leather jacket, so she has no idea. "Just don't try and hold me back."

Gabriel has the lieutenants pass out metal handled torches and N95 respirators. "Don't light the wick until the signal. The torches are green poplar." Gabriel moves among his attentive troops. "That means, they will create a lot of smoke, which is what we want. We need it for cover. And we don't know how many people he's infected or what we might walk into, so stay alert. Listen for each other. There are far more of us than of them. Don't break the line."

The SUVs spread out from Featherton territory, no headlights, no sound. Peyton rides with Shane and two guys he doesn't know. One of them, super built with shoulders wider than Peyton's and green hair, jumps in the front beside Shane. The dude in back with Peyton looks a little punk with eyeliner and deep purple bangs hanging in his face. He reminds Peyton of Vanessa. None of them introduce themselves. Shane smokes a cigarette as he drives and hangs it out the window after each puff.

The burly kid in the passenger seat cringes whenever Shane takes a drag. "Shane, man, keep that away from the sticks, okay?" He clicks his tongue. "The ends of these torches are soaked in kerosene. They'll go up in flash, man."

As soon as the engine cuts out, Peyton emerges, squints into the dying light, searching out their contact. Some kid with a magenta Afro. *Okay. There.*

Peyton points his unlit torch at Shane and the other guys, gestures for them to follow him through the yellowed, broken cornstalks. Their boots crunching the dried leaves and dropped cobs makes enough noise that they could have just driven the fucking Land

Rover right over the field. In the settling darkness, he can see the ranch house all lit up in a grove of redbud trees.

"Down," Shane orders, and they all duck low. Magenta Afro slinks off to Peyton's right, and Shane and the others fan out to the left. Peyton puts on the respirator. So do the others.

A low whistle—*Feathertons surround the house and barns.*

A second whistle. Peyton pulls the lighter from his pocket. Magenta Afro keeps pulling up his hoodie and then shaking it off again. *No hoodies. No hats.* They need to recognize each other if it gets chaotic. He's glad Case didn't try and rinse out the purple.

The third whistle. Peyton flicks the lighter and touches it to the end of the wooden torch. Flame jumps into the air, like the whole thing might go up in a blaze. But it settles to a steady burn as Peyton moves forward in synch with the other Feathertons. "*Step!*" Shouted down the line. "*Step!*" A shrinking prison of fire. Colton's base in its center.

42 Bailey

Colton drags the tip of the needle down over Bailey's cheek and against his neck. He's hoping to freak Bailey out, get him babbling about the location of some big storage facility when one doesn't even exist. Behind him, the feral boy struggles against the pole that holds him down, and the red-haired teen starts to moan. Both just kids. Trying to survive in this unsurvivable world.

"We don't know anything!" Cecilia pleads behind him.

Bailey locks eyes with Colton.

Before Colton knows what's happening, Bailey catches the needle against his skin, lets it pierce into his neck. The needle burns as it goes through his muscle.

Colton jerks the syringe in shock—Bailey feels the liquid drive into his neck.

"Bailey!" Cecilia sobs.

Colton's upper lip curls as he kicks Bailey away, and Bailey sprawls on his back. The syringe, still half full in Colton's hand, drips a shivering gold drop of the infected fluid onto Bailey's cheek, and it trails down like a tear. Guys like Colton, they don't like when their victims push back. Bailey laughed at him, inviting infection instead of giving up Featherton secrets. He called bullshit on Colton's intimidation tactics. Bailey waits for another kick, fists, one of the guns to fire.

A siren wails.

Not the pulsing high-pitched creature sirens they use in the suburbs but something constant and flat. An old-fashioned alarm. Colton and his men rush from the barn, latching their captives inside. Bailey's arms shake as he pushes himself up from the dusty cement. The darkened barn transforms all of them into cowering shadows. Underneath the alarm, Bailey can hear a keening noise. *The little creature is free.* He scrambles to find the pole and leash Colton used to control the little boy. His searching fingers close onto the thick leather strap, then the metal rod. He pulls it in front of him as he stands.

The creature child stays on the ground, face down, blond curls matted with dirt and straw as he moans. He doesn't realize Colton's boot no longer holds him in place. When Colton returns, he'll plunge another needle into the boy's skull. Colton will use the feral little boy to make more just like him. *Unless... Even though he looks and sounds like a child crying, he won't ever be that again.* Bailey raises the pole.

"I'm sorry. I'm so, so sorry." He brings it down on of the boy's head with a powerful smack. The little creature jerks once, makes a gurgling sound, and falls limp. At first, Bailey can only hear his own guttural breathing as he fights against the tears. Then, sparking yellow light flashes through the barn's wooden slats, and the alarm cuts out… Demolition takes its place. Splitting wood, shattering glass. Shouting. The roar of an engine.

Feathertons. Bailey starts to tremble. *They came.*

13 PEYTON

Three of Gabriel's biggest trucks break through the ring to dash for the house and a row of trailers—Colton's stores. Unlike Gabriel, Colton concentrated all his supplies in one central location to guard. *Stupid.* One place to attack. Peyton's breath pants hot and moist inside the mask, and his eyes water. All the dead and dying cornstalks create smoke thicker than any fog he's ever gone through. Gabriel's plan is designed to work fast with only Peyton and a chosen few going for the barn where Colton holds prisoners. Shane snaps his mask up to yell, "Go now!" Then to the others, "Don't break the circle!"

Peyton races away from the closing ring, has to dodge when Moltov cocktails hit a ramshackle guard tower, and it teeters over. One of the Featherton trucks crashed right into the storehouse and candy-colored heads already pick their way into the rubble. Shouting. Gunshots. Clouds of smoke bounce the firelight in flashy patterns across the mayhem. Magenta Afro kid collides into Peyton as a horse gallops past him to escape the smoke and fire, the explosion of the fire bombs.

In the chaos, Peyton misses the weight of his chained club. He'd gotten used to the heft of it in his right hand. Instead, he reaches for the deadly bulge under his shirt—the Glock.

Someone slams into Peyton from behind. He pulls the gun up to shoot.

No creature or man grabs at him though. In the flickering strobe of the fire, Peyton finds Case, luminous dark eyes, mass of wild curls.

"It's me. Peyton, it's just me." Case yanks Peyton by the hand and hauls him forward. She tosses the torch away, and darkness swallows them. "I followed Colton back inside the ring. He tried to escape, but then, he went back in and…" Case gestures toward the gleaming aluminum sided elevator building. "He went in there."

44 Bailey

In the heavy shadows of the barn, Cecilia and the other teenager recoil against the wall. The boy's dark eyes glitter at Bailey. "Keep away from us," he says. He has the metal line that connected them earlier—he lashes it in front of himself like a whip. "Stay back!"

The boy grips Cecilia's arm, hauls her with him as he sidesteps against the wall. They angle for the barn door. Even though they all heard the bolt thud into place when Colton left, one side looks crooked. Like a good kick might pry it loose.

"I…I'm not going to…" Bailey says, the words come out a breathy whine. "I had to kill him…" The tears still in his throat making it hard to speak and breathe at the same time. "He was… Colton was…"

Cecilia won't meet his eyes. "Stay there, Bailey. Don't come closer." She makes a sobbing noise, but her eyes are dry. "You're infected!"

The virus.

Bailey has been living with it for weeks now inside of him, but she didn't know. No one knew. She only, just now, saw the needle prick his skin, the plunger empty some of its deadly liquid inside of him.

The boy strikes out toward him with the metal cable. "If you come any closer, I'll kill you!"

"I'm not… Cecilia, I'm still me."

The boy beside her thrashes the thick wire faster, screaming, too. But not at Bailey.

Behind him.

Bailey whirls around.

The red-haired boy curls from the floor, stands in a shaking crouch. His eyes dart around the room, the whites showing through the dim light. A long string of drool dangles from the corner of his mouth down to the distinctive clawed fingers. And trapped between a newly popped creature and a whipping metal wire…Bailey.

"Set down that fucking cable. You're going to scare him." Bailey tries to keep his voice calm and low, not panic the creature boy.

More glass shattering. Then, the rear wall of the barn erupts into flame. The red-haired creature boy turns toward Bailey. Stares at him with addled comprehension. Bailey takes a slow step back from him. "You're okay—"

Splintering glass echoes through the barn, and firebombs flare through the wood walls. A chunk of the roof groans and drops to the cement floor, burning lumber spraying outward like a bomb. Heat sucks at Bailey's clothes and skin. But still, the wire rips through the air, impeding his way to the barn door, forcing him back toward the flames. Forcing the red-haired creature back as well.

"I'm not sick yet. I'm still—" Bailey sucks in a gasp just as the tip of the wire cuts across his right arm, through his t-shirt to the skin. He grabs at the slice in his bicep. Blood streams down his arm toward his wrist. Beside him, the creature leaps. It tackles the other boy to the ground, clawed hands grabbing him, drawing him closer, jaw opening. He tears into the meat of the other boy's face, rips his nose away, and bites again.

Cecilia screams. The barn doorway collapses, leaving a gaping dark mouth on the burning barn.

Bailey races across the room before he has time to think, crushes Cecilia to his chest. "Cecilia."

One of the long wooden support beams topples half the barn.

"Please, Bailey, I want out of here." Searing flames in red and yellow flash from the darkness at every point. Should they run toward the fire, through the dark gaps between flames? Choking black smoke and searing red heat surround him. Bailey rubs at his stinging eyes. *Wait...there.* Several yards ahead...another structure, metal and gleaming with a wide door in its side. The grain elevator, standing untouched, glowing from within. "Look," he points toward the door, but Cecilia doesn't follow.

She sways on her feet from fear and exhaustion, crying and passive. Bailey hefts Cecilia up into his arms. *Hide from Colton. Take care of Cecilia.* He doesn't know how long he has until he loses his mind like the red-haired boy. Colton's syringe had only pricked the muscle of his neck, not the crucial resting point at the base of the brainstem.

If he starts feeling confused...

He doesn't want to turn into the red-haired boy, blood running down his face, panicked enough to attack.

If he starts feeling confused... *I'll run.*

15 PEYTON

So close now. Peyton can't wait any longer and sprints forward through the smoke toward the tall silo and elevator buildings, their aluminum walls reflecting orange flame and shifting black smoke. Case stays with him, one hand gripping his jacket not to lose him in the smoke.

The barn is gone.

Supporting beams frame a massive red and yellow blaze. Peyton grinds to a stop. *Bailey was in the barn.* "Gabriel said Bailey would be in the barn. Where's my brother? Where—"

"But, Colton went in there." Case points toward a hanging metal door. "Maybe, Bailey—"

"Come on." Using both hands, Peyton holds the gun in front of him the way he's seen cops do on television. "Colton better hope I find Bailey before I find him."

***

Inside the grain elevator, metal bins and tubing glitter like treasure in the haze of smoke. The building creaks and moans. Peyton's skin broils in the heat wafting in from the burning barn. "Bailey!" Case lunges toward him to cover his mouth.

Right. Right. Sneak up on him.

Peyton nods understanding, Case lets go. His hands feel slick on the gun. *Point and pull the trigger.* Gabriel made him shoot twice against the brick privacy fence in a quick lesson, then they called it good. Even if his aim sucks, Peyton's got enough bullets to kill Colton. Screw the plan.

He shoulders Case aside. "Bailey!" he bellows again. Machinery pillars run floor to ceiling in a cluster around the door, shining cylinders to move grain around the building.

"Dammit, Peyton!" Case hisses. She clutches the back of Peyton's jacket.

As the roof burns, ash sprinkles down on them. "Bailey, I'm here!" When Peyton comes around the forest of metal cylinders, he finds his brother crouched over the body of Cecilia Vu. She looks dead. Bailey's wide gray eyes brim with tears, his dark blond hair coils from sweat against his neck and cheeks. He looks beat up, exhausted.

"Peyton?" Bailey's bottom lip trembles.

Peyton drops his arms, gun pointed at the ground. "Bailey, get—" Something moves in the tubing behind his brother, and Colton lunges forward. He clamps a thick hand onto Bailey's neck, hauls him up and against his barrel chest. In his free hand, he brandishes a sawed-off shotgun.

Peyton brings the Glock up again, bracing it with both hands, "Let him go!" How many times had he heard someone say those same words in movies, on television? And Peyton always yelled, *"Just shoot!"* at the screen. But now, he understands why the characters never did what he told them. He doesn't trust himself not to hit Bailey. Even if he'd practiced making a million shots instead of only the two.

"They really did come looking for you, didn't they?" Colton's spit hits Bailey's cheek. "Don't you pop on me, yet." He shakes the fist that circles Bailey's neck and mimics a nod.

Behind Peyton, the wall groans with a shuddering noise, and he makes a quick glance back. It cranks up like a garage door and lets in the sounds of shouting, of destruction, of smoke and heat. And with it, a flash of candy color in his periphery. Feathertons rush inside, flank him.

"Look what I've got here!" Colton shouts, gaze moving over Peyton's shoulder, behind him. "I found him in your house... I've had spies on you, ya know." Colton laughs, but it's forced and desperate sounding.

From behind Peyton, "No, I don't think you have, Colton." Gabriel's voice. Undaunted and calm. "At least, none that stayed loyal to you. Fear doesn't keep people loyal once they are free of the source of that fear. Any people you sent to infiltrate the Feathertons were turned. I don't let my people starve. I don't threaten them with the virus. I don't kidnap their children when they disobey me." Gabriel steps closer with every word until he stands at Peyton's right shoulder. He might have his voice under control, but his hands— clasped behind his back—clench so tight that his fingers have gone white. "On the other hand," Gabriel says, a smirk at his lips. "I've had spies crawling up your ranks since the beginning. Your drinking buddy's daughter. Your nephew, Beau. They're helping unload your stores into my trucks as we speak."

"Well, I've got something, too!" Colton forces Bailey to his knees. Peyton's eyes dance from his own aim on Colton, to his brother's pale, angry face. *Thank God, the welling tears have dried. Thank God, Bailey doesn't look afraid.*

"Let him go, and you can walk out of here unharmed. Most of the country has emptied out, you could start over…a second chance."

"You think you can kick me off my own land?"

"You came on my land and hurt my people. You took them from my home." Gabriel grits his teeth but then releases his jaw. "But I also know that none of that was your idea, so I'm willing to let you go…as long as you don't harm that boy."

"No. This is *my* land!" Colton pulls Bailey in tighter. Pushes the gun harder into the side of his head.

Peyton feels Case press into his back, her warm and solid presence offering support.

Gabriel's voice turns soothing, "Come on, Colton. You can find better land." He takes another careful step forward and opens his arms. "The whole country is full of empty land."

Sweat runs down Colton's face. He blinks against it, mouth hanging open. "And you'll let me leave? I'm supposed to believe that?" Colton's hand shakes, but he drags the gun lower. The cut barrel inches down from Bailey's temple, down to his cheek, down his neck. Then, it points at the ground.

Peyton doesn't even think. He raises the Glock, squeezes the trigger, the recoil vibrating up his arm. Colton's head snaps back and explodes.

Gabriel spins around to glare at Peyton, but Peyton only really sees Bailey, pulling himself up from his knees and trembling. *He's okay. He's alive.* Peyton stares, trying to accept it—*he's alive.*

Another beat, and Gabriel stands at Bailey's side, one hand brushing the curling dirty hair from his forehead. Peyton's brother gasps. The anger on his face gone, his eyes wide and wet. Gabriel steps back to let Bailey curl over to the floor like he might vomit.

Then, one of the creatures launches itself toward him, a flash of red blood and black dirt…the white and gray of rot. Peyton reaches for the phantom of his club.

He finds the gun instead.

Case reaches around him. "Peyton, no!"

Another shot, and the creature falls in an explosion of gore. "Got it." Peyton likes this gun. He wants to ask Gabriel if he can keep it. Someone must have more ammo squirreled away… Gotta stomp the neck, though. Peyton strolls toward it. "Get the fuck up," he grumbles at Bailey.

Bailey doesn't rise from the floor. He crawls toward the mutilated creature…a girl with pale blood-streaked hair, wearing a dirty white shirt. Bailey's hands shake as he scoops her into his arms. Dark eyes open but unseeing, her face tipped up toward Peyton.

Cecilia.

"You're going to be okay. You're going to be fine…" Bailey tells her. Blood pours from the back of her skull like water from a pitcher, and still, Bailey keeps talking to her, telling her that she'll be fine. Maybe, he doesn't see? The upper left side of Cecilia's head is gone.

gratitude

46 Bailey

After the shooting stops and the last Molotov cocktails crumble the barn to embers, Gabriel orders everyone to dig a burning pit. No one points out that Colton and his men don't have the virus, don't need cremation.

He rounds up four captured men, puts them on the ground like criminals. His Featherton soldiers grind them into the dirt with their steel toed boots. Gabriel gives them the choice he gave Colton. "Leave. Leave, *now*. Don't come back."

"Or what?" scoffs one of the rednecks. A muscled, greasy man Bailey recognizes from the attack on the mansion.

"Gabriel?"

The cold blue eyes snap onto him. "He was at the mansion. He's one of the men that…hurt…Cecilia…" Bailey swallows, working up to saying it… Rape. *They raped her.* Fucking animals.

But he doesn't get the chance to even form the words, before Gabriel spins back to face the smirking hick. He pulls a gun—*the same gun Peyton used?*—from inside his jacket and shoots.

Colton's remaining men have no problem deciding after that. Those three run. Some got away, took off during the fight, but the rest died in the explosions, and the black gritty soot of their burning bodies melds with the lighter, curling smoke of winter grass and wood.

Bailey watches them swirl together. Chills crawl up his spine. His head hurts, throbs. *How long did Ashley have those same symptoms?* She went home with a cold on Friday. On Saturday, she sounded confused on the phone and then… Shit. *It's starting.*

He uses the tail of his shirt to wipe away the soot and sweat from his face. He could have gone back to the mansion, but Bailey needed to move, to work, so he stayed to help clear brush and dig. Non-stop demanding physical labor to burn off his shock, his horror, his trembling fear. Until the handle of his iron shovel rubs his palms raw and stains the wood with his blood. Infected blood. He'll need to toss the shovel into the fire with the bodies when no one is looking.

"Dude, don't touch it." A boy with canary yellow dreadlocks pushes a girl away from a tangle of burnt arms and legs

"Oh shit—is that guy popped?" The girl scrambles backward, tripping over a stack of wood.

Behind Bailey, someone laughs, "Did he eat that other guy's face? What the hell? That's so crazy. Shane, come look at this."

Gabriel's buffed up guard comes forward and pokes at the entwined bodies with the tip of his boot. "Hey, someone get a tarp over here. There's two more." The guard looks familiar, stocky and tall. Maybe Bailey knew him before he got that silver buzz cut, those steel toed boots, the leather jacket. The same uniform that Peyton wears. He notices Bailey watching him. "Are there any more of these things?"

These things. "About six feet farther in, another one." Bailey flaps his arm in a weary gesture. Then, he adds, "He was a little boy. He was sick. Not a *thing.*" The silver-haired guard just shrugs.

Cecilia's tiny body doesn't go into the pit. Gabriel carries her to one of the flatbed trucks, gently lays her inside. Her brother Lawrence gets in beside her, Cecilia's father, too. They cradle her body between them. Then, the head of Feathertons orders everyone away, leans against the truck while he speaks privately to the Vu family.

Cold wind sweeps Gabriel's hair around his face, making him look like some kind of romantic hero from a period drama. At one point, he places a hand on Lawrence Vu's shoulder. Cecilia's father nods. Then, two of Gabriel's people get in the truck cab and drive away down the road and the boss of Feahtertons looks right toward Bailey.

Watching from the edge of the fire pit, Bailey leans on the heavy shovel, sinks it into the ground as Gabriel makes his way toward the pit. Billowing smoke makes him cough, grab at his stinking tattered t-shirt to wipe his eyes.

"Bailey?" Gabriel saunters toward him. He steps close enough to whisper, to touch, and wraps his long fingers around Bailey's right wrist. "You're alright?"

"No," Bailey says. "Not at all." He sucks in the gritty air. "How could anyone be alright after this? After *all* of this? What Colton did to those boys. Threatened to do…" *I wish you had shot the other men, too. I want them all dead.* The vicious thought leaves Bailey breathless. No. He won't start thinking that way. Like a Featherton. Like Peyton.

"When anyone challenged Colton, he took someone important from them. A parent, sibling…one of their children…" Gabriel's fingers jitter against Bailey's wrist, then clench, and his hand drops away.

God—Bailey thought something like that happened, but it sounds so much more horrible when spoken aloud. How can Gabriel stand to know these kinds of things, to plan for them? "So, those kids who attacked The Greens, they'd been prisoners. Just like me." A shiver creeps down Bailey's body. "I heard that Peyton slaughtered them."

"Hmmm… I didn't want you to know about that. Someone told you?" Gabriel squints over Bailey's shoulder at Shane and the other two Feathertons searching through debris for the missing body. He still has that gun tucked away inside his jacket.

"No one had to *tell me*. That's all they've been talking about tonight." Bailey squints at the sky. "Like he's a hero." While he helped dig the fire pit and drag bodies toward it, the night felt like it would never end, like the sky would remain dark forever. But dawn has begun to break on the edges of the horizon. "Where *is* Peyton, anyway?"

"I sent him back to The Greens. He needs to smooth things out with his Neighborhood Watch." At Bailey's incredulous look, Gabriel sighs. He pinches the bridge of his nose. "Which was a stupid decision."

"He's going to get angry and just make it all… I need you to take me there." But that can't happen. As the two of them talked, Shane, the silver haired guard returned. Now, he stands a respectful distance away, waiting to speak to the boss. Two girls queue up behind him, also wanting Gabriel's time and direction.

"Can *someone* drive me?" Bailey's stomach tightens again. He needs to hold on. Just a little longer. *Come on.* "Don't…say no. I'll be with Peyton. If I pop, he won't let anything happen to me. He won't let anyone…"

Gabriel cups Bailey's face in one hand and tilts his head near as if looking for evidence of the virus creeping into Bailey's eyes. But, he holds him there, his own gaze intense and searching. "I promise that you will survive this Bailey."

The laugh hurts his chest because it wants to turn messy and tear-filled. "Okay. I'll hold you to that." A gust of wind churns the smoke around them, cocooning them together for a few seconds, then dissipating.

Gabriel goes cold and brusque again, drops his hand. The mask of aloof control back in place, as he becomes the head of the Feathertons once more. "Fine. I'll have someone drive you." As soon as Gabriel turns and steps away, the waiting, bright-haired lackeys swallow him up.

17 PEYTON

A knot of neighborhood men waits on the driveway of Peyton's house. He watches them from the shadows of the front room, bottle of Cruzan Single Barrel Rum dangling from his fingers. It tastes disgusting warm, straight, and stale. But Spencer claimed he couldn't find anything else in the storehouse. The kid has a healthier respect for the inventories than Vanessa does...*did*. "Fuck, Vanessa, I'm... I should have... Fuck." Peyton takes another swig of the rum as a Featherton Jeep pulls up. Bailey climbs out the back. *What the hell? Gabriel sent Bailey here to calm things down?* After all the shit Bailey just went through... Spencer told Peyton the booze would "chill him out," but as his grip on the bottle tightens, it starts to feel like a weapon.

"Peyton! I want to talk to you!" Mason's voice bellows from the kitchen.

"Do you?" Sour acid churning through his stomach, Peyton swaggers away from the window. "What do you want... *Dad?*"

Mason wears the same golf shirt and pressed pants as always, like the outbreak never happened, like Lucy never disappeared, like Peyton doesn't have to kill monsters to get the family things they need. His father has his arms folded over his chest as he leans one hip against the kitchen table. "I expected so much more from you, Peyton. But look how you've turned out."

Peyton laughs before slamming the bottle down on the table. "So, now that the neighborhood has turned on me, you aren't so willing to ignore all the things you hate about your son. Is that the gist of it... *Dad?* "

Mason's face flushes dark red, his moist lower lip juts out. "Getting drunk isn't going to help anything, Peyton. Don't think I haven't noticed that this is how you cope with all your problems lately."

The front door opens and closes, but his father just keeps on with the lecture. "Now, we have the Neighborhood Watch saying they're going to ask Gabriel to replace you! What will you do then? What will—"

Bailey walks into the kitchen. Dark circles ring his eyes, and Peyton doesn't miss the shudder that runs through his brother, the sweat on his forehead.

Mason jolts backward, feet sliding on the kitchen tile. Like any second Bailey might pop. "What is *he* doing here?"

"He's here to make sure I don't go on a killing rampage." Peyton smirks and waves the tequila bottle at his brother. "What the fuck does Gabriel think he's doing sending you?"

"He didn't send me, you moron. I came to help you, Peyton." Bailey rubs at his forehead with both hands, closes his eyes. "You need to go outside and talk to them, explain yourself. Let them know you still plan to run this neighborhood for Feathertons." His index fingers press into the inner corners of his eyes, and he rubs hard. "My fucking sinuses are going to explode!"

From the far side of the kitchen, their father gasps, flattening himself against the counter. "Bailey, I think you should go. Peyton, don't you think that Bailey should leave?" Mason glances to the rear hallway, to the back door. He inches closer that direction.

"He's afraid of you, Bailey." Peyton can't hold back his laughter. Drunken, angry laughter that ends with him gripping the back of a kitchen chair for balance. "You fucking coward," he spits at Mason. "You worthless piece of shit."

Bailey throws a hand in front of Peyton's face, blocking their father's skulking form. "Stop it—Leave him alone for once. It's normal to be scared!"

One of Peyton's earliest memories washes over him right then. Sledding on the golf course when he was three, maybe four years old. His father tucked Peyton between his legs on a blue plastic disc, dizzy snowflakes whipped all around the two of them. Peyton remembers crying because his fingers burned from the cold. So, his father stripped off Peyton's wet mittens, curled his small frozen hands into his own, and breathed warmth back into them.

A door slams. The sound snapping through the three of them like the crack of a gunshot. "Are you boys fighting again?" Lila rounds the corner into the kitchen, staggering as she drags her sheets and comforter out onto the floor with her. "Ssstop fighting."

Great. Perfect. "Mom, I think you took too much of your medicine again. Why don't you go back to your room and sleep it off?" Peyton's eyes flick to Bailey and away again.

Lila shuffles to the table, the swathe of bedcovers giving her the appearance of a giant moving chrysalis. "Peyton, I told you to take care of your brother." She cants her head to wipe her dripping nose on her upper arm. Snot smears across her cheek. "Can't you see that Lucy is sick?" She has most of the covers bundled in front of her. The creepy little girl wrapped inside. "Peyton, you have to watch after Bailey. Lucy needs me right now."

"What's going on?" Bailey steps around Peyton toward their mother. "Who is that?"

"This kid from the road, one of the refugees. Her brain's fried or something."

Mason clears his throat, "Now remember sweetie, you have to make those pills last now that..." Even though his voice feigns cheerfulness for his wife, Mason throws a look of disgust toward Peyton. "Well, we just need to make them last."

"You gave her pills?" Bailey gapes at Mason. He looks between his brother and father. "She needs help, not..." Bailey moves closer toward Lila, as if drawn to her misery. *Too sensitive, too soft.*

"She doesn't want any help." Peyton gestures at her. "Just look at her, she's a mess. It's hopeless."

Lila ignores them, pulling the sheets and puffy white comforter tighter. "Poor Lucy. Mommy's here...shhh..." The bundle moves. Part of it kicking free from Lila's arms, a small pale hand emerging.

Clawed fingers.

Missing fingernails.

Peyton takes a step closer, reaches out, pulls at the tangle of bedding in his mother's arms, reveals the snarling face of the girl, her wild rolled back eyes. Baby teeth chewing at her ragged lips. "She popped."

48 Bailey

"Jesus—" Bailey's dad scrambles backward.

Once the sheet drops fully off her face, the little girl makes a low whining sound, fixing her feral stare on Bailey. And he feels Peyton grasp hold of his shirt, fisting the loose fabric and yanking. He sends Bailey sprawling behind him.

Peyton's other hand tips the liquor bottle up like a bat and tequila spills out onto the floor. "Lila, drop it," he orders. His mother blinks at him, confused. "Mom, that's not Lucy. Throw that thing on the ground."

The back door snicks open, and both of them turn. "Dad?" Mason has one hand on the doorknob, his back to them, shoulders tight underneath the knobby pink cotton of his golf shirt.

"Mason, where are you going?" Lila's eyes have a moment of lucidity. Outrage at her husband ignoring her. "Get back here. Lucy is sick. I can't take care of all these children by myself!"

But Mason doesn't look back.

Bailey doesn't understand. They'd all been a family. "Dad? Where are you going?"

His father opens the door just far enough to angle his body through. Peyton steps in front of Bailey, blocking his view. "If you fucking leave right now… If you leave me with all this shit to deal with, then you better hope you never see me again."

Mason pauses only a second. He doesn't turn around to face his son, either of them, just slides through the narrow opening. Shuts the door behind him.

"Peyton?" Bailey looks up at his brother. Wants Peyton to make sense of their father leaving, their mother holding a strange sick child. "Peyton what's going on?"

But all his brother's attention stays on the back door, where their father left. "Don't come back, asshole. Don't ever come the fuck back!"

Peyton raises the heavy glass bottle in the air. Bailey follows the smooth practiced arc when Peyton brings it over his head and down. All the talent his brother had once shown in sports, now honed into killing. The force of his swing bashes the tiny creature from their mother's arms. All the sheets and the comforter heave with the frenetic struggle of the little girl wrapped inside them. Peyton pivots, raises a leg, stomps down with his steel toed boot onto the back of the girl's spindly neck, crushes the little skull on the tile at their feet.

Their mother screams. The hoarse, ragged scream of an animal. Her scream sputters, and her jaw goes slack, and her back spasms. Her eyes roll, her nostrils flare.

"Get back, Bailey. Get out of here."

"What? No. No way! I'm not going to leave!"

Peyton lunges forward, grabs one of the dining chairs with both hands and slams Lila in the chest, knocking her backward.

"Peyton, don't!"

"Let me handle this. Just go." Lila looks toward Peyton now. She tries to run, but between the spill of sheets and dark blood oozing from the crushed girl at her feet, she can't get purchase. She balls up, then uncurls into the telltale crouch, shoulders hunch, finger's curl, mouth drops open. She prepares to charge as Peyton hoists the chair, braces his arms.

"No!" Bailey darts toward their mother. For one heart-stopping second, he thinks Peyton will bring the chair back down over his head. But his brother isn't that far gone in the haze of a fight. Bailey shoves Lila, slides her backward several feet. "We can push her back to her room."

"Bailey. Stop. She won't survive this. You know that, right?"

"I know, okay. I *know*." His eyes brim with tears. "Just please, Peyton—!" Bailey turns his back on Lila to plead. *Don't turn your back on them. Don't ever turn your back.* Peyton must have drilled it into him a million times, but it never sticks. "Shit!" Bailey jumps out of the way.

Peyton raises the chair again, but now, he only uses it to block Lila, knocking her backward as he herds her out of the kitchen and into the back hallway. "Open the door—open the door to her room!"

"Okay!" Bailey rushes past Lila and throws open the door. The room is a mess, the bed ripped apart and stinking. After glancing inside, Bailey flattens himself against the hallway wall.

Peyton continues to advance on Lila, pushing her with the chair, the way Bailey has seen animal trainers hold back tigers. He drives her backward into the master-bedroom. Once Lila crosses the threshold, Bailey slams the door.

"Bailey...she's not Mom anymore..."

"I *know*. I *know that*. But if you killed her—I didn't want you to kill her. For you, Peyton. Not for her. *For you*."

remembrance

"You just keep your mother's shit together through this. Can you do that?"

"I don't know, man."

"You have to. Peyton, you have to."

***

The phone in Peyton's back pocket had vibrated on the way home—Gabriel transferring money to him. Keeping his word to fund rehab for Lila. *I can do this.* Mason had looked smug, packing his bag, deciding to cram in a game of golf between leaving his wife and picking up his mistress for the big escape he planned. Once Lila got her shit straightened out, Peyton would see to it that she took every dime from his father. *Let's see how long Mason can hold onto a spoiled bitch like Pauline Featherton without any money. Ha!*

"Mom?" he called as he slammed into the house. "You awake?"

Probably not. Probably taking her usual Vicodin enhanced morning nap. "Mom. Sleep time is over for the day," he yelled and made for the kitchen for ice. No need to be quiet with Lucy gone to the soccer tournament and Bailey engrossed in video games in his room.

He tasted the blood in his mouth from Gabriel's punch, his fingers found the cut and came away dripping red and pink from his split lip. *God damn, Gabriel.*

Lila kept the Band-Aids and antibiotic gel in the master bath, a holdover from when Peyton and Bailey scraped their knees on the pavement, pinched fingers, bumped foreheads. "Mom?" The sheets and down comforter made a lump in the bed, pillows heaped over the form of his sleeping mother. Peyton kicked the corner of the bed as he passed by it. "Get up."

In the master bath, plastic shattered under his shoe…an empty pill bottle. "Jesus, Mom." At his feet, another caramel-colored empty bottle rolled across the white marble tile.

Peyton slapped at the light switch on the wall, and the long strip of vanity lights blinked on above the mirror. Three more empty bottles in the bathroom sink. Peyton looked back at the mound of covers in the bed. He pivoted and rushed back into the bedroom, dug both hands into the comforter and blankets and jerked them from his mother's limp body. *What have you done?"*

Her face and hands looked purple and bruised, but Lila's eyes opened to slits. A smile worked slowly across her mouth. "It'll be okay."

Peyton grasped her shoulders and pulled her up, tried to get her on her feet, but her legs and arms flopped boneless and useless. Her eyes rolled back, even as the loose slow smile stayed in place. "Don't…worry…is gonna be fine…"

Peyton snatched the phone from his pocket and pressed Gabriel's name.

"What is it? Peyton?"

"Please Gabriel. She overdosed."

"Who—? Oh, your mother, that stupid bitch." Peyton heard the chime of the car door on Gabriel's Lexus, the purr of the engine starting. "Where does she keep getting the drugs?"

"I don't know! I don't…" Peyton's throat had tightened, choking his voice.

"I'm on my way," Gabriel said. "Keep her breathing."

50 Bailey

Lucy had left for the soccer tournament, and Ashley couldn't go to the movie because she had a cold. Neither Bailey nor Ashley thought of Super Flu—that happened in faraway places to other people—not here, not in their perfect suburban paradise.

Bailey came down the stairs from studying. Chem homework, so boring.

He'd heard retching, the sound of running water, and moaning. *His brother's hangover kicking in? God, Peyton!* Bailey followed the strange noises like a trail toward the kitchen and stopped short. His mother, her face dripping water onto her shirt. Vomit on the ends of her hair. She turned a glassy-eyed blank look in Bailey's direction. Then, Gabriel's hand cracked against her cheek.

Bailey jumped. "What—?"

Peyton pushed him back from the kitchen entryway. "Get out of here, Bailey!" His brother's arms crossed over his chest, and he barred Bailey's view of the kitchen. *Why does Peyton look like that?*

He's afraid, Bailey realized. "Peyton?"

Gabriel pushed Lila's neck over the sink. Gabriel also looked off…sweat dampening his hair, weariness dragging at his features, pale eyes sunken into dark sockets.

Bailey froze. Nothing about the scene made sense to him.

"You heard me," Peyton growled. "Go. Get out of here."

God. Bailey threw up his hands. "Okay, I'm leaving."

He found his bike in the garage, and he got on it without thinking, wanting to get away, to forget the weird scene back at home. He rode along the wide swath of pavement winding down toward the golf course. Cut grass and pesticide in the air. Manicured lawns—the Kentucky Bluegrass unnatural to their region, gobbling water to make plush carpets that served no purpose. Grand entryways to each front door, the five models of homes identifiable beneath little touches—a bay window on the two-story open plan, a stucco facade to the ranch style, an expanded garage on the luxury family model like Bailey's own house. He biked round and round streets named after golf resorts far more famous than the sprawling, rolling course they circled. Glen Mills, Cypress Point, Shinnecock Hills, Oakmont, Gatlinburg, Crystal Downs... At the neighborhood entrance, spring daffodils swayed in the chilly late-February air. They'd sprouted up early in the flowerbed splitting Augusta Drive at the entrance gate.

5/ Bailey

No more flowers. They'd dug it up to make the neighborhood's pit.

Bailey watches the bundle of his mother's body and the little girl roll down into the red embers at the bottom. His eyes squeeze shut as the bloody sheets catch.

Eight months earlier, when Gabriel stood over the sink with Lila, he'd had the virus racing through his blood, amassing in his brainstem, getting ready to pop. But, instead of heading to his father's hunting cabin to hide, he'd helped clean up the mess Lila had made of herself, for Peyton...for Bailey.

Beside him, a grim-faced Case tugs the back of his jacket. "Time to go." After they'd closed Lila into the bedroom, Bailey could only think of one person to turn to for help. Well, maybe two...but Gabriel had just doubled the size of his territory, and Case lived right next door. Sweat dampens her shirt and skin. Bloodstains speckle the bottom of one pant leg. The only remaining traces of what he had asked her to do.

She cocks her head to Peyton, standing across the street, where just the tendrils of pit smoke reach. He leans against one of the black

Featherton Jeeps with braced legs and folded arms, with rigid anger as his expression.

"He lied to me—kept things from me. About my mom. Maybe things about our dad, too."

"He was protecting you. You and Lucy are his younger siblings. Via treats...*treated*...me the same way, taking everything on her shoulders." Case swipes a hand over her neck, flicks the sweat from her fingers—hard work killing and burning—worse with someone you know. "It's not the same as lying."

"Yeah? Well, I didn't *want* him to protect me. I didn't *ask* for it." Peyton's protection feels the same as all those times Bailey tried to run as fast, or kick as hard, or climb as high as his older brother, only to fail and be laughed at, made to feel pathetic and weak and inferior.

"You didn't need to." Case shakes her head. "Listen, Bailey, all I know is—"

"What?"

Case shakes her head. And they make their way to Peyton, who gets in the driver seat and starts up the Jeep. The passenger side door is open and waiting for Bailey.

"All you know is *what*, Case?"

Around them, the neighbors have started to retreat back to their homes. *Show's over.* Two little kids linger, watching the Jeep, waiting to see it pull away, like they might have marveled at a firetruck in the world before the Super Flu.

"All I know is that this world is too messed up not to cut people slack. Okay?" She watches him buckle himself inside.

"Ready?" Peyton asks.

"I guess." A memory floats in on the smoky air. His brother on the football field, the year Memorial went to State. They'd all nearly froze in the frigid night air, under the false bright heat of the stadium lights. It was during the time that Case and Peyton dated, and she'd sat beside Bailey with Lucy on her lap. The air smelled of burning wood—maybe left from the bonfire the night before. Bailey couldn't remember much else, just the final winning moments of the game. Peyton spiking the ball in the end zone, raising his arms in a V, the crowd cheering, clapping wildly. And Bailey jumping to his feet, mimicking Peyton's V from the stands.

acceptance

52 PEYTØN

At the mansion, Peyton pulls a gas can from the garage. No one stops him when they look his way. Peyton supposes that nerdy little Spencer Clarkson will take his place today. He has no idea who will fill Vanessa's spot.

Not his problem anymore.

He loads the gas can into the Jeep. Like almost all the houses in Olde Town, Gabriel's home garage doubles as a staging area for emergencies, the walls lined with shelves of rope, canvas, tools, water jugs—really anything practical that someone might need in a siege or evacuation. Peyton eyes it all and tries to mentally jigsaw puzzle it into the Jeep. He grabs a coil of rope and throws it over one shoulder.

Gabriel's voice. "Take the extra water jug."

Peyton jumps a little, his nerves still frayed from letting Case into the house that morning. While she did it, he'd gone upstairs rather than wait with Bailey outside. Despite what his little brother thought, Peyton didn't care that much about Lila's death. He just couldn't take any more of Bailey's expression, the resignation plain in his stormy eyes. Somehow, Peyton had let Bailey down in every way that mattered, and he didn't know how to fix it.

"There's a hunting knife and a spear taped under the work table. Take those, too."

"You could let me keep the Glock from the raid."

"No."

Peyton shrugs. "Fine. I'll get by without it."

"You can stay. I can station you at Colton's, and you'd work outside…you might like it better."

"No. I want to go. I need to leave. I need to…" Peyton stops. Clears his throat, "After my mom…" His expression twists, so he turns away. "I don't want to be here when it happens…to Bailey." Peyton strangles the rope in his hands. "I guess that makes me a coward or at the least a shitty brother. But I just can't see him…like that."

"Fine," Gabriel answers as he makes a brisk pacing inspection of the Jeep. He looks the same as ever in his immaculate clothes and clean, shining hair, polished shoes. "If you're going to leave anyway, then you can do a job for me. Something long-term, and you would have to leave the suburbs but still be in touch."

"You dick. Of course, you want something. You always want something." Peyton slits his eyes at Gabriel. "No. I'm done with this shit. I'm just done." No matter what Peyton thinks of Gabriel, he trusts him to take care of Bailey. He'll continue to do that for Peyton, or for Bailey—Peyton doesn't care. He'll continue.

But it doesn't look like Gabriel intends to accept that resignation. He moves to stand between Peyton and the Jeep, a human barrier. "You'll do this job for me because you are going to come back," he commands. "Bailey will want you to come back."

"I'm not running away," Peyton counters. *But yes, he is…* He just now admitted it. He scrubs his hands against his face.

"He'll recover," Gabriel says it the way he gives orders, like there's no room for negotiation. There's his way, or there's nothing.

Peyton takes a long time to finish loading the Jeep. What Gabriel wants from him, wants him to do, is more a mission than a job, and he's not sure he wants a mission right now. Killing, looting, drinking himself to sleep sounds like a much better plan to keep himself from thinking about his brother.

Once he's done with the Jeep, he stares at the door leading into the house for an even longer time than it took to load up. *Go inside. Tell Bailey you're leaving. That you just don't have the guts to watch him pop into a monster. To watch him die.* He leaves the door untouched. He doesn't really know how to say any of the crap that needs to be said.

When he backs out the Jeep, he glances one last time at the house. *Goodbye.* In the top window on the right, Bailey looks down at him.

Hands choking the steering wheel, Peyton forces himself to hold Bailey's gaze. *He knows I'm leaving.* Peyton lifts his fingers from his white-knuckled grip in a half-assed wave. *You'll be okay, Bailey.* His foot comes off the brake, and the Jeep lurches onto the street. *Please be okay.*

53 Bailey

The oily soot from the burning pit still clings to Bailey's skin. Ash from Colton, from his mother. He can hear Gabriel shuffling at the door. "It's your room, come inside. I just wanted to see him. Before he left."

"Your brother will come back. He just couldn't—"

"I know. I know," Bailey cuts him off. His fingers leave behind smudgy prints on the curtains. "My headache is better, so that's good." He plucks at his shirt. "I need a bath."

"Take your time."

***

The Featherton mansion still gets hot water, and Bailey turns the knob all the way before getting in the wide marble tub. Steam coats his aching lungs. He scrubs at his arms and legs with a loofah and soap. He pours out the last of a bottle of shampoo to lather his hair and dunks beneath the water's surface, eyes squeezed tight, ears muffled from the outside world.

Only when he springs up, choking for air, does he realize that everything stays muffled. Bailey slaps at his ears, heart speeding, lungs unable to suck in enough air. *Calm down.* His vision goes wonky, tunneling, colors blurring. A jarring quake spreads down the back of his neck and spine. All the diagrams and descriptions made real.

"Gabriel—" Oh, God, the inside of his head buzzes like a trapped mosquito, the vibrating hum of an alarm. "Gabriel, help—" His stomach clenches, and he launches himself half over the tub's edge. Vomit boils up from his stomach, burns his throat, sprays over Gabriel's plush white bathroom carpeting. A cool hand on his back.

"Try to calm—"

"I can't—I can't!" The virus is inside of him, eating him. Every thought chokes inside a tight band, a ring of pain. It pushes down on him, an overwhelming sensation of mental and physical pressure squeezing at his body, at his mind. "Gabriel?"

"You're strong. You can survive this."

"Are you really here?"

"I'm here. I won't leave you…" Someone is holding Bailey, hugging him. *"Focus on my voice."*

But the squeezing ring on his brain won't let him focus. His heart thumps, every beat like it will push itself right out of his chest. He aims all his awareness on that pulse inside, curls his body in toward it. Arms curling inward. Fingers curling inward.

My heart. My heart.

He tries to hang on. Just enough…just…

please review this book

Reviews help authors more than you may think, so if you enjoyed *Survive the Streets*, please consider leaving a review at Goodreads or your favorite retailer. I would greatly appreciate it.

about the author

Alex Timothy writes urban science fiction and fantasy stories, YA and angst. An ex-dancer with a sugar addiction and an overactive imagination, Alex spends a lot of time drinking coffee and pacing the room while muttering. It's hard to find what matters in this chaotic world.

objective

1 Renée

As soon as she walked into the showy suburban party, Renée could pick out all the elements of her brother's planning. The spotless white of this soot-free mansion, when fire and ash covered every inch of their apocalyptic world. Those towering stacks of food—oranges, plates of imported cheese. Even bananas! *Where the hell did you find those, Gabriel?* Eight months into the worst pandemic the world had ever known, and her brother decided to host the government patrols, to serve them Camembert and fruit. *Very impressive showing, little brother.*

And then all these admiring children he surrounded himself with, their crazy dyed hair. He recruited them to his gang and named them all after himself. "What does he hope to accomplish here?" she muttered under her breath. Gabriel hadn't changed at all from the eccentric and idiotic boy she'd grown up with. "Feathertons…" she scoffed, touched her fingers to the pearls at her neck. Granny Featherton's pearls. What would that snobby old woman have thought of Gabriel labeling his criminal empire with their family name? *Daddy's name.* A flash of memory…Granny Featherton telling an eleven-year-old Renée not to talk so loud, not to throw her head back when she laughs. "It's not how a lady acts," she said and touched her wrinkled fingers to the same pearl necklace. *That old bitch, I wish she could see this.*

Of course, Gabriel himself hadn't shown yet. Not to make a dramatic late arrival, like everyone here assumed. *Everyone but me.* Renée knew the truth, that her brother would need to minimize his exposure to the crowd, the noise, the influx of sensation inherent to a party. Same weak, volatile *freak.* Gabriel couldn't risk a breakdown in front of his devoted followers. He needed to impress the adults who controlled the remaining bones of infrastructure. "It won't work, little brother." These men would simply take what they want before they'd even acknowledge some suburban teenage gang and its leader. All he'd manage to do was incite their greed.

Dandridge and Lanson came up to flank her on either side. "Those hillbillies haven't shown yet," Lanson griped.

"Those hillbillies are the last hope of civilization in this mess outside the city," General Dandridge countered. "You'll do well to remember that, Lieutenant." Dandridge had been a commander on the army base before the outbreak, before the virus decimated it. Close quarters, too many men just outside of the survival range of fifteen to twenty-five... The young survivors weren't inclined to stay in place while the world around them, around their families, imploded. "Nothing here but these delinquent kids running wild. Someone should step in and take charge of this mess."

"Yes, sir." Lanson's jaw tightened. He was younger than Dandridge by at least twenty years. Twenty crucial years when it came to surviving the virus. Like Renée, Patrick Lanson had worked in a position of obscurity until all the people between him and his highest aspirations fell to Super-Flu. Renée wondered if Lanson looked forward to Dandridge catching the virus as much as she did.

Renée made a vague noise of agreement. Dandridge and Lanson and the rest of their entourage had no idea that she was the same age as these "delinquent kids." When the outbreak began, she had worked as a paid intern to the governor. Gradually, as everyone with legitimate power died, she became the last connection to the remnants of legitimate government. And she'd always looked older than her age. Men only noticed her face and body, the expensive clothing she wore. *Mother would be so proud.* The bitter words in her head made Renée wince. She followed it with a mantra of her father's, *"Whatever it takes to gain power."*

A blaring car horn and blast of music shook the windows on the back of the house—the only warning before Colton's people barreled into the back yard, driving their oversized pickup trucks.

"Is that them?" Lanson didn't hold back his disgust.

"Yes." Renée had expected this dramatic arrival. After all, she'd given that disgusting piece of work, Jaxon Colton, this idea to upstage her brother's party. She'd counted on Gabriel's complete inability to understand normal social interactions, to understand people. "Oh, he'll host an impressive party with all kinds of black-market food and booze and music…" she'd told Colton, ignoring his eyes as they roamed her breasts and legs. "But, my little brother has no understanding of fun or entertainment. Bring something for everyone to do—something they can't resist and won't forget," she'd told him.

Stupid, Rénee. She'd underestimated the psychopathic cruelty of someone like Colton. She'd meant for them to round up creatures they found on the highways, people who had ceased to be human long ago, staggering bodies with the virus fully in control. Not the feral sick that Colton's people started to throw into the empty swimming pool. Newly popped, newly infected—*these people have a chance of recovery.* But, Colton bound their arms and hands to ensure the fight stayed in the favor of anyone willing to jump down into the pool crater. "Creature Cracking"—a term used to describe anyone who went searching for the sick, to kill them for fun. The feral sick rarely attacked first.

At last, she spotted her brother.

Gabriel. His tall, thin frame outlined by the LED spotlights on the back deck. He'd dressed formally, all in black, just as she had. His height, bright red hair, and high cheekbones—inherited from their mother—made him stand out in the crowd. But, Renée saw past this glossy, superior version of her brother to a little boy with trembling lips and a snotty nose. Pauline Dufort Featherton called her son "broken," and she cringed away from Gabriel's many, many meltdowns.

Renée nodded toward where Gabriel stood, completely still, frozen in the center of unruly partygoers. *You must be barely keeping yourself together, little brother.* "That's him," she pointed Gabriel out to both Dandridge and Patrick Lanson. "My little brother," she sneered. No one would guess that she meant he was younger in minutes instead of years. "We weren't raised together," she added, a lie just to distance herself further.

As twins, they had spent their early years side-by-side, closed inside a spacious nursery with blue-and-white striped walls, a white rocking horse that neither of them played on, a string of nannies who spent more time fawning over their direct-to-video movie star mother than paying attention to her sullen twins. "I barely know him." Another lie. She knew her brother like a part of herself. She knew his frail nerves, his explosive temper. She knew his spoiled nature. Even if Pauline rejected him, Gabriel had always been their father's favorite. *Daddy's golden child.*

Kids hung off the deck railing and screeched to the brawling in the pool. Pulsing music blared around them, a wild post-apocalyptic rave. And even though Colton instigated the chaotic, frenzied atmosphere, it only highlighted the undisciplined youth of Gabriel's followers. Before the outbreak, someone would have called the police to break it all up. But this was Featherton territory now.

From her vantage point diagonal to him, Renée could see Gabriel's entire body poised in rigid control over his fight-or-flight response. How many times had she seen her brother fall apart in similar situations? He would crumple, squeeze his eyes shut, cover his ears, and shake. What would these military and government men think of him then? What would his *followers* think?

Then, something grabbed her brother's attention, the curly-haired boy she'd stopped earlier who'd looked at her with a deer-in-headlights expression. The boy had buckled over in a faint, and Gabriel swung into action to rescue him. Her brother threw his arms around the skinny kid and dragged him from the thickest part of the crowd, back into the empty kitchen. *Lucky break, little brother.* Looked like Gabriel found a perfect excuse to get out of the mob.

"This is outrageous and a waste of time," Lanson griped. "No one participating in this frenzied bloodlust and chaos deserves our respect."

Renée took another look at the people bludgeoning down the victims of the virus. "I suppose you're right," she said, hardly able to hold back her smile. "We should give up the idea of working with them." She looked one last time at the writhing, bound, sick people getting thrown into the empty pool, the candy-colored heads of the kids fighting them.

In the center of the melee, swinging a baseball bat dripping with chains and gore, she recognized Peyton Tyrone. Tall, muscular, his golden blond hair with blue-dyed tips flew back from his strong features, square jaw. *"He's beautiful,"* she almost said it aloud. *How had a freak like Gabriel managed to befriend this flawlessly masculine boy before the outbreak?* The outbreak had twisted his perfect American high-school-hero image into something vicious…dangerous. And Renée couldn't help but admire the result. *If I could have someone like that at my side…*she could take whatever she wanted. She could rule the entire city and everything surrounding it.

She could create an empire with someone like Peyton Tyrone at her side.

2 Gabriel

Don't fidget. You are in control. Gabriel has his hands folded in front of him on his father's desk. Willpower keeps his legs and fingers still. "It has to be you," he tells Case.

She refused the seat opposite him, so now Gabriel has the unpleasant experience of her standing over him with her folded arms and angry eyes, still blaming him for Peyton's monthslong absence. It makes his skin crawl. *You are in control.*

Case Bell does not look happy. "And you want me to tell her I'm going behind your back?"

"Yes. That's exactly what I want. Tell Renée you have side business—that you'll go behind my back to get her an extra tanker every four days. In exchange, you want meds that you plan to trade here in the territory."

Huffing disapproval. "So, not just defying you, but also betraying Feathertons."

"Correct. Those are my orders." *You are*—the fingers of one hand start drumming against the surface of the desk, rapid muted tapping. Gabriel springs up, thrusts his hands into his pants pockets. He paces to the fireplace. "Take the delivery and make the trade. Then report back to me. Shane will tail you for backup, but you won't see him."

Behind him, Case makes another frustrated noise, and the study's French doors creak open.

Finally. But, when he spins around, she's still there. Looking guilty of all things. "Why are you still here? I told you what to do. Now leave."

The round expressive eyes widen. She takes a deep breath. Gabriel knows Case Bell dislikes him, dislikes the Feathertons organization on principle, dislikes him personally because she still loves Peyton, and she suspects Gabriel sent him away. But Gabriel still values Case's honesty and bravery. He trusts her not to fumble this assignment and not double-cross him.

That he's ordered her out, snapped at her, doesn't seem to register at all. Case catches and releases the door handle like she's thinking of leaving but can't seem to do it. "I think I should tell you… There are a lot of rumors about what really might be going on here in the compound."

Every muscle tenses. *Stay still. Don't move. Don't change expression. Don't change your breathing.* "What do people think is 'really going on here' despite the entire compound being accessible to anyone in my organization?"

"Accessible…maybe. But you're the only one who really knows what's behind every door, and you're the only one who knows every plan."

Because it would be extremely naïve to let that information be common knowledge—to guard every door that mattered, or to let Feathertons' resources and needs… He stares her down stone-faced, but even the breath inside him wants to tremble in frustration. *You are the one in charge, in control, and you don't have to tell her anything. You can say nothing at all.* He says nothing at all.

"There are rumors that you might be doing experiments on people, and trying to find a cure…or something worse."

"They suspect I'm keeping Bailey Tyrone alive, I already know this. Once he recovers, they'll be ready to hear me out on my ideas for an infirmary. We don't have to kill every person who *pops*." He can't hide the disgust in his voice at the slang term for those who reach the acute stage of the virus. "Once everyone sees that Bailey has survived, any rumors like this will end. He's young and healthy, so it can't be much longer."

Case steps closer, brow furrowed. "There's more."

Gabriel admires this about her, too. She doesn't shy away from speaking her mind if something needs to be said. "What *more?*"

"People think that you made him sick. That you tricked him into living here and then infected him on purpose. After what Colton did, turning people just to kill them for fun, use them as weapons…it isn't that hard to believe."

That people believe him capable of terrible things doesn't bother Gabriel, it's an unfortunate part of trying to keep his territory in line and protected. But that anyone would believe him capable of hurting Bailey is intolerable, excruciating. He has killed, destroyed, and suffered for Bailey. "Who is saying this?" His voice shakes. *You are in control. You are—*

Case's round dark eyes soften, and she bites at her lower lip. "Too many people, Gabriel."

"It doesn't matter. Once Bailey recovers, the rumors will stop." He turns to stare into the glowing embers of the fire. *You are in control.*

"I know you wanted to help Bailey," Case says. Gabriel can't turn around if that means facing Case's soft eyes and kind words, just the thought of her behind him with all her tender sympathy makes him want to scream out his rage.

"I know you wanted to help," she repeats. "But it's been months and—"

"Just *go* and stop wasting my time with all your gossip and…your *concern,*" he spits out. He remains still, afraid to breathe, to look anywhere but into the fire. "One of the brothers will drive you home." Since Colton's attack on the mansion, Hugo and Felix Mageo both live in Gabriel's home with him. Shane, Gabriel's head of security, insisted on it. One of them, they look enough alike to be identical twins, pokes his head into the study. *Listening at the door.*

"I'll take you, Case."

"Take your brother with you, I want to be alone."

"Sure thing, boss."

Gabriel waits to hear the front door snick closed…and then he bolts from the study for the basement door. Trembling fingers key in the code on the lock.

I just need to see him. To see that he's still alive. Still here.

***

Down a flight of stairs in the dark and cool of the underground room is the barred cage. Two small plug-in nightlights near the stairs are the only illumination. Creatures abhor bright light. "Bailey?" he whispers into the shadows, clears his throat. "Bailey, it's Gabriel Featherton. Do you recognize me?"